DREAMLAND

ROBERT L. ANDERSON

HARPER TEEN
An Imprint of HarperCollinsPublishers

Geographical disclaimer:
Fielding and its environs, including Marborough, Pellston, and, farther
afield, Wapachee Falls, and DeWitt, are entirely my own creation.
I imagined Fielding to be some miles outside of Bloomington, Indiana,
which is, of course, a real place. I've found it useful to drop imagined
towns into a very real landscape and then pass between them, much
in the same way that Dea passes in and out of our known reality,
but I apologize for any confusion that may arise as a result.

HarperTeen is an imprint of HarperCollins Publishers.

Library of Congress Cataloging-in-Publication Data
Anderson, Robert Luis.
    Dreamland / Robert Luis Anderson. — First edition.
        pages   cm
    Summary: "Odea Donahue has been able to travel through people's dreams
since she was six years old, but when Dea breaks the rules, dreams start to
become reality"— Provided by publisher.
    ISBN 978-0-06-233867-9 (hardback)
    [1. Dreams—Fiction.   2. Fantasy.]   I. Title.
PZ7.1.A53Dr   2015   2014047863
[Fic]—dc23   CIP
                                                                AC

15 16 17 18 19   CG/RRDH   10 9 8 7 6 5 4 3 2 1
❖
First Edition

To Stephen Barbara,
for your ultimate bad-assery and your belief in this book.

PART ONE

All *that we see or seem*
Is but a dream within a dream.

—*Edgar Allan Poe*

Afterward, Dea blamed it all on Toby. She knew it wasn't nice to blame a cat. It was definitely immature. But that was life: one big chain reaction, a series of sparks and explosions.

Always, explosions.

If Toby hadn't clawed through the screen door, she would never have met so-and-so, she would never have said such-and-such, she would never have done blah, blah, blah. She'd still be slogging through dumb algebra homework in Fielding, Indiana, getting picked last in gym class and ignored in the cafeteria.

Funny how Fielding, Indiana, didn't seem so bad anymore. Or maybe it just didn't seem important. Not after the cops and the disappearance. Not after the men with no faces and the city in the sand.

Not after the monsters started showing up in the mirror.

Definitely not after Connor.

ONE

"Freaks." An empty can of Coke ricocheted off Odea's backpack and landed in the dirt. Inside the car, several girls laughed, a sound like the distant twittering of birds. Then Tucker Wallace's truck continued grinding and bumping down Route 9, kicking up dust and exhaust.

"Thank you!" Gollum shouted. She scooped up the can and dribbled a few drops of soda in the dirt. "Thoughtful," she said to Dea. "Too bad they forgot to leave us anything to drink."

"I'm sure it was just an oversight," Dea said.

"You know, for an evil hell spawn, Hailey's got pretty good aim. Maybe she should try out for the basketball team."

Dea laughed, imagining Hailey Madison, whose sole form of exercise came, according to rumors, from showing off various parts of her anatomy to different horny senior boys beneath the bleachers, running up and down a basketball court. She liked that about Gollum, arguably the only person in Fielding more unpopular than Dea was. She couldn't be fazed. She turned everything into a joke.

Gollum always said it was because she'd grown up on a working dairy farm, dirt poor, with *five* brothers. *After you've shoveled shit at five in the morning in December,* she always said, *you learn how to keep things in perspective.*

They kept walking. It was hot for September. The fields were full of withered corn and sun-bleached grass and the occasional spray of white wildflowers, floating like foam on the surface of a golden ocean. The sky was pale, practically white, like someone had forgotten to vacuum the dust out of the blue.

Even by Fielding standards, the Donahues' house was in the middle of nowhere. There were only four properties within shouting distance: a house that belonged to an ancient alcoholic Dea had never seen; Daniel Robbins's house, which was bordered on all sides by a chicken wire fence and bore a dozen No Trespassing signs; the Warrenby Dairy Farm, which sprawled over three hundred acres ("all of them useless," Gollum liked to say); and a large brick colonial almost directly across the street that had been vacant since Odea and her mother had moved in.

But today, as Odea and Gollum got closer, Dea saw the yard of the colonial house was littered with cardboard boxes and furniture sheathed in plastic. There was a big U-Haul truck parked in the driveway. A woman was standing on the front porch, sorting through cartons as though looking for something specific. She straightened up, smiling, when she spotted Dea. She was wearing jeans and a short-sleeved white T-shirt and she had blond hair tied neatly in a ponytail. She was just the right amount of fat for a mom.

Dea felt a sharp stab of jealousy.

Before the woman could say anything, a man's voice called to her from inside and she turned and entered the house. Dea was relieved. She would have had nothing to say by way of greeting. *Welcome to Fielding, pimple of Indiana. Watch out for roadkill.*

"Think they got lost?" Gollum asked, adjusting her glasses. Everything Gollum owned was a hand-me-down or picked from the Salvation Army, and was either a little too big, too small, or just slightly out of fashion. Gollum, real name Eleanor Warrenby, had earned her nickname in third grade, when she'd made the mistake of wearing her older brother's *Lord of the Rings* T-shirt to school too many days in a row. When she'd first explained this to Dea, Dea had been stupid enough to ask why she hadn't just worn a different shirt. Gollum had looked at her like she was insane, squinting from behind her too-big glasses.

"Didn't have any," she'd said matter-of-factly, and Dea had been ashamed.

"Think we should tell them to run?" Dea said, and now it was Gollum who laughed, a honking laugh that belonged to a person way bigger than she was.

They'd reached Dea's gate, which was crowded with climbing leaf and honeysuckle, so much of it the small bronze plaque nailed to the wood was almost completely concealed: HISTORICAL LANDMARK SOCIETY, BUILT 1885, RESTORED 1990.

"If you're bored this weekend . . ." Gollum trailed off, like she always did, leaving the invitation unspoken: *I'm right down the road.* Gollum and Dea had been walking to and from the bus stop together since January, when Dea had moved to Fielding in the middle of sophomore year. They sat next to each other in class and ate together at lunch. But they'd never once hung out after school, and Dea hadn't seen Gollum at all except in passing over the summer.

Dea's fault. Dea's *problem.*

And she could never, ever explain why.

"Bored? In Fielding?" Dea pretended to be shocked. "Never." She didn't want to have to make up an excuse, and Gollum never pushed her for one, which was one of the things she liked best about Gollum.

The Donahues' house was the exact replica of a farm that had existed there over a hundred years ago. It was restored to look completely original—silo and all—even though not a splinter of the original house remained. For two decades, the house was a museum, but by the time Dea and her mom rented it, the place had been shuttered for a few years. Dea figured no one wanted to walk through a past that looked exactly like the present, and vice versa.

A *simulacrum*: that's what it was called when something was made to resemble something else. Dea's mother had taught her the word. Her mother loved simulacra of any kind: plastic sushi designed to look like the real thing, kettles concealed within the plaster model of a roosting chicken, clock faces that were actually cabinets.

As usual, her mom had locked all three locks on the front

door, and as usual, Dea had a bitch of a time getting the keys to work. In Cleveland, in Chicago, even in Florida, Dea could understand her mom's obsession with locks and barriers, escape plans and worst-case-scenario talks. But here, in Fielding, where the biggest crime was cattle tipping, it made less sense.

Then again, her mom had never made any sense. Dea occasionally imagined that scientists would come knocking on the door and drag them both to a lab for experimentation. They'd isolate the gene for crazy—an inherited twist in the double helix, an unexpected sickle shape.

The hall was cool and dark, and smelled like rosemary. Other than the *tick-tick-tick* of a dozen old clocks, it was quiet. Dea's mom was a nut about clocks. They were the only things she insisted on keeping, the only possessions she bothered to take with them when they moved. Sometimes Dea felt like that crocodile in *Peter Pan*, like a ticking clock was lodged in her belly and she couldn't escape it. Every so often, her heart picked up on the rhythm.

Dea didn't bother calling out for her mom. She was usually gone during the day, although Dea was no longer sure what, exactly, she did. There'd been so many jobs triumphantly attained, then quietly lost. A quick celebration—*I'm a receptionist now!*—a rare glass of champagne, a spin through the local mall to buy shoes and clothes that looked the part. Sometimes Dea thought that's why her mom got jobs in the first place: so she could dress up, pretend to be someone else.

Inevitably, after a week or two, the sensible, flat-soled shoes were returned to the closet; the car would remain in the driveway well past nine a.m.; and Dea would find a laminated ID card bearing a picture of her mom's smiling face under the words *Sun Security Systems* or *Thompson & Ives, Attorneys-at-Law* discarded in the trash, under a thin film of rotting lettuce. Then the weeks of scrimping began: microwavable meals purchased from the gas station, sudden relocations to avoid overdue rent, pit stops in cheap motels mostly populated by drug addicts. Dea was never sure what her mom did to get fired. She suspected that her mom simply got bored and stopped showing up.

In the kitchen, Dea excavated some pickles from the back of the fridge, behind a bottle of crusty ketchup and a chunk of moldy cheddar cheese, and took the jar out to the back porch, her favorite part of the house. She loved its broad, white railing set on a curve, like the swollen prow of a ship, its sagging rattan furniture, and beat-up iron tables. She settled down on the porch swing, relishing in the Friday feeling: two whole days without school. She liked to think of the weekend as a geometric shape, as a long wave. Now, she was just riding up toward the first swell, at the very farthest point from the dumpy shoreline of school.

Sometimes, when she was sitting on the porch, she liked to imagine another Odea, an alternate-girl who lived on an alternate-farm, maybe back in time when it really was a farm. She imagined her sitting on the porch swing, using one leg for momentum, as Odea did. She enjoyed imagining all the different people and lives that had been played out in the same space, all of them packed together and on top of each other like Styrofoam peanuts in a carton, and at the same time preserved in their separate realities.

She wondered whether alternate-Odea liked pickles, too.

She was startled by a sudden rush of wings. A black bird landed on the railing, hopped a few inches, and cocked its head to look at her. It had a big red splash across its belly, as though it had recently been plucked out of a paint can.

"Hey." Odea wrestled a pickle out of the jar. She had no idea whether birds liked pickles but decided to give it a shot. "Want one?"

The bird hopped away another few inches. Its eyes were like two dark stones.

She liked birds. Birds were *harbingers*—another word she'd learned from her mom. The dictionary defined *harbinger* as *a person who goes ahead and makes known the approach of another; herald. Also an omen; anything that foreshadows a future event.*

In dreams, birds were very important. Dea often depended on them to show her the way back out of the dreams she walked. Dreams were confusing and ever changing; sometimes she turned and found the passage she had come through blocked by a new wall or a sudden change in the landscape. But birds knew the way out. She just had to follow them.

"Hungry?" she tried again, leaning forward, reaching a little closer.

Suddenly, a dark blur of fur rocketed past her. The bird startled, let out a scream, and went flapping into the air just as Toby made a clumsy lunge for it. Toby thudded down the stairs, belly thumping, and plunged into the garden, as if hoping that the bird might change its mind and fly directly into his mouth.

"Toby!" She stood up quickly but Toby had already disappeared into the garden. She followed him, swatting aside heavy branches dripping with flowers, clusters of chrysanthemums, fat bunches of zinnias that crowded the walkway. Her mother's garden always reminded her of dreams: the colors slightly too vivid to be real, the perfume so strong it was like a lullaby, whispering for her to *sleep, sleep*.

She spotted Toby slinking under the low, rotted picket fence that divided her property from the road. It had been too long since she'd walked a dream—a week, maybe longer—and she was getting weak. She was sweating already, and her heart was beating painfully in her chest, even though she wasn't moving very fast.

Toby took off again as soon as she was close enough to grab him, and it took another ten minutes before Dea could corner him at the edge of Burnett Pond, which was technically the border of Gollum's family's property, although Gollum always said her family used only a quarter of their land.

"Got you, asshole," she said, and snatched Toby up. He was heavy, like a fat, warm rug. "Good thing you're cute," she said. "Otherwise I'd chuck you in the pond." He licked her chin.

She stood for a moment, trying to catch her breath, careful not to stand too close to the water. They were sheltered from the sun by a heavy growth of pine and sycamore trees, a rare break from the wide fields, burnt and withered, stretching all the way from horizon to horizon. The pond was covered with deep purple and green shadows.

She was about to turn back when she noticed a pair of red shorts—a guy's—and some flip-flops carefully laid out on the bank. She scanned the water and saw a ripple at the far side of the pond, and a dark shape she had originally mistaken for an animal. An arm pinwheeled out of the water. Then another.

She was temporarily mesmerized, as she always was when

she saw someone swimming. Slowly, the boy carved his way through the water, creating a small wake. Then, abruptly, before she could turn away, he surfaced.

He had a nice face—good-looking without being *too* good-looking. The water had turned his hair into spikes, and his nose was crooked, like maybe it had been broken. His chin was pronounced, probably a tiny bit big, and it gave his whole face a stubborn expression.

"This is awkward," was the first thing he said.

"Sorry," she said quickly, realizing she probably looked like a weird stalker or a pervert. "My cat . . . I wasn't watching you."

"No, no." He made a face. "I meant . . . well, my clothes."

Then it hit her: he was swimming naked. He was naked, right then. Which meant she was having a conversation with a naked boy.

"I was just leaving," she said.

"Wait! Just wait one minute. Just . . . turn around and close your eyes, okay?"

She heard sloshy water sounds, and then the rustle of fabric. She tried to think of something other than the fact that a boy was pulling on clothes less than three feet away from her: a large hall of statues, cool, full of echoes. An image she had seen once in a dream.

"You can open your eyes now," he said.

She did, and was surprised to see that he was taller and skinnier than he looked in the water—probably at least six foot two. He had a swimmer's build: long arms, broad shoulders, skinny waist.

"I don't want you to think I'm some kind of nudist," he said. "I didn't know anyone came down this way."

"No one does, except for this guy." She hefted Toby in her arms, glad her hands were full and she didn't have to figure out what to do with them. "He got out."

He reached out and scratched Toby on the chin. Toby stretched his head to the sky. As he purred, his body vibrated in her arms.

"What's his name?" he asked.

"Toby," she said.

He kept his eyes on Toby. "And what about *your* name?"

She hesitated. "Odea," she said. "People call me Dea." This wasn't exactly true, since most *people* didn't speak to her or address her at all. But her mom called her Dea, and so did Gollum.

"Connor," he said. There was an awkward pause, and then they both spoke simultaneously.

"So, you live around here?" he said.

Just as she said: "You new?"

He laughed. He had a nice laugh. Nice teeth, too. "You first."

"Yeah. The farmhouse," she said, jerking her chin to indicate the direction from which she'd come.

He smiled. Suddenly, his whole face was transformed. The slightly-too-big chin, the crooked nose, and eyes maybe spaced a centimeter too far apart—all of it became perfect, symmetrical. Beautiful. She looked away, suddenly embarrassed.

"We're neighbors," he said. "We just moved in across the street."

"I figured," she said. He raised his eyebrows, and she clarified. "Everyone knows everyone around here. I figured you were the new kid. I saw the moving truck."

14

"Busted," he said. "You go to Fielding? I'm a transfer." When she nodded, he said, "Maybe you know my cousin. Will Briggs?"

Even thinking the name brought a foul taste to her mouth, like rotten gym socks and watery beer. Will Briggs was huge and dumb and mean; rumor was that his dad, who worked for the police department, had once cracked him over the head with a guitar, and he'd been screwed up ever since. Nobody liked Will Briggs, but he was good at football and his dad was a cop, which meant that no one messed with him either.

Apparently he was the one who'd started calling Gollum *Gollum* in third grade, probably the only vaguely creative thing he'd ever done.

"No," she lied. In Dea's opinion, Will Briggs was radioactive material: anyone associated with him was contaminated.

He was still smiling. "I thought everyone knew everybody around here."

"Guess not." She squeezed Toby tightly, burying her nose in the soft scruff of his fur. Connor would get to school on Monday and hear from his cousin that she was Odor Donahue, friendless freak; then her new neighbor would turn suddenly unfriendly, and make excuses to avoid looking at her when they passed in the hall.

It had happened to her like that in Illinois. The summer before freshman year, she'd spent two months hanging out with a girl, Rhoda, who'd lived down the block. They'd spent hours looking over Rhoda's sister's yearbook and giggling over cute upperclassmen. They'd shopped for their first-day-of-school outfits together. And then, as always, the rumors had spread: about Dea's house, and the clocks; about how she and her mom were crazy. On the third day of school, Rhoda wouldn't sit next to her at lunch. After that, she would make the sign of the cross when she saw Dea in the halls, like Dea was a vampire.

In fact, Gollum was the only semi-friend Dea had had in years. And that was only because Gollum was weird. Good-weird, in Dea's opinion, but definitely weird. Besides, Gollum couldn't really be counted as a friend, since she knew hardly anything about who Dea really was—if she had, Dea was pretty sure even Gollum would go running.

"I should get back," she said, not looking at him.

"See you Monday," he called after her.

She didn't bother responding. There was no point. She already knew how this whole thing would go.

TWO

Dea was six years old the first time she ever walked a dream.

It was an accident.

They'd been living on the outskirts of Disney World then, in a large condo meant to look like a castle, with turrets on the roof and flags hanging above the doorway. Inside, however, it looked nothing like a castle. The carpeting was green and smelled like cat pee, and the elevators were always out of order.

There was a central courtyard, basically a paved deck with a pool in the shape of a kidney bean, surrounded by sagging lawn chairs and straggly plants overspilling their planters. There was a tetherball pole, and a small outdoor pool house that held a bunch of moldy umbrellas, an old bocce ball set, and a foosball table whose handles had been palmed smooth.

Dea was sick a lot back then. She had an irregular heartbeat. Sometimes she couldn't feel it at all, and she'd find herself gasping for breath. Other times, it raced so hard, she thought it might fly out of her mouth. It was as though her heart were tuned to the rhythm of a song she couldn't hear.

Her mom had forbidden her to swim—she wanted Dea to stay away from the pool entirely—and Dea was too weak to play tetherball. But she killed at foosball. When her mom was away at work, she spent hours playing both sides of the table, watching the ball spin between the plastic players.

There was a girl, Mira, who lived in 7C. Like Dea, she was too sick to go to school. She had bad asthma and legs that were kind of collapsed, so she walked really slowly, knees crooked inward, dragging her feet. She was one of Dea's first friends. Dea and Mira made up elaborate stories about the other residents of the condo, invented a new language called Inside Out, and buried treasure in the potted plants so that aliens would someday find it.

The day it happened, they'd spent the morning pretending to be scientists, inventing names for every flower they could think of, drawing them carefully with crayons in a big book of heavy-duty artist's paper Mira's dad had bought her, of which Dea was insanely jealous. She was jealous, actually, of everything Mira's father did, even stupid things, like coming down to the courtyard and telling Mira when it was time to come up for dinner, standing with one hand on the door, looking impatient.

She was jealous that Mira had a dad at all.

It was hot. Even the pool was too hot to give much relief, not that Dea would have swum or even known how. Instead, Mira had the idea to drag a lawn chair into the pool house, next to the foosball table, where there was a fan. At some point, they fell asleep, lying next to each other in their shorts and T-shirts, their feet just touching.

And Dea found herself walking down a narrow stone corridor, open to the air on both sides and half collapsed, as in a castle gone to ruin. As she moved forward, the stone shifted and re-formed into individual doorways.

Later, she learned from her mom that this wasn't uncommon. The dreamer, sensing an intrusion, builds walls, buildings, sometimes whole cities, to prevent the strange element, the walker, from getting in—kind of like the body releases white blood cells to the site of an infection.

But Mira's mind wasn't very practiced, and so Dea passed easily through one of the doorways and ended up in the open, standing on a vivid stretch of green grass. Walking someone else's dream was like moving through a stranger's house. Everything was unfamiliar, and Dea knew instinctively not to disturb or touch anything.

On a tennis court several hundred feet away, Mira was playing. She was running back and forth on legs that were both strong and straight, and each time her racquet connected with the ball, there was a satisfying *thwack*. Then, midair, each ball turned into a bird and soared away. Soon there were dozens of birds, circling overhead, as though waiting for something.

Even at six, Dea knew that she was trespassing on something very private.

All at once the birds converged and became an enormous kite, so large it blotted out the sky. Then the court was swallowed in shadow and she knew it was time to wake up.

Outside the little pool house, it was raining. And for the first time in Dea's life, her heart was beating normally.

Her mom knew what she'd done. At the time, Dea didn't think that was strange. She was *Mom*. She knew everything. She knew how to make the perfect chicken soup by adding cream and tomato to a can of Campbell's. She knew how to catch a single raindrop on her tongue. She knew mirrors and open water were bad, and clocks were good.

That day, Miriam sat at the kitchen table, gripping a mug of tea so tightly Dea could see individual veins in her hand, and explained the rules of walking.

The first rule, which Dea had already intuited, was that she must never try to change anything or intervene in another person's dream.

The second rule, related to the first, was that she might walk as many dreams as she wished if she was careful, and followed all the rules, but she must never walk the same person's dreams more than once.

And the third rule was that she must never, ever be seen.

Her mother explained other things, too—that birds were harbingers and would serve as guides, that mirrors and water were places where the boundary between the worlds was the thinnest, that clocks would keep them safe from the other side—but Dea had barely listened, so disappointed was she by the list of rules, especially the fact that she was forbidden from entering Mira's dreams again.

"Why can't I go back?" Dea had asked.

Dea's mom reached out and took Dea's chin. "I won't let them find you," she said. Her eyes were very wide; she was looking at Dea as if trying to beam a secret message to her, and Dea knew her mom was afraid.

Then *Dea* was afraid. "Who?" she asked, although she felt she already knew the answer.

"The monsters," Miriam said simply.

THREE

At six o'clock and every six hours afterward, even on Saturday, the clocks started. First a half dozen, then a few more, then a handful more. Dea and her mom had more than two dozen clocks, at last count, many of them fitted with chimes and bells, gongs and whistles. Miriam liked them, said they comforted her. She liked how they pulled her into morning with a song of gears and mechanics.

Dea was used to them. The clocks had come with them to all the houses they'd lived in. Often, Dea managed to sleep through them. Today she was jerked awake and, for one confused second, couldn't remember where she was, which house, in which town, in which part of the country. As soon as the last clock stopped chattering, she rolled over, pulled the sheet over her head, and went back to sleep: deep and dreamless, like always. Like how she imagined it would be to swim, to sink into dark water.

When she woke up again, sun was streaming through the paper blinds. It was after eleven a.m. She could hear her mom padding around the kitchen downstairs. She loved that about this house: the space, the sense of separation. She hated Fielding, and missed living in cities like Chicago and even Houston—but there they'd lived on top of each other, sometimes sharing a single bedroom.

She pulled on clothes without paying attention to what she was wearing, then moved to the closet and extracted a small mirror from behind the jumble of sneakers and boots and flip-flops worn down to paper. Her mom allowed absolutely no mirrors in the house. Whenever they moved, the first thing Miriam did was dismantle the bathroom cabinets. Dea had a growing collection of forbidden mirrors, all purchased from yard sales: tarnished silver handhelds, makeup compacts obscured with a thick coat of ancient powder. Sometime in the spring she'd told Gollum in passing that she collected mirrors, and for Dea's birthday Gollum had presented her with a pretty chrome handheld, obviously antique, so heavy it hurt Dea's bicep to lift it. Dea had nearly cried, especially since she knew Gollum's family had hardly any money.

"Don't worry," Gollum had said, in that ridiculous way she had of being able to read Dea's mind. "I stole it."

She was kidding, obviously. Dea was embarrassed and humbled by Gollum's generosity, especially since for Gollum's birthday Dea had just gotten her a leopard-print Snuggie (to be fair, Gollum was obsessed with Snuggies, or at least the idea of them). The chrome mirror, along with the picture of her father displayed in the living room, was one of the few physical possessions she actually cared about.

She checked her reflection. Hair: enormous. Skin: clear. Her one good feature. Eyes: pale blue, the color of ice. She made a monster face, then put away the mirror.

"Feeling better?" her mother said, as soon as she came downstairs. As usual, Miriam could tell that Dea had walked.

"A little." Dea nudged Toby out of the way and moved toward the coffeepot.

A week earlier she'd pocketed a cheap plastic hair clip Shawna McGregor had left on a bench after gym. She knew it would be difficult to use—the best doorway objects were the ones that were cherished and closely guarded, like jewelry or wallets. Her mom speculated that it had something to do with the way that the mind transforms the objects we love best into extensions of the body. Touching someone's favorite necklace was nearly as good as holding hands—and made it so much easier to get in.

The night before, she'd had to grip the hair clip for nearly an hour before she could push her way into Shawna's dream.

She'd been in and out relatively quickly, before the dream had time to change. It was a dream of a standard basement party, the kind of gathering that Dea had never experienced in real life—lots of sweat and bodies packed close and plastic cups, as boring as she'd always imagined parties like that would be, filled not just with the standard assortment of high school kids but also with strangers, including a boy who looked like he'd stepped out of a fairy tale. Maybe he had. Maybe he was Shawna's Prince Charming.

Hanging back behind one of the walls of the overstructure—a decaying castle hung with moth-eaten tapestries and pictureless frames—Dea had watched him, drawn to him without exactly knowing why. His hair was a dark tangle and fell to his jaw. He was tan, as if he'd spent a long time in the sun, and wearing strange clothes and an old-fashioned belt fitted with a knife. And while everyone else was dancing to an inaudible current of music, he was perfectly still—observing, just like Dea was, as if somehow the rules of Shawna's imagination didn't apply to him.

Then, suddenly, he started to turn toward her. Dea had ducked quickly away.

Dea's mom came over and gave her a squeeze. Even through layers of clothing, Dea could feel how thin her mom was.

"What about you?" Dea said.

"I'm fine." Miriam pulled away and reached for the coffeepot.

"You look tired." Miriam looked worse than tired, but Dea didn't want to say so. Her skin was so pale, Dea could see individual veins running through her wrists and neck. Her eyes—big and beautiful, the color of storm clouds—looked huge in the narrow hollow of her face.

Dea's mother walked dreams too. Dea had known that since she had known what walking dreams was, but Miriam hardly spoke of it except in generalities. Dea had asked her once whether her grandparents had walked too, thinking it might be some genetic aberration. But Miriam just said no and Dea didn't press it. That was another thing they hardly ever spoke about: family, or why they didn't have any, and where they'd all gone.

The single picture of her father, positioned prominently on top of the living room mantel, was a snapshot from probably twenty years earlier, when he was young and wearing a cheesy red polo shirt and laughing, petting a dog. She didn't know if it was his dog or her mom's, or when the photo was taken, or where. In some ways she didn't like to ask, because then it would ruin her ability to imagine.

And she did imagine. A lot. That he'd been a firefighter who'd perished heroically during 9/11. That he worked for the CIA and had been captured during a dangerous mission, but would someday reappear, having escaped from prison using only a pair of tweezers. That he'd been framed for a crime he didn't commit and would remain hidden until he could clear his name.

Anything but the suspicion that crept up on her sometimes, surprised her when she wasn't paying attention: that he'd simply gotten tired of them, and walked out.

"Are you sure you're okay?" Dea asked. She knew that her mom went as long as she could between walks, until she was so sick she could barely stand.

"I'm positive. Let me do the worrying, Dea." Her mom finished pouring the coffee, and added exactly three seconds' worth of milk. "Coffee?"

"In a minute." She sat down at the table and reached absent-mindedly for the newspaper, which trumpeted headlines about record heat and a murder all the way down in Aragansett County. She felt good. It was Saturday and sunny and she had forty-eight hours before she had to be back in school.

"I was reading that," her mom said quickly, moving to stop her.

It was too late. Several real estate brochures slipped out from between the folds of the paper. Each of them featured nearly identical pictures of happy-ever-after-type families: Greenville, North Carolina. Tullahoma, Tennessee. St. Paul, Minnesota.

Dea's whole body went cold. "What is this?" Dea pushed back from the table, as if the brochures might come alive and bite her. "What are these?"

Dea's mother was stirring her coffee. She didn't look up. "There's no need to shout, Dea," she said. "I'm just looking."

"You said no more moving." Dea's stomach rolled into her throat. The blond-haired teenage boy on the cover of *St. Paul, Minnesota*, smirked at her.

"You don't even like it here," her mom said.

"I won't like it there, either," Dea said. It was the same every-where; she knew that by now. New kids, same old rumors. At least here she had Gollum. Weirdly, the new boy's face flashed in her mind—the way it had transformed when he smiled. "I mean, come on. Minnesota?"

"I said, I'm just looking." Finally, Dea's mom looked up. Her eyes were signaling a warning. But Dea didn't care.

"You promised," she said. She stood up, feeling shaky. "You absolutely swore—"

"Things change." Miriam cut Dea off, slamming her coffee cup down on the counter, so a little liquid sloshed over the rim. They stood in silence, glaring at each other. Then she sighed. "Listen, Dea," she said. "Nothing's certain yet, okay? It's all preliminary."

"I won't do it," Dea said. "You can't make me."

"Of course I can," Miriam said, frowning a little. "There are things you don't understand, Dea. Things much too complicated for you to—"

There was a sharp knock on the front door. Miriam jumped; Dea, too. Toby began to yowl. No one ever came to the front door, except for the Domino's guy and sometimes a Jesus freak pushing repentance and offering to sell a bible for $3.99. Gollum and Dea met every morning at the gate, and said good-bye every afternoon there too.

"Who is that?" Miriam looked almost afraid. She quickly shuffled the brochures back under the newspaper, as if they were evidence of a crime. Which, to Dea, they were. "You're not expecting anyone, are you?"

Dea didn't bother to answer. She was still furious.

Toby followed her down the hall. She pinned him against the wall with a foot so he wouldn't run out, and then unlocked all three locks. She hadn't bothered to look out the window. She knew it would be a Bible thumper.

But it was Connor.

"Hi." He lifted a hand and waved, even though they were standing only about a foot away from each other.

Dea was so shocked that for a moment, she nearly said *go away*, which is what she would have said to a Bible guy. Toby wiggled away from her and darted out onto the porch. Connor bent down and grabbed hold of him.

"Not so fast, little guy," he said.

"Thanks," Dea said, when Connor passed Toby back, holding him delicately, as if Toby might shatter. When she turned around to place him back in the house, she saw a quick movement down the hall: her mother, retreating into the kitchen. Dea stepped out onto the porch, closing the door, so her mother couldn't stand there and gape—so Connor wouldn't accidentally get a view of a dozen clocks and the faded silhouettes of mirrors removed from the wall, too.

"What do you want?" she said, which sounded rude, but it was too late to take it back.

"Happy Saturday to you, too," Connor said, but nicely, as a joke. Dea thought he was expecting her to say something but didn't know what. "Um . . . can I come in?"

"No," she said. She wished suddenly she'd paid more attention to her outfit. She was wearing flip-flops, ragged cut-off shorts that revealed the paleness of her legs and the smattering of freckles on her thighs, and a faded blue T-shirt with a Mr. Clean logo stretching directly across her boobs. She hadn't even brushed her teeth. "So what's up?" She crossed her arms and tried not to breathe too hard.

Connor smiled wide. She wondered whether his smile was like a negotiation technique, to get people to say yes to him. She wondered whether it worked with other girls. "I thought you might want to hang out," he said easily. "Give me a tour. Show me the Fielding sights."

"Trust me," she said. "There's nothing to see."

He shrugged. "I thought you might want to hang out anyway."

For a split second, Dea felt as if she must still be walking a dream. Boys like Connor—good-looking, sporty, prom-court kind of boys—weren't nice to girls like Dea. It was a fundamental rule of nature, the same way that panthers didn't get chummy with groundhogs unless they were hunting for their next meal. Any second Connor's face would fracture and he'd turn into her math teacher. Or the scene would dissolve, and the front porch would turn into a rolling ocean, and Connor would disappear entirely.

But no. Connor was still there, on her porch, looking extra boy: old jeans and worn black Chucks and a band T-shirt, his hair a little messy, his smile a little crooked, definitely the cutest boy who had ever spoken to her or stood close enough that she could smell the fact that he was chewing gum.

"I don't know anyone else," he said, almost apologetically.

"What about your cousin?" she said.

He made a face. "I hate that guy. Always have. Do you know when we were kids he used to amputate frogs' legs for fun?"

"That's sick," Dea said, although she wasn't surprised. Last year, Will Briggs had shoved Carl Gormely into a gym locker and left him there for a whole day. The janitor finally let him out when he was making rounds after school and heard banging.

"Tell me about it." Connor was looking at her with an expression she couldn't decipher. "Come on. What do you say?"

She wondered, then, what kind of dreams he had. They were probably sun-drenched and happy, full of pinwheeling flowers and girls in bikinis and rivers of Coors Light. Normal dreams.

She half suspected this was some kind of trick. And she knew, definitely knew, that it couldn't last.

But maybe, just for a day, it wouldn't hurt to pretend.

"I'll get the keys," she said.

Dea's first real crush was on a guy named Brody Dawes, back in Arizona. All the sixth-grade girls liked Brody. He was in eighth grade and had long sandy hair he was always sucking into his mouth, especially during tests. He skateboarded to school every day and carried around a dingy army-style backpack covered with patches for bands no one had ever heard of. When he wasn't sucking on his hair or a pen cap, he was picking at one of the patches, looking bored. He always kept his backpack in his lap, like he was ready to make a quick exit.

One day, Dea sat behind him at a schoolwide assembly. She hadn't planned it that way. She was sandwiched in the very back row of the risers when he came and plopped down right in front of her. His friends soon joined him and for forty-five minutes she sat motionless, afraid to move or even breathe, afraid he might turn around and tell her to leave. When he stood up, she saw that one of his patches had fallen off his backpack: red and black with the words *Turkey Army* embroidered on it. She pretended to be tying her shoelaces and pocketed it.

Getting into his dream was easy. His mind barely put up defenses at all—just a series of curtains, many of them torn, fluttering as though in a breeze. Just beyond the line of flimsy fabric was a patchy yard and a cheap, aboveground pool. It was the kind of sunlight that exists only in dreams: it came from every direction at once, so it felt like being on the wrong side of a magnifying glass.

He was in the pool, not more than two feet away from Dea, shirtless. She could have threaded her hand past the curtains and touched his shoulders or run her fingers through his hair. She could have climbed into the pool with him. She could have leaned over and pressed her lips to his, like she'd seen Mishti Barns and Mark Spencer do every morning before homeroom. She wanted to, desperately.

But it was against the rules.

The water broke and Hillary Davis surfaced soundlessly, looking even better than she did in real life. Her skin was golden and her teeth were the white of bleached bone. Her hair shimmered in the sun and her boobs floated like overturned cups on the water.

Then they were kissing. Dea stood there, not two feet away, mesmerized. She could hear the suction sound of their lips and the lapping of their tongues and the whisper of his fingers on her back and shoulders. She stayed there until the curtains became iron walls and she knew Brody was waking up. She had just enough time to slip out of the dream before she felt a sudden, jolting pressure in her chest and she was back in her room, in her body, touching her lips with one cold hand.

Still, to this day, Dea had never been kissed.

FOUR

The Donahue house was a good seven miles outside the commercial center of Fielding. On the way toward town, Dea spotted Gollum riding her ancient Schwinn. Dea jerked the car off the road, sending Connor careening against the passenger-side window.

"Thanks for the warning," he said. But he laughed.

"Sorry," Dea said. Gollum spotted Dea's car and came to a stop by dragging her feet, kicking up a cloud of pale dust. She didn't get off her bike but stood up, straddling it, gripping the handlebars.

Gollum was dressed in her typical style: an assortment of

clothes no doubt inherited from one of her older brothers, which she'd tucked and pinned and rolled so that they would at least somewhat fit. Her blond hair was pulled back, but a crown of wisps had escaped from her ponytail, giving her the look of a deranged angel. For the shortest second, Dea was embarrassed by her and wished she hadn't stopped. Then, furious with herself, she rolled down the window as Gollum looked up, her eyes practically shooting out of her head.

"Connor," she said. "This is my friend, Gollum." She pronounced the word *friend* emphatically, still angry at herself for her moment of mental treachery. "Gollum, this is Connor. He's the one who just moved in."

Gollum stooped down to peer past Dea. Her mouth opened, and then closed. Dea had never seen Gollum speechless before.

Luckily, Connor took the lead. He leaned over the center console, his shoulder bumping Dea's. "Gollum," he said. "Cool name."

"Thanks," she said, still staring at him. "Cool . . . face."

Connor burst out laughing. Gollum turned roughly the color of beet juice.

"Sorry," she said. "My mouth isn't always hooked up to my brain."

Dea reached out and squeezed Gollum's hand. She was filled with a sudden sense of warmth. She was driving in the car with a boy who had a cool face, and her friend—they *were* friends, even if they didn't really hang out outside of school—was standing there, blushing, and the whole scene felt like it could have been lifted straight out of any teen movie.

Which made her, Dea, the star.

"That's okay," Connor said. "Neither is mine."

Once again, Dea had a momentary suspicion that Connor must be tricking them. Or maybe he was secretly a freak. Maybe he was hiding a third and fourth nipple, or a secret *Star Wars* addiction.

"Want a ride somewhere?" Dea asked. "You can throw your bike in the back."

Gollum made a face. "I gotta go home. Besides, the Beast would never fit." She patted the handlebars.

"I'm getting the grand tour of Fielding," Connor said, still smiling.

Gollum's face had returned to its normal color. She shoved her glasses up the bridge of her nose with a thumb. "Should be the most mediocre five minutes of your life," she said, and thumped Dea's door. "Have fun. Don't forget to swing by the dump. It's one of Fielding's most scenic attractions." When Connor wasn't looking, she mouthed, *Oh my God* and did the bug-eyed thing again.

Now Dea was the one blushing.

Gollum wasn't exaggerating: It took approximately four minutes to get from one end of Fielding to the other. The commercial district was just two intersecting roads and a heap of buildings in various stages of decay. On Main Street there were two gas stations, a church, a liquor store, a hair salon, a fried chicken spot, a mini-mart, and a mega-mart. On Center Street was a diner, a pharmacy (now shuttered), a 7-Eleven, another liquor store, and Mack's, the only bar in town, which everyone always referred to by its full name, Mack's Center Street, as if there were another somewhere else. Two miles past Center

35

Street, after a quick patchwork of fields and farms and houses that were falling slowly into the dirt, was the Fielding School, serving grades kindergarten to dropout.

They didn't even have a Walmart. For that, you had to drive all the way to Bloomington.

"Voilà," she said to Connor when they reached the Fielding School. The parking lot was mostly empty. In the distance, she spotted a bunch of guys from the football team running drills. "Tour complete. What do you think?"

"I think the mega-mart was my favorite," Connor said. "But the mini-mart's a close second." One thing that was nice about Connor: he didn't fidget. He was way too tall for Dea's mom's car, another simulacrum: an exact replica of the original VW Beetle, with its engine in the back and everything. Even though Connor was squished in the front seat, knees practically to his chest, he looked perfectly relaxed. He didn't even press Dea about the fact that the rearview mirror was blacked out with masking tape, even though she'd had an excuse ready: the glass had shattered and they were waiting on parts to replace it.

"I told you there was nothing to see," Dea said.

"Depends on your perspective," Connor said, looking at her in a way that made her suddenly nervous. She put the car in drive again, and rumbled slowly out of the parking lot. Plumes of red dust came up from the tires. The sun was so bright, it was hard to see. She was glad, at least, that the air conditioner was the modern kind.

"So. Anything I should know about F.S.? Trade secrets? Words of warning?" he asked.

"All schools are pretty much the same," Dea said. "Don't

backtalk the teacher. Don't touch the hot lunch. Try to stay awake during history."

He laughed. He had a great laugh—just like his smile, it made him about a thousand times more attractive. "You been to a lot of schools?"

"Half a dozen." Actually, she'd been enrolled at ten different schools, and lived in twelve different states. But no point in launching into a monologue about it. "My mom likes to move around," she added, when he made a face. "How about you?"

He hesitated for a fraction of a second. "My dad got laid off," he said. "My uncle—that's Will's dad—is a cop down here. He hooked him up with a landscaping job. Dad was a teacher before. My stepmom has some family nearby."

So the woman she'd seen unpacking was his stepmom. Dea waited for him to mention his real mom but he didn't, so she didn't press.

He was quiet for a minute and Dea started to panic. She couldn't think of anything to say. Then he blurted out, "It's too open here. Too much sky." Almost immediately, he laughed again. "I guess I'm used to the city."

She knew exactly what he meant—the sky was like a big mouth, hanging open, ready to swallow you whole. But she just said, "Where'd you move from?"

"Chicago," he said.

"I lived in Chicago for a while," she said. "Lincoln Park."

He turned to look out the window. "That's where we lived," he said. Then, "Where to now?"

She got a flush of pleasure. *Don't trust it*, a voice, her logical voice, piped up quickly. *You know you'll only be disappointed.*

Maybe not, another voice said stubbornly. *Maybe he's got those four nipples after all.*

It was so absurd: she was actually hoping that the boy next to her had extra nipples.

"We could go to Cincinnati," she said. "It's only two hours." She was joking, of course. But Connor's reflection, overlaid across a plain of brown and gray, smiled. "Drive on," he said.

Dea found it easy—almost too easy—to open up to Connor. In less than an hour, she'd told Connor more than she'd told anyone in years—way more than she'd ever told Gollum. They shared likes and dislikes, words neither of them could stand to hear, like *cream* and *moisture.* They'd hopscotched from Dea's love of old junk to her hatred of bananas to the months she'd spent living next to a military base in Georgia. Her mom had a boyfriend then, the only boyfriend she remembered.

"So it's just you and your mom, then?" Connor asked. She appreciated that he didn't just straight-up ask her about her dad. Not that she would have anything to say, except *he looks good in a red polo shirt.*

She nodded. "What about you?" she said. "No siblings?"

A muscle twitched in Connor's jaw. "No. Used to, though." His fingers drummed against the dashboard, the first time he had shown any sign of discomfort. Dea tried to think of something to say, words of comfort or a question about what had happened, but then he was smiling again and the moment, the impression of past pain, was gone. "You really hate bananas?"

Dea felt vaguely disappointed, as if she'd missed an opportunity. "Despise them," she said.

"Even banana bread?"

"Even worse." She made a face. "Why ruin bread by putting banana in it? It's like a banana sneak attack. I like them out in the open, where I can see them."

He laughed and chucked her chin. "You're a piece of work, Donahue." But the way he said it made it sound like a compliment.

Connor plugged in his iPhone and played her some of his favorite songs—stuff by Coldplay and the Smiths, plus a bunch of songs from bands she'd never heard of—but he never stopped talking over the music. He didn't like the color red ("too obvious"), or raw onions ("it's texture, not taste"), or highways. "They look the same everywhere," he said. "Back roads are way more interesting. They have flavor. Except," he quickly added, "for this beautiful highway, of course."

He gestured out the window; they were passing an industrial farm. Dea knew only one way of driving to Cincinnati, on IN-46. The view had been the same since they'd left Fielding. The three *F*s: farms, flatlands, firearm ranges.

Connor had been a swimmer in Chicago and was "decent—good for state, not good enough to go national." He hated football and mozzarella cheese ("it's like weird alien skin"). He believed in ghosts—really believed. Scientifically.

"Are you serious?" Dea couldn't help but say.

He spread his hands wide. *"There are more things on heaven and earth, Horatio, than are dreamt of in your philosophy."* She was impressed that he'd memorized a Shakespeare quote, and didn't want to tell him she disagreed. There were plenty of things that were dreamed about, more things than you'd believe.

He'd been a vegetarian for four years, which was weird, because he didn't seem like one. When she asked him about it, he shrugged and said, "I really like dogs."

"We don't eat dogs," she pointed out.

"Exactly," he said cryptically. "Anyway, I'm not vegetarian anymore. One day I went crazy at a steak buffet. It wasn't pretty." He had to rearrange his whole body to turn and look at her. He reminded her of a puppet whose strings aren't working all together. "What about you?"

"I'm not vegetarian," she said.

"No." He laughed. "I meant what about you? Weird quirks? Dark secrets?"

For a split second, she thought of confessing: *I walk other people's dreams. I get sick if I don't. Mom is afraid of things I don't understand. That's why three locks. That's why no mirrors. She's probably nuts, and I might be nuts like her.*

"I don't have any," she said.

Something flickered behind his eyes—an expression gone too soon for her to name. "Everyone has dark secrets," he said.

They went on a hunt for billboards. The weirder the sign, the better. She got three points for spotting LAVENDER'S: INDI-ANA'S LARGEST EMPORIUM FOR XXX TOYS, VIDEOS, AND POSTERS. Connor got a point for THE FIREWORKS FACTORY and two points for a faded billboard featuring an enormous Jesus on the cross and the words: MEET JESUS FACE-TO-FACE! In smaller letters: RESULTS NOT GUARANTEED.

They'd crossed over the Ohio border when Connor shouted. Dea nearly drove off the road.

"Pull over, pull over!" he said, so she did, barely making the exit. A big billboard, faded from the weather, was staked into the dirt: OHIO'S LARGEST CORN MAZE. In the distance, she saw it: golden walls of corn, stretching toward the horizon.

"Really?" she said.

He was still gazing at the sign, enraptured. "It's the largest, Dea. We have to." He turned to her and put a hand on her thigh just for a second. Her heart went still. But then his hand was gone, and her heart started hammering again, even though she'd walked a dream the night before.

The last time Dea had been in a maze of any kind was in Florida. That one was made of walls; it was part of an amusement park called Funville, which was only thirty miles from Disney World but smaller and older and cheaper, the dollar store equivalent of the amusement park industry. Dea's mom hated crowds but she loved mazes because they reminded her of dreams: that same twisty kind of logic, the same sense of being suspended in time, moving forward without moving forward at all. She especially loved the maze at Funville, which was all white, made from cheap plastic studded with glitter so it looked kind of like snow, especially if you lived in Florida and didn't see snow very often. In Dea's memory, the white walls were the size of skyscrapers.

Dea and Connor climbed out of the car. Dea had been expecting a crowd but there was no one around—no parents and kids rushing in and out of the maze. The ticket booth was padlocked and marked with a sign that said CLOSED. There was just a bleached fence and a gap in the corn where the maze began, and the high white sun staring down impassively.

At least it was cooler inside the maze. The ground was dark

with shadows. Connor suggested they race to the center. Dea quickly agreed. She didn't know if it was the heat or the maze or Connor, but she was feeling a little dizzy, almost drunk, like the time at Christmas in Houston when her mom made eggnog with too much rum and let her have a full cup, and they ended up outside in their bikinis, tanning until the sun went down, and she woke up with a headache and a slick tongue and a bad sunburn.

"On your mark, get set, go!" he shouted.

After a single turn, she'd lost sight of him. Two more turns and she couldn't hear anything but the occasional gust of wind through the dry corn. Another two turns and she hit a dead end. She backtracked quickly. Her heart was going hard, skipping a beat here and there, then trying to compensate, spilling together into a constant thrum. It was too quiet. Even the clouds had stopped moving.

She was seized by irrational fear: what if, somehow, this was all still a part of Shawna McGregor's dream? What if she had never woken up? What if the conversation with her mom and seeing Connor and all of it was just a subplot, a random spool unraveling in Shawna's brain? Maybe this was the part where Connor disappeared and instead she found herself alone in a maze with Morgan Devoe or Keith, the bus driver. Or maybe no one would come. Maybe the sky would start melting and the corn would fall down around her like a series of dominoes.

She knew it was stupid, but she couldn't shake the idea. It was so bright. She started running. She hit another dead end. Not a whisper of breeze. She forced herself not to call out Connor's name. If it was a dream, it would end eventually. All dreams ended.

She didn't want it to be a dream, though.

She turned a corner and ran straight into Connor. Same T-shirt, same smile, same hair falling over his eyes. Not a dream, then. She nearly grabbed him to check.

"I found you," he said.

"I found *you*," she corrected him. "I guess we tie." She realized they'd made it to the very center of the maze. The sun was almost directly above them.

If Connor noticed how hard she was breathing, he was too nice to mention it.

"If I ever needed a place to hide out, I'd come here," he said, as they wound their way back to the parking lot.

She raised an eyebrow—or tried to. Gollum was teaching her but she hadn't mastered it yet. "Are you planning to go on the run?"

"Think about it! A maze is even better than a moat. It's like a built-in security system. No one would ever find you."

"Except for the tourists," Dea said.

Connor grinned. "Yeah. Except for the tourists."

A few miles away from the corn maze, Dea spotted another billboard, this one just after a sign pointing the way to DeWitt: THE RAILROAD DINER: WORLD-FAMOUS MILKSHAKES.

"You hungry?" Connor asked.

"I don't have to be *hungry* for milkshakes," she said. "That's like asking if I feel like breathing."

They pulled over and got milkshakes (vanilla for him, strawberry for her). The diner looked like it had come straight out of a billion years ago. There was even an old cash register made of brass. The waitress, Carol, who seemed just as ancient as her surroundings, warmed to Connor right away and even let

43

him open the drawer and press a couple of the buttons when he asked. Dea realized that Connor was that kind of person. He could get away with anything. He belonged.

He made her feel like she belonged, too.

Next up was a fifteen-mile detour to Ohio's largest rubber ball.

"We're never gonna get to Cincinnati, you know," Dea said.

"It's the journey, not the destination," Connor said, making a fake guidance-counselor face. "And come on! Indiana's *largest rubber ball*." He tapped her thigh with every syllable. "How could we punk out on that?"

By the time Connor had finished snapping pictures at the Biggest Rubber Ball in Ohio—which, true to its name, was enormous—the sun had rolled off the center of the sky and the fields were striped with purple shadows. As they headed back to the car, a dusty minivan pulled into the parking lot and a family poured out: mom dad kid kid kid, all of them wearing some combination of visor and shorts and flip-flops. Dea imagined, briefly, what she and Connor must look like to them. They probably thought Connor was her boyfriend.

It was after three, and Dea knew they should turn around. But she didn't want to. She felt fizzy with happiness, like someone had uncorked a giant bottle of soda inside of her. For once, she was glad she didn't have a real cell phone, except for the crappy pay-as-you-go one she'd bought one winter with the savings she pocketed from scraping off people's windshields. Her mom didn't even know about it, which meant that she couldn't call Dea and bug her to get home.

Miriam owned nothing: no cell phone, no property, no bank account even. She kept all their money in bricks of cash, elastic-banded together, concealed in shoeboxes in her closet, stashed in the passenger seat of the car, camouflaged in a tampon box beneath the bathroom sink. (That was the emergency fund: when even the tampon box was empty, Dea knew, it was time to move.) The money came in spurts, like blood from a new wound, and Dea didn't ask where she got all of it, like she didn't ask why Miriam was so afraid and who Miriam thought they were running from.

"We're like wind," Miriam always used to say, running her fingers through Dea's hair. "Poof! We vanish. We disappear."

It had never occurred to her that someday Dea might grow up and wish instead to be visible. That she might want a cell phone and friends to call, apps and pictures and customizable ringtones. That was why Dea had bought the phone, even though it was plastic and cheap and she hated to bring it out in public and half the time she forgot to charge it: she wanted to feel like everybody else.

But for once, Dea wanted to do exactly what her mom always talked about: vanish. If no one knew where she was, maybe she wouldn't have to go back.

"Where to next?" she said. *Don't say home,* she tried to telegraph in his direction. *Anywhere but home.*

Connor's eyes clicked to the dashboard clock. "I bet we can still make it to Cincinnati and back before dark."

She put the car in gear. Her cheeks ached from smiling.

When they reached the outskirts of the city, Dea turned off the highway and onto local roads with no clear sense of where they were going. Houses clumped together, like water beading into a narrow stream: a blur of dingy white Cape Cods and low-rent trailers and patchy yards and garages fitted with old basketball nets. Connor spotted another sign, this one handmade on poster board, propped against a telephone pole: RUMMAGE SALE!! 249 WARREN, RIGHT ON ROUTE 9. SPORTING EQUIPMENT GOLF CHINA TOYS KITCHEN TOASTERS.

"Let's stop," Connor said. "Maybe I'll find an old toaster."

"You want a toaster?" she said.

Connor leaned over.

"Listen to me, Dea," he said solemnly, like he was about to recite a pledge. "You can never, ever, have too many toasters."

She laughed. "Freak," she said.

"Thank you," he said, still smiling, touching his fingers to an imaginary hat.

A dozen folding tables, the kind found in school cafeterias and at cheap weddings, were set out on the lawn in front of 249 Warren. Behind one of them, a girl a few years younger than Dea sat slumped in a lawn chair, punching her iPhone with a finger. Two barefoot kids made circles around the lawn, shrieking, smacking around a Wiffle ball. An overweight woman, sweating through her dark T-shirt, was manning a cash box and periodically yelling at them to stop. A dozen people, mostly women, were picking through plastic bins filled with old lamps and lunchboxes, picture frames and plastic toys, with the same attentiveness of children searching the beach for the best seashells.

"Jackpot," Connor said, gesturing toward one of the tables, where two rusted toasters were wedged next to an old microwave and a grimy coffee pot.

Dea felt a quick lift of happiness, like the soft rise of a moth's wings in her stomach.

She loved rummage sales—the strangeness of things grouped together that didn't make sense: children's clothes next to old smutty paperbacks next to kitchen equipment next to lawn mowers, like a long and glorious sentence full of mixed metaphors. She'd always liked to imagine belonging to a family that dug through its closets and basement and garage once a year, and carted up all the broken and stained and useless things, expelled them like a disease. Dad would complain about giving up his golf clubs; Mom would point out he never played. Little sister and brother would refuse to give up a beloved toy, even though it had long been retired to the bottom of a mothball-smelling trunk, underneath the winter sweaters.

If Dea and her mom had a rummage sale, practically everything they owned would fit in a single bin.

Connor pretended to be fascinated by the toasters, hamming it up to make Dea laugh and asking the heavy woman—who had succeeded in wrestling away the Wiffle ball from her younger children, and was trying to compel them to go wash up for dinner—questions about whether the toasters could be counted on to make toast crusty or just crunchy.

"Both. Neither. Whatever you want," she said, pushing her hair from her eyes with a wrist.

Dea picked a bin at random and began flipping through it, sifting through the kind of miscellany that accumulated at the bottom of kitchen junk drawers: coins, scissors, unopened cans of rubber cement. She found a knitted potholder shaped like a hen, soft and often handled, and she wondered briefly whether she should pocket it, use it as a door to get into the fat woman's dreams. But in the end she dropped it and moved on.

The next bin was full of random housewares: old whisks and lightly stained tablecloths, bronze candlesticks and a snow globe featuring a figurine of a topless girl in a grass skirt, who wiggled her hips as the snow came down. Hawaiian vacation, she decided, or maybe Florida. The mom had always hated it, and had finally convinced the dad to trash it, or had done it behind his back. *She's topless, Don. What message are we sending the kids?*

She shoved aside a tablecloth and froze. All of a sudden, she felt like she did in those floundering moments of dark and cold when she was fighting her way into someone's dream—as if she were falling, weightless, into nothing. For several long seconds, her heart didn't beat at all.

Two identical cheap laminate picture frames were stacked together at the bottom of the bin. Her father's smile beamed up at her from both of them, his teeth dentist-white above his red polo shirt. His dog was turned partly away from the camera, looking almost apologetic.

An advertisement. A stock photo used to sell cheap plastic frames. *Man Posing with German Shepherd.* How had she never seen it before?

The world came back in a blast of noise and heat. She could smell the bubble gum the girl with the iPhone was chewing, the booze-breath of the man rifling through an assortment of cutlery next to her, charcoal smoke on the air, sweat. She was going to be sick.

What had Miriam said when Dea had asked her what Dad's dog was named?

I don't remember. Then: *Daisy, I think.*

She thought of the other things her mother had told her

over the years, vague references to her father's importance, to his severity, to his sense of duty. Nothing specific—but ideas, suggestions that Dea had clung to for years, trying to wring meaning from them.

Lies. All lies.

"Find anything good?" Connor was behind her. She dropped the photos quickly, and shoved the tablecloth on top of them, as if they needed to be smothered.

"No," she said. Little spots of color flickered in the edges of her vision. Her heart had lost its rhythm entirely. "I need to go."

Connor's face got worried. "Is everything okay?"

"Fine." She couldn't stand to look at him. She started speed-walking toward the car. "I just have to get home, that's all."

Connor caught up to her quickly. His legs were much longer than hers. For a moment, he was quiet. "Did something happen?"

"I told you, no." More seconds when her heart cut out totally, like a song interrupted by a power outage. Then a sudden flare and it was pounding high in her throat.

"Because you seemed happy, and then all of a sudden—"

"You don't know me," she said. She knew she was acting like a crazy person, but she didn't care. She *was* a crazy person. It was genetic, inherited. All lies. He might as well know it. "You don't know whether I'm happy or not."

That made him shut up. They drove back to Fielding, all one hundred and thirty-two miles, in silence.

FIVE

The light was long gone by the time Dea reached Connor's house. Through the windows, she could see his dad and stepmom moving around the dining room table, clearing away boxes, occasionally stopping for a kiss. There was a tight belt of fury across her chest.

"Listen." Connor spoke for the first time since they left the yard sale. "If I did something to, I don't know, piss you off—"

"You didn't." She willed him out of the car, sick with jealousy, sick with guilt. It wasn't his fault. Obviously, it wasn't.

"All right." Connor sounded tired, or maybe disgusted. He got out of the car without another word—*see you later* or *that was fun* or *thanks for the tour*—and at the last second she had to force herself not to call out after him.

She jerked the car into her driveway, climbed out, and slammed the door so hard it rattled. Good. She hoped the whole piece of shit fell apart. An illusion on top of an illusion.

It took her a few tries to get the key into the first lock. Her fingers were shaking, her heart still doing its jerky dance in her chest: she pictured valves opening and shutting desperately like the mouth of a dying fish. She slammed the front door, too.

"Dea? Is that you?" her mom called out, as if it could be anyone else.

Thick as thieves, Miriam always said, putting her face right up to Dea's, nose to nose—practically mirror images.

She'd been lying forever.

"I didn't think you'd be out so late. Did you remember to lock the door?" Miriam was sitting in the rented living room, on a rented leather sofa, listening to music on the crappy rented stereo. She straightened up when she saw Dea's face. Her mug of tea had left rings on the rented coffee table. They might as well just be renting space on this planet. "Dea? Is everything okay?"

The photograph of the man who was supposed to be Dea's father was sitting on the mantel above the defunct fireplace. Every time Dea and her mom moved, Miriam made a big show of swaddling the photograph, safe, at the bottom of her suitcase. *So it won't break,* she always said. And then, when they got to their new place, still smelling of paint and plaster or maybe of the old tenant, like cat urine and burnt coffee, she removed it carefully again, untucking it like a baby from a diaper. *Do you want to find a place to put Dad, Dea?*

Dea was across the room before she knew she was moving.

She grabbed the picture from the mantel.

"Dea?" her mom repeated. Then, more sharply, when she saw what was in her hands: "Dea."

"Tell me about this photo, Mom," Dea said, struggling to keep her voice steady.

Miriam's eyes went wary, watchful, like the eyes of a wild animal when you get too close. "What do you mean?"

"I mean, I want to know the story. Where were you?"

"Oh." Her mother pronounced the word exactly. *Oh*. If she were smoking, a perfect ring would be on its way to the ceiling. "It was a long time ago."

"What were you wearing?" she said. "Whose idea was it to pose?"

Miriam's hand fluttered to her hair, then returned to her lap. "It was your father's idea, I think. Really, I can't remember. . . ."

"Why this picture, and only this picture?" White spots were eating the edges of her vision and her heart was stopping for whole blank seconds, stretches of silence when her body hung, suspended, between alive and not. One time when Dea hadn't walked a dream for a month she felt just like this; she collapsed in the bus as she stood up to get off at her stop. She was hospitalized for two days and got better only after she stole a nurse's crucifix and pushed into a dream, hot and disorganized, of hospital rooms and babies crying behind every door.

"Your father didn't like photographs," her mother said. There was an edge to her voice now. "I don't understand the point of all these questions."

"The point, Mom, is that you're a liar." The words came out in a quick rush and left Dea feeling queasy—like throwing up when you really didn't want to. "This isn't my dad. This isn't anyone. This is some random picture of some cheesy model you found in some cheesy discount store."

For a second Miriam stared—white-faced, almost sullen. Then she cleared her throat and folded her hands on her lap, one on top of the other.

"All right," she said calmly. That was the worst: how calm she was. Dea desperately wished her mother would yell. Then she could yell too, do something with the anger that was clawing its way into her throat. "You got me."

Just those three words. *You got me.*

Before Dea could regret it, she hurled the photograph across the room. Her mom screamed. The glass shattered. The frame thudded to the ground.

"God, Dea." Now her mom *was* shouting. "Jesus. You nearly gave me a heart attack."

"You. Lied. To. Me." Dea could barely get the words out.

"I had to." Miriam sounded impatient, as if Dea was the one being unreasonable. "There are things you don't understand, Dea. I've told you over and over. . . . There are things you'll never understand. . . ." She turned away. "And it wasn't all a lie. Not all of it. Your father was—is—a very powerful man."

Dea ignored that part. More lies, probably, to make her feel better. "Oh yeah?" She crossed her mind. "So who is he? Some big shot lawyer? Some random guy you screwed?"

"Odea Donahue." Her mom's voice got very quiet. Dea knew she had gone too far, but she couldn't stop.

"I don't even know my real last name. Maybe Brody Dawes was right about you," she blurted out. "Maybe all those people in Arizona were right."

Her mom flinched, as if Dea had reached out and slapped her. But it was too late to take the words back so Dea just stood there, breathing hard, fighting the desperate open-shut feeling in her chest, pressing down the guilt.

Her crush on Brody Dawes had ended when, halfway through sixth grade, she was shocked to hear Brody say her name. For a second, she nearly fainted from joy. Then she realized what he was saying. *Donahue's mom's a whore. She gives it out in the parking lot of the Quick-E-Lube.* No one could figure out how Dea's mom was making her money that year—she'd been laid off at the insurance office—and the rumor had spread quickly. It was a small town.

Miriam opened her mouth, then closed it again. Her whole face was like a scar: pinched and white. "Go to your room," she said, forcing the words out. Dea was grateful for the excuse. She couldn't stand to look at her mom anymore.

Upstairs, Dea tried once again to slam the door, to make a big statement, but the house was old and its joints swollen and instead she had to lean into the door just to get it to close. Toby looked up, blinking, from his position right in the middle of her pillow.

She lay down on the bed and let herself cry, feeling sorry for herself about everything, even the fact that Toby didn't move or lick her face, and instead just sat there purring like a motor on her pillow.

Practically, she knew it changed nothing. She'd never had a dad. But at least she'd been able to pretend. She had studied his image and cut-and-pasted it into memories so he was there, in the background, watching her tootle along on her three-wheeler in a cul-de-sac in Georgia; beaming from the front row when she won a spelling bee in second grade in Virginia; nodding with approval while she flew down a soccer field in New Jersey, the one and only time she had been stupid enough to join a sports team. She'd been Photoshopping her past, tweaking it, aligning it just a little more closely with normalcy.

Why would her mom lie—why would her mom spend years lying—unless her real father was horrible, a criminal or a drug addict or someone who trafficked kiddie porn? Unless Miriam didn't know herself. Dea had never seen her mom with a guy except for in Georgia, but that didn't mean anything. She remembered plenty of nights she'd woken, thinking she heard the muffled sound of the front door closing, as though her mom had been out and just reentered. And her mom spent hours out of the house every day, working shit jobs, and would still show up sometimes with wads of cash, take Dea on a shopping spree to the local mall, spend three, four hundred bucks, like it was nothing.

She felt cold and her head hurt, as it always did when she cried, like she'd somehow snotted out her brains. She shook her bag out on her comforter—bad idea, it was full of old coins and petrified pieces of gum, lint balls and crumpled receipts and, mysteriously, some sand—looking for a pack of tissues her mom always stole from drug stores while they were waiting to pay. (That was another thing about Miriam—Dea didn't feel like thinking of her as Mom anymore—she stole. Stupid things, little things, but still.)

Connor's iPhone had somehow ended up in her bag. She must have grabbed it and shoved it automatically into her bag when they'd stopped at the rummage sale. She reached for it slowly, as if it were a grasshopper that might bound away if startled. Phones made great doors. Pictures, texts, music—all of it was *personal*. Using his phone to walk would be like opening up his brain.

She knew she should go over to his house right away to return it, but she also knew she wouldn't be able to face him. Not yet. For the first time, she realized how shitty she'd been to him on the drive home. He was the first person who'd been nice to her in forever, and she'd totally screwed it up.

She swept the junk from her bed back into her bag, slapping the comforter to shake off some of the dirt. She shoved Toby over and he got up, yawning, before settling down again six inches from where he'd last been sitting. Then she turned off the lights and got under the covers, shorts and T-shirt and bra still on, not even bothering to wash her face or brush her teeth. She couldn't face going out into the hall, in case her mom decided to come upstairs. And she definitely wasn't going to eat dinner, even though she was starving. She hadn't eaten anything since the milkshake at the Railroad Diner in DeWitt.

Instead she lay in the dark, clutching Connor's iPhone, imagining it was a line that tethered her to him. She must have lain there in the darkness for at least an hour before she felt it—a softening of the boundaries of her body, and an opening, as though her bed had become a hole and she was dropping, or she was the hole and the world was dropping toward her. For a moment that could have been seconds or minutes or longer, she felt nothing but swinging, as if she wasn't a person any longer but just sensation and vertigo. This was the in-between space, an awful space, untouched by thought, where nothing could exist. From the time she had started walking she had been terrified that one day she would get stuck here.

Then there was a parting, as of a curtain, and Dea felt a soft sucking pressure on her skin and suddenly she *had* skin again, and ribs and lungs expanding inside of them. She came out of the dark like surfacing after being underwater and she was in. She'd made it.

She was in Connor's dream.

She was standing in an empty apartment. She recognized it right away as a hastily constructed overstructure, not an element of the dream, exactly, but Connor's instinctive response to her intrusion. The details weren't filled in. The furniture was missing, and there were soft petals of plaster drifting from the ceiling, as though the whole place were in danger of collapse. The windows were missing, too, although as she approached, panes grew up out of the empty sills; the glass knitted itself together elegantly, like ice forming over a pond. He was trying to keep her out.

She estimated she was on the third or fourth floor: across the way, she could see four- and five-story apartment buildings, wedged together, and lights in several windows. Christmas music was piping from somewhere, a tinny sound, like the music that gets played in Hallmark card stores. Chicago. She knew it right away. She could *feel* it, could feel it in the cold air that made the glass chatter ever so slightly and see it in the wind, which spiraled a plastic bag down the block and made the street signs sway.

Below her, a Lotto sign was blinking in a deli window.

Colored Christmas lights dangled limply from its blue awning. It was dusk—there was a faint red smear on the horizon, like a small cut in the fleshy clouds knitted across the sky—and the light had a strange charcoal quality, like a drawing that had gotten smudged. Then she realized it was snowing. But the flakes were dirty, gray looking, almost like ash.

She wondered where Connor was. She assumed he would appear soon on the street, blowing into his hands, maybe, or trying to catch a snowflake on his tongue when he thought no one was looking, and was surprised when instead he appeared in the window of the apartment directly across from her. She ducked quickly. She counted to thirty before she risked peeking over the windowsill again. He was gone. Instead, she could see a brown-haired woman—his mom? Not his stepmom, definitely—hanging ornaments on a Christmas tree. The room was warm looking, practically glowing, and Dea had a momentary suspicion that she was *supposed* to be serving as witness to this: to the perfection of it, the completeness. That Connor knew she was there, somehow, and wanted her to see. But she dismissed the idea just as quickly.

Before she could second-guess what she had come to do, and decide it was a really fucking stupid idea to break the rules, she found the stairs leading down to the street level. Her footsteps were very loud, as they often were in dreams: Connor's mind was too focused. He was zeroing in on the room, on his mom, on the ornaments. There weren't neighbors to shout or cars to honk or babies to cry.

Outside, it was a dream kind of cold: it didn't hurt, didn't knock Dea's breath from her chest or make her hands swell and stiffen. This, too, was because of Connor's focus. He wasn't putting enough energy into the world outside of his apartment. Her feet crunched on the accumulating snow as she jogged across the empty street. She kept glancing up at his window, paranoid that he might look outside and see her again.

That would be very bad. That was majorly against the rules. And even though she was technically, *technically*, about to break the rules, she didn't see how this would hurt. He wouldn't know she was responsible.

She stopped in front of the deli, stretched onto her tiptoes and curled her fingers around one end of the Christmas lights. One sharp pull, and they were down, blinking in her hand. She would have to hurry. She had no idea how long this dream would last. Any second, it might morph into something else, and she might find herself on a battlefield or in the middle of an ocean.

She knelt. Moisture seeped into her jeans. It gave her a small thrill. She loved the way Connor's unconscious mind expanded, reacted to her presence, pushed back and made things difficult.

It took her a while to get the Christmas lights just right. The wires were stiffer than she'd expected, and in the end she had just enough material to work with. She straightened up, her knees now aching and her shoulders sore. She imagined Connor moving to the window again and seeing the words she'd written out in blinking letters, nestled in all that gray snow.

I'm sorry.

SIX

She woke up to simulated church bells, one of her mom's favorite clocks sounding dolorously through the house. Sunday. The down part of the wave. The shore was hurtling toward her— Monday, seven thirty a.m., first bell—and she couldn't do anything to stop it.

Overnight, the seasons had shifted. Summer was gone. Rain was pounding the window, as if it were trying to get in, pasting blackened leaves against the glass like flattened palms. Dea could hear the wind, like the distant whistle of a teakettle, and the air was cold. The shimmer of gold was washed out of the fields, replaced by a dull, flat monochrome, a wet mulch-y color. When she went to the window, she could see Connor's dad make a quick dash from the front door to the car, sloshing through puddles, holding a paper over his head as a makeshift umbrella.

She pulled on jeans and her favorite sweatshirt, which she'd had since Chicago—even though there were now two fat holes at the elbows and a coffee stain by the hem—hoping it might serve as good luck. She finger-combed her hair. When she checked her reflection, she saw she looked good, rested and relaxed, and felt a brief moment of guilt. Sometimes she felt like a giant leech: she fed on other people's dreams.

She wasn't speaking to Miriam. She'd decided that, definitively, this morning. Since her mom was the primary person Dea talked to, it seemed like a drastic measure. But deserved. She didn't even want to *see* Miriam, but she was starving and she could already hear Miriam banging around in the kitchen, like she was trying to startle Dea into forgetting she was mad.

Dea's mom looked good, too—she looked as if she'd gained weight overnight. Her skin was smooth and her eyes were clear. Dressed in a big cashmere sweater and leggings and big socks, she looked like a model from a magazine about Healthy Mountain Living. She was almost through a plate of eggs. Dea knew that meant that Miriam had walked a dream the night before—her mom never ate in the mornings unless she had—and felt even more resentful. After their fight, after Dea had called her out on being a fraud, it was a direct reminder of how screwed up everything was.

Of how screwed up she, Dea, fatherless dream-walker, was.

"Dea?"

Dea didn't answer. She banged the cabinets loudly when she got her cereal, which she ate plain, shoveling it into her mouth with a serving spoon.

"Don't you want some milk with that?" Silence. "I can make you some eggs. Why don't I make you some eggs?" Her mom sighed and rubbed her forehead. "Listen, Deedle"—an old nickname—"I know you're angry at me. But you have to know that everything I do—everything I've always done—is for your own protection. You have to believe that. I love you very much. You're all I have."

Dea clattered her bowl in the sink.

"Come on, Dea."

It was awful to ignore her mom but also gave her some sick pleasure—like when she flossed too hard and her gums bled a little. In the hall, she shrugged on a Windbreaker and stuffed her feet in an old pair of rain boots.

"You can't ignore me forever!" her mom called.

Dea stepped out onto the porch and slammed the door behind her. Her breath steamed in the air. Rain poured off the overhang, a solid sheet of water that distorted the view, and turned the world into a wash of browns and grays.

Strange how quickly the weather turned here, in this vast bowl in the middle of the country where nothing ever happened—like the sole reminder that the world was actually unpredictable and wild.

Seasons turn. Patterns get broken. People change.

She had successfully made it out of the house without saying a single word to her mother.

* * *

As soon as Connor opened the door, Dea saw that he'd forgiven her, and felt a small thrill. She wondered if in some dark corner of his unconscious, her message to him was still blinking: *I'm sorry.*

"Jesus," he said, as soon as he saw her. "Come in, before you drown."

He shut the door and the noise of the rain was suctioned out. His house was cool and half-dark. Most of the lamps weren't set up yet, although several of them stood, encased in thin plastic, like alien birds. She stood awkwardly just inside the door, overly conscious of the fact that she was dripping onto the wood floor.

But Connor didn't seem to mind. "Is it always this nice in Fielding?" he said.

"Just be grateful it isn't snowing." She crossed her arms and her Windbreaker squeaked, a tiny farting noise. She quickly uncrossed them. "Last winter, Toby got out and nearly froze in a drift. Thank God his ears are so long. Otherwise I would never have found him."

Connor laughed. The noise was loud and echoed. Most of the furniture wasn't set up yet, and all the rugs were bundled in a corner. But Dea could imagine, already, the shape that the living room would take: the comfy leather couches, worn in from years of Super Bowl viewing parties and Sunday afternoon veg-out sessions; the big flat screen TV and the just-shabby-enough throw pillows and the family photos, clustered across every available surface, sprouting like weeds on side tables, mantels, bookshelves.

Dea reached into her bag and took out Connor's iPhone. She couldn't look at him. "Here. I must have grabbed it accidentally."

"Hey, thanks. I was about to put out an Amber Alert." Connor was wearing track pants and a soft-looking T-shirt. It occurred to Dea that he was wearing his sleep clothes. That she had gotten him out of bed. Then she thought about *being* with him in bed and immediately had to think of something else. Ice cubes. Poison ivy. Heat rash. "Listen, about yesterday . . ."

"That's why I came by, actually," she jumped in. "I wanted to apologize."

"You don't have to," he said.

She already had, of course. But she plunged on, "I do. I'm sorry. I freaked out." Then, without planning the words before she was speaking them: "My dad loved rummage sales. We used to go, when I was little." The lie was immediate and convincing. She latched onto it, coaxed it into life. "I guess sometimes I just get . . . overwhelmed."

"What happened to him?" Connor asked.

"He died." She had a bad taste in her mouth, like the lie had soured there. But she dismissed the feeling of guilt. Her dad probably was dead. Might as well be, whoever he was.

"I'm sorry," Connor said quietly. He reached out and touched her arm. "My mom died, too." The words came out kind of strangled, as if he wasn't used to saying them. Dea thought of the pretty woman in his dream, stringing lights on a Christmas tree.

The idea flashed: now they had something in common. The second she thought it, she felt ten times worse. What kind of fucking person was she?

"I'm sorry," she echoed.

"Thanks." For a second, Connor just stood there, awkwardly fiddling with his phone, as though verifying it still worked. He

64

looked so cute in his track pants, and Dea couldn't think of a single thing to say that wasn't stupid. But then Connor looked up. "So . . . you want a tour or something?"

"Are you trying to pay me back for yesterday?" she asked.

He smiled, and his face did that puzzle-piece-rearranging thing again. *Click, click, click,* and it was perfect. "I can't promise you Ohio's largest corn maze," he said. "But I can promise you an excellent view of a whole lot of boxes."

"Sounds great," she said, happy for the excuse just to stay a little longer.

They moved through the downstairs, which was big, and seemed even bigger with hardly any furniture. Everywhere, Dea saw signs of a normal family growing out of the soft, mulch-y boxes, the way mushrooms sprout from dirt. And the more she saw, the more she wished that what she'd said about her dad was true; and the more she wished it, the more she could imagine it. Her dad. A lawyer. No—a doctor. A cardiologist. Flattened by a heart attack one day. Ironic. He shouldn't have worked so hard, but he just loved saving other people.

Connor took her from room to room, showing off random features of his home, acting as if Dea were an interested buyer and he was a broker, and making up ridiculous terms like "scrolled spigoting" and "twentieth-century post-modernist classicism" to describe the sink and the toilet. In the kitchen, he actually showed off the inside of the refrigerator, which so far contained nothing but milk, several Chinese takeout containers, and three family-size bottles of ketchup.

"What's with the ketchup?" Dea asked. The house phone had started ringing—a shrill, startling sound—but Connor ignored it. "You preparing for Armageddon?"

"You can *never* have too much ketchup," he said. "I think that's written in the Constitution somewhere."

"Hmmm. I don't remember that part from history class."

The phone stopped ringing, but a second later the voice mail kicked on, making Dea jump.

"Hello," a woman's voice said; amplified by the speakers, her voice seemed to be coming from several places at once, *"this is Kate Patinsky again, from the graduate school of criminal justice at Howard Jay University. I've tried several times to reach—"*

Connor practically leapt across the room and punched off the answering machine. "Courtesy call," he said breathlessly. "I keep telling my dad and stepmom we should just chuck the phone out the window."

"Where *are* your parents?" she thought to ask. They left the kitchen and started up the stairs to the second floor.

"Church," Connor said. Even though he was walking ahead of her, Dea could sense the eye roll in his shoulders.

"You got off the hook?" she said. Everyone in Fielding went to church, at least on Christmas and Easter. Everyone but Dea and her mom.

"I don't believe in God." Connor had reached the top of the stairs and he turned around to look at her. His face was in shadow, but she could tell he wasn't smiling.

"You believe in ghosts, but you don't believe in God?" She tried to make a joke out of it. She didn't know whether she believed in God—but the way he looked, with his face carved out of darkness, and his hand gripping the banister, made her suddenly uneasy. "'There are more things on heaven and earth' . . . ?"

"I don't believe in heaven, either." For a second, his voice sounded alien. Then he reached out and turned on a light, and his face reappeared. Now he was smiling. "Plus, I like sleeping in on Sundays."

She thought of Connor asleep, his legs tangled in navy blue flannel sheets—and a quiet snow falling in his dreams.

"Welcome to Casa Connor," he said, pushing open a door at the end of the hall. She followed him into his bedroom: a small, pretty room with three big windows that would let in lots of light, when there was any light to let in. The rain drummed against the glass like thousands of tiny feet making a run for something better.

There were boxes heaped on the ground. One of them was filled with old sports trophies and swim team medals, another with video games and wires and a few water-warped books. Clothes were piled on the desk—mostly balled-up sweatshirts and jeans, from what she could tell—and the room smelled like new paint and pine trees. Dea nearly burst out laughing when she saw navy blue flannel sheets. Maybe, somehow, walking his dreams had brought them closer. Maybe she understood him, at least a little bit.

The idea came to her, immediate and overpowering: she needed to walk his dreams again. Tonight. As soon as possible.

But she had already disturbed the course of his dream— touched something, made something. Walking a person's dream more than once was majorly against the rules.

Who cares? a little voice in her head spoke up. *Why does it matter?*

"What's so funny?" Connor flopped down onto the bed, leaning back on his elbows. Dea suddenly realized that she was alone with a boy—a cute boy—in his bedroom. She had no idea whether this was a thing—whether he'd asked her up here for a reason. What would Gollum tell her to do? Probably to go kamikaze-style on him, hurl herself into his arms and try to kiss the cute off his face.

Instead, she stood, stiff-backed and awkward, by the door.

"Nothing," she said quickly. "I like it."

"Thank you." Connor actually looked pleased.

"I should probably go home, though," she said, and then didn't know why she'd said it: because there was a pause that went on a fraction of a second too long; because she didn't know whether to keep standing or sit on the bed. Because she wished she could slip into his dream and move around in safety and write a new note: I want to kiss you.

"Really?" Connor sat up. Now that she'd looked at him longer, she decided his chin was her favorite part of his face: it was a chin that no one would mess with. "You don't want to watch a movie or something?"

"A movie?"

"Yeah." Connor smiled. "Popcorn, couch, a movie. Sunday classic."

"All right." Dea thought about her mom, who would probably be pacing the house, peeking out the windows, waiting for Dea to return. Planning her next lie, and what she would say to get Dea back on her side.

"Awesome." Connor stood up. "I don't have any popcorn, though. We'll have to pretend. I'll even buy you a pretend soda."

"How chivalrous," she said. "But I'm a modern girl. We can go dutch."

They watched an action film, sitting side by side on the couch, their thighs just pressing together. She couldn't understand one of the leads, who had an Irish accent, and couldn't follow the plotline—but she decided it was the best movie she'd ever seen. When Connor's dad and stepmom came home, Connor introduced her as his friend. The word sounded sweet to her, like a long, sunny dream about a picnic.

Before she left, she pretended to get lost on the way to the bathroom and pocketed one of Connor's swim medals. Just in case.

SEVEN

She had two friends now. It was a new reality; it was as though gravity had lessened and everything had become easier, lighter.

Instead of waiting with Gollum at the bus stop for Morgan Devoe or Hailey Madison to peg them with empty soda cans, Dea and Gollum were riding to school in Connor's Tahoe. At lunch, she, Connor, and Gollum split french fries and debated whether mayonnaise was an acceptable condiment. (Gollum was a yes, Connor a firm no.)

They went to the homecoming pep rally together, all three of them, and sat together on the bleachers huddled under an enormous blanket that Gollum had found in the horse barn (it still smelled like hay). They ignored the game, and instead pretended to be sociologists witnessing alien social groups and arcane mating rituals. By group consensus, they vetoed the dance and instead drove Connor's car to the middle of an abandoned farm, and had a midnight picnic in the field with corn chips and spiked hot chocolate Connor had brought in a thermos. On Halloween, they dressed up like a peanut butter and jelly sandwich. Gollum was the jelly and wore all purple. Dea was the peanut butter and wore all brown. And Connor didn't wear anything special, but kept squishing them into enormous bear hugs and shouting, "Sandwich!"

Connor either didn't notice that he'd made friends with the two biggest losers at Fielding, or he didn't care. He never teased Gollum about her clothing or the fact that she was on the subsidy program at lunch, although he teased her about everything else—shipping Harry and Hermione ("how obvious"), listening to Led Zeppelin, refusing to pee in public restrooms. And he never said anything about the rumors, which Dea was sure he must have heard: that Dea and her mom were cannibals. That Dea and her mom were zombies. That they sucked the blood out of local animals, and worshipped the devil. He never asked her why she had to sit out in gym, either, or why she sometimes lost her breath even if they hadn't been walking fast.

Connor made no secret about hating Fielding almost as much as Dea and Gollum did. When he passed his cousin, Will Briggs, in the halls, Dea noticed that they barely spoke to each other. Will sometimes muttered hi. Connor sometimes nodded. That was it.

She was happy. She didn't worry too much about it. She

didn't wonder why Will Briggs almost seemed afraid to meet Connor's eyes, as if Connor might hex him.

She didn't hear the rumors about Connor—whispered stories about what had happened to his mom and baby brother all those years ago; rumors that it was Connor's fault. That he'd done it and only made up that crazy cover story afterward, of the intruder he hadn't seen. That his dad had orchestrated a cover-up to keep Connor from getting shoved in a mental institution. That some woman was writing a book about it and was going to tell the truth.

She didn't hear any of it. How would she? Connor and Gollum were the only two people she talked to.

PART TWO

Once upon a time, there was a pregnant woman who dreamed of a woman, also with child. The woman who dreamed was very sick. The doctors said she was dying. She hadn't woken in two whole days, hadn't spoken or stirred.

But only dreamed, and dreamed, and dreamed.

And as she lay in her hospital bed, sheathed in sheets as cold as a thick layer of ice, she dreamed of the other woman, belly taut and round as a bowl, lying in the middle of a field of snow. But the snow drifted like feathers, and warmed, too, and the dream woman was laughing, her mouth open to the sky, her pink tongue exposed.

And the real woman could feel the tickle of the snow, the drumming of the dream-woman's heart, the stirring of the dream-child in the dream-world of snow as soft as kisses.

"I'll save you," the dream-woman said, opening her eyes, and sliding a hand inside her coat, onto her swollen belly, where a tiny dream-heart drummed and drummed. "We'll save you. Just let us in."

Then the snow became a river of plastic, sliding down her throat, and the snow broke apart into white walls, and the whole world became a scream.

Two screams.

Then the woman who was supposed to have died woke up, and found she had given birth to a beautiful child, with eyes the blue of new ice and skin the color of snow.

EIGHT

In the weeks since Dea and Connor had met, she had walked his dreams four times. She couldn't stop. She didn't want to. For the first time in her life, she could sympathize with addicts. She was filled with a near-constant ache, an itch that seemed to come from *inside* her, as if her blood were infected. She got relief only when she walked. The guilt—knowing that she was breaking the rules, that she was doing something wrong—made walking his dreams feel even more delicious.

Each time she entered his dreams, she found them softer, more pliable, more responsive to her. The overstructure was crumbling.

The second time she walked, she arrived in the middle of a crowded wharf in what looked like the 1920s, except that the deckhands were checking off lists of passengers by administering math homework. The third time, she ended up above an old racetrack that Connor and his dad were endlessly circling in separate cars, trying to get the advantage. In the distance, she spotted a single other spectator leaning against the chain-link fence that divided the car track from the fields beyond it, dark hair hanging to his jaw, hand up to his eyes to shield them from the sun so that his face was in shadow. He struck Dea as somehow familiar, but she was too far to make out what he looked like clearly.

The fourth time she walked, she found herself in a set of high bleachers bordering an indoor pool. The air stunk of chlorine, and people were cheering. Above them, a cracked-glass ceiling was webbed with condensation. Connor was swimming, his arms circling soundlessly, his body sleek as an animal's. Birds raced above the water, casting shadows on its surface, occasionally submerging to sweep up the flashing belly of a fish.

Dea had sat alone in the very back row of bleachers, cheering for Connor along with everybody else, knowing he wouldn't see her.

"Do you ever miss swimming?" she'd said to him the next day, at lunch.

He looked up, startled. "Yeah," he said after a minute. "Yeah. I do." Then he'd reached over impulsively, grabbed her hand, and squeezed, and Gollum smirked in a way that made Dea both embarrassed and deliriously happy.

All of the reasons she had never walked Gollum's dreams—it

was intrusive and weirdly intimate; she didn't want to do that to a friend; what if she saw something terrible?—she was quickly able to dismiss when it came to Connor. She knew she was invading his privacy, feeding on his innermost thoughts and using them, but no one cared about privacy anymore; everyone knew that. Connor was on Facebook, after all—that was almost just as bad. (Last year, Greg Blume had hacked Coralie Wikinson's profile and switched her profile picture out to a blurry camera shot of her . . . Dea didn't even like to think the word. Her mom still called it the "flower pot," which for years she had heard as "flour pot," a misunderstanding that had made the act of baking cookies very embarrassing.) And it wasn't like Dea would use the knowledge *against* him.

The fifth time she walked, she was back in Chicago.

There was the usual swinging feeling, the sensation of darkness and an imminent fall. But she was through it quickly; navigating the in-between space was getting easier, too. The darkness broke apart and she stepped through it. She was standing among mounds of broken-up cinder blocks and concrete ruins, the remains of the apartment complex that had once been Connor's mind's protection from her intrusion. There was a sign staked to a chain-link fence nearby: COMING SOON, WHOLE FOODS. Dea almost laughed. It was a nice touch.

It was snowing again—the same ashy gray snow, accumulating in thick, silent piles, far faster than normal snow. The Christmas lights were still blinking on the awning of the deli across the street. Light overspilling its big window turned the snow a sickly shade of green. She scanned the windows above her, noting the bedroom she'd identified as Connor's, which was fitted with funny blue curtains patterned with giraffes. She saw a shadow pass the window and wondered if it was Connor or his mom. She imagined the big Christmas tree behind them, covered in tiny glass ornaments, like a coating of frost. She wished, for a moment, she could go upstairs, knock on the door, invite herself in.

But she knew that Connor must never see her in his dream. Miriam had always emphasized that rule especially. Dea wasn't even sure what would happen if he did. Maybe he'd die from shock or something. Then she'd be stuck here, in his dream, forever. Or maybe she'd die with him.

Instead she crossed the street and repeated her trick with the Christmas lights, tearing them down with one hard yank. Her hands were shaking a little, and her mouth was dry. Funny how even her dream-self got anxious.

She knelt in the snow, enjoying the slice of the cold in and out of her lungs, her breath steaming in the air. She worked quickly, her fingers red, stiff from the cold.

She was nearly done before she realized something was wrong. It shouldn't be so cold. Connor never filled in the details like that. And it was only getting colder. Now each breath felt like inhaling glass. The snow fell so thickly, she could hardly see. The construction site across the street was almost completely obscured by a thick veil of gray snow, like a vast shadow stretching from the sky to the earth.

The dream shifted almost imperceptibly, like the ground right before an earthquake. But suddenly she was aware of the vast silence of the streets and the darkness of the skies and a waiting quiet, as of an animal holding its breath to avoid attack, and she knew that this wasn't a dream anymore.

It was a nightmare.

She felt them even before she turned around.

There were two of them coming down the street—men, she thought at first, but as they drew closer, she saw she was wrong. The urge to scream worked its way from her chest to her throat and froze there.

They had no faces. No eyes, no noses, no cheekbones or foreheads: just a swirl of flesh-colored skin, barely patched together, like some horrible painting left to bleed in the rain. But they did have mouths. Dark mouths, gaping open, toothless, like long dark tunnels. They were sucking the air in-out, in-out through their mouths. Tasting it.

Looking for someone.

She felt as if the wires that kept her body and mind connected had been cut. She stumbled toward the door of the deli, slipping in the snow, barely managing to right herself. She threw herself inside—a bell tinkled overhead and she was furious, in that moment, that this, of all details, was intact, the stupid, fucking bell—and slammed the door, wishing it had a lock. The deli was empty, thank God. The cash register was barely sketched in. It kept blinking in and out, like the awning lights, now half-buried in the snow.

The lights. They would see the lights and know she had interfered.

They would find her.

She remembered what her mother had said all those years earlier: she must follow the rules or the monsters would find her.

Dea's heart was going so fast it was like the rush of water. She thought she might pass out. She didn't know whether that was possible—to pass out or die in someone else's dream. Maybe, if her own heart just stopped. She'd have to ask Mom.

Why hadn't she listened to Mom?

On the street just outside the deli, the men with no faces stopped. Even through the glass, Dea could hear the sucking drag of their breath. *In-out.* She dropped into a crouch, partially concealed behind a display of Miller Lite. Now she was hot—sweating, nauseous, feeling like she might be sick. *Please,* she thought. *Please. Go away. Keep moving. Please.*

She felt as if she'd been crouching there for an infinity. Her thighs were cramping. She wanted out. She wanted to be back in her bed, safe, with the rhythm of her mom's clocks ticking reassuringly in the darkened hall. *In-out.* Her chest ached from holding her breath. She was afraid they would hear her, though they had no ears, either—just bits of melted flesh where ears should have been.

Then they were gone. They continued past the deli, and she was so relieved that for a moment she didn't register that they had gone into Connor's building—that they must have. She straightened up. Her legs were shaking. Hands, too. The snow outside had turned black; she would have mistaken it for rain, if it hadn't been falling soundlessly. She could barely make out the silhouette of a blackened church across the street—the construction site was gone.

The dream was changing on her. Her body was tight with terror.

She had to get out before the men—the *monsters*—came back.

The deli was mostly empty of food. Even as she watched,

she saw bits of the room begin to evaporate and blur, as though someone was taking an eraser to them, and she knew Connor's attention was now fixed elsewhere. Electric fixtures in the ceiling became smudgy coronas of light; cereal boxes vanished off the shelves, dissipating like liquid in the heat; the shelves themselves began to melt. She grabbed a roll of paper towels before it could disappear and shredded open the plastic with her teeth.

She imagined she could still hear the men breathing behind her—*in-out*—and feel the pressure of hot breath on her neck.

She tore off a square of paper towel, but her hands were shaking too badly and her first bird came out lopsided. It barely lifted off the ground before fluttering shakily directly into the wall and collapsing, inert, only half-changed: a small pale beak and one feather were visible within the folds of paper.

She tried again. This time she managed it: it was an ugly bird, rudimentary, but it should work.

Birds are harbingers. She remembered sitting at the kitchen table when she was six or seven, in front of vast piles of paper birds. Her mom was making cranes, crows, swans—her fingers moving quickly, practically a blur, until the whole table was covered with them. Was that in Delaware? St. Louis? She remembered a river sparkling in the distance; she was never allowed to go near it.

Dea launched the bird into the air. For a second, it fluttered unsteadily, just a scrap of paper towel in the stale air of an old deli.

Then it changed. Its wings stiffened and sprouted white feathers. Its tail unfolded.

Dea pushed open the door as the dove swooped out into the

street. She plunged into the cold. The snow felt like tiny bites on her skin. There was no light left in the street—no light from anywhere in the world, except for the small window high above them. Connor's house.

Dimly, she heard screaming. But it was worse than screaming. Explosions so loud they made colors pop behind her eyes. *Boom.* She ran, stumbling, following the dove as it wove through the air, wings speckled with black snow. *Boom.* She didn't turn around, didn't look back, didn't realize she was crying. *Boom.* She left Connor behind, left the screaming behind, left the Christmas lights still blinking, earthbound, beaming up a message to the sky: *Kiss me.*

Boom.

She sat up, breathing hard, fighting back a scream. Her room was cold but she was sweating. She groped for the light on her bedroom table, and could have sobbed with relief when suddenly her room was revealed—all hard angles and planes, nubby carpet and water-stained desk, faded curtains—real, real, real.

Boom. She jumped. But it was only her mom, pounding on her door. The sound must have reached her even in Connor's dream.

"Dea? Dea? Are you awake?"

She was so shaken from the nightmare, and the vision of men with no faces, that she forgot that she and her mom weren't speaking. She shoved Connor's swim medal under her pillow, as though Miriam would see it and know what Dea had done. She swept her hair back into a ponytail and checked the clock on her bedside table. Six thirty a.m. She wondered, briefly, whether

Connor was still in the middle of that nightmare.

Where had those horrible monsters come from?

"Unlock the door, Dea. I need to talk to you."

Her legs felt sore, as if she'd actually run a long distance in the snow. As soon as she unlocked the door, she crawled back into bed.

It had been a while—at least a month—since Miriam had been in Dea's room. She entered cautiously, as if afraid that the piles of clothing on the floor might conceal a deadly snake, and stopped a few feet from Dea's bed.

"What is it?" Dea pulled her covers to her chin.

"Are you all right?" Miriam said. She looked pale and pinched and worried, as if the past few weeks had worked on her like a gravitational force, sucking out her center. "I heard you cry out."

"I'm fine," Dea said.

"Were you walking?"

"No," Dea lied. And then realized it was a stupid thing to say. She and her mother didn't dream. Why else would she have cried out? "Yeah," she said. "Something stupid. There were bugs. Why'd you wake me?"

"I need to go take care of a few things," Miriam said, turning to the window. She parted the curtains with two fingers and peered out into the darkness, and Dea had a sudden moment of terror: the men would be there, breathing their ragged breaths onto the glass. But of course, there was no one. Just the reflection of Dea's room in the darkened windowpanes.

"At six thirty in the morning?"

Miriam let the curtains drop, but didn't turn around. "Start packing your things. It's time."

Dea took a deep breath. Her lungs ached, as if the cold from Connor's dream had infected her. "You aren't serious."

"There's no point in getting angry. It won't change anything." Miriam picked her way through the clothes back to the door. She didn't even look sorry, or embarrassed, or anything but faintly impatient, as if the conversation were keeping her from more important things.

Dea closed her eyes and reopened them. How many other mornings had her mom woken her up saying the very same thing? *I have some things to take care of. Start packing. It's time.*

She didn't know if she was angry or not. She couldn't think straight.

"I won't go," she managed to say.

"Yes, you will," Miriam said matter-of-factly. She paused with her hand on the doorknob. For a second, Dea thought she might apologize. But she just said, "Your suitcase is in the attic," and passed into the hall, closing the door behind her.

Dea sat in her bed for a long time. She heard the front door close and the locks turn, one after another. She heard the growl of the car engine. She heard Toby, mewling to be fed. She didn't have the energy to move. She didn't have the energy to cry.

Eight o'clock. Toby yowled a little louder, and clawed Dea's door. Thin shafts of sunlight, fine as silk, passed between her curtains. It was going to be a nice day. She, Connor, and Gollum were supposed to go to Lesalle to check out the Fright Festival, a cheesy Halloween-themed carnival that would last all the way until Thanksgiving. Connor had promised to win them each a stuffed goblin from one of the shoot-'em-up booths.

By nine o'clock, she'd made a decision.

She got out of bed. Toby was still mewling outside the door, but she ignored him. She didn't have that many clothes, and many of the clothes she did own were scattered across the bedroom floor. In both closets there were maybe a dozen sweaters and ratty thrift store sweatshirts, a few skirts she never wore, and a dress her mom had given her a few Christmases ago, which was shaped like an inverted martini glass and had beaded skulls embroidered all over it. She'd never had anywhere to wear it.

She could have worn it to prom. Maybe Connor would have asked her officially, like as a couple.

She pulled down all the clothes, and the hangers, too, for good measure. She dumped them all on the floor, kicking a pair of jeans under her bed, tossing a sweatshirt over the radiator. In the hall, she nudged Toby out of the way with a foot.

She hardly ever went into her mom's room. Whenever she did, she felt like she was seeing the stage lights come on after a play, and suddenly noticing all the bolts and screws keeping the whole thing together: a sense of awe and also of embarrassment, because the deception had been so easily believed. The room was spotless, as always. Two clocks hung side by side above the headboard and clucked their tongues at Dea. Two suitcases, already half-filled, were open on the bedroom floor. The closets were empty. The bed was stripped, the comforter rolled back to reveal the mattress.

She inverted the suitcases onto the floor, kicking and hurling the neatly folded clothing into various corners of the room. She pulled the comforter and pillows off the bed. She shook out the contents of her mom's vanity drawer—used tubes of cream, nail files, sample perfumes from department stores—onto the rug. In the bathroom, she found two plastic ziplock bags filled with toiletries. She squeezed the toothpaste all over the sink and uncapped an old tube of her mom's lipstick.

I'm not going, she wrote on the bathroom wall, where a mirror had once hung.

Feeling slightly better, she went downstairs and fed Toby. Instead of returning the cat food to the pantry, she shook the bag out all over the kitchen floor. Toby watched her, uncertain, crouched over his bowl. She knew she was being immature, but she didn't care. If her mom wanted to leave, fine. But Dea was sure as hell not going to make it any easier for her.

"Go nuts," she said to Toby, once the kitchen floor was covered with a surface of hard brown pellets, so it was impossible to walk without crunching. She didn't bother to throw out the empty bag—just tossed it in a corner. The kitchen clock sounded nine-thirty, dinging shrilly, as if in protest. For good measure, she wrenched it off the wall, tossed it onto the kitchen counter, and smashed it to pieces with an old meat tenderizer that had been abandoned by the house's previous tenants. It let out a faint whine before it died completely, like something alive.

Feeling all the way better, she went upstairs and took a long shower. It took her a while to sort through the clothing on her floor to find her favorite pair of jeans, a thin T-shirt, and an oversize cashmere sweater with leather patches at the elbows, which always made her feel like she should be living on a real farm and not just an imitation of one.

Outside, it was cold, clear, and very bright: one of those days that looks like a child's drawing, the sun shooting daggers at the ground out of a radiant blue sky. She jogged across the road, her breath steaming in the air, pushing aside a sudden memory of Connor's nightmare—the cold, the snow, the men with no faces.

Connor was shirtless when he opened the door, and wearing only a towel around his waist. She was momentarily too distracted to speak. He smelled like soap, even from a distance of three feet, and his chest was beaded with water. She thought about the lights she'd arranged in the snow of his dream: *Kiss me*.

"You're early," he said. He didn't look like he'd been kept awake by nightmares. He looked the same as he always did— easy, smiling. Maybe a little more tired than usual, but not much.

She knew she was early, and she knew he would comment on it, and she'd planned a few funny responses in her head: *Fried dough is a great motivator* and *The Ferris wheel waits for no man*. The kind of things that the lead girl would say in a romantic comedy.

But confronted with Connor in a towel she just said, "I know," and tried very hard not to look at him.

"Give me ten minutes." He stepped back to let her inside.

She'd been over to Connor's house a few times—because they were friends, she reminded herself, never tiring of the way the words sounded in her head—and every time it was closer to perfect: carpets unrolled, lamps perched prettily on side tables, potpourri poured into wooden bowls, filling the house with a faintly spicy smell. She never got tired of admiring how much Connor's family owned, how much they'd accumulated together. She thought again of her father—her real father, not the stranger in the red polo shirt—and wondered whether he was somewhere out there, and living in a house like Connor's, filled with coffee tables and pretty statuettes, candlesticks and porcelain vases. For one delirious second, she imagined tracking him down and showing up on his doorstep, imagining he'd be happy to see her.

Her mom would be so pissed.

Connor went to get dressed and Dea waited in the living room and looked at the family photos, which had been newly set out, partly so she wouldn't have to think about Connor naked upstairs. There were pictures of Connor at every age—one where he was grinning, practically toothless, in front of an enormous cake with two candles on it; one where he was standing, scrawny and proud, in front of a pool with a medal strung around his neck—and several photos of Connor's dad and step-mom and various other old people Dea assumed were relatives or friends.

In the very back of the arrangement of photographs, Dea spotted a photo of an infant wrapped in a blue blanket decorated with giraffes. She felt a quick shock of recognition: she'd seen that pattern before. She'd seen it in Connor's dreams, on the curtains in one of his windows. She picked up the photograph, squinting.

"That's my brother." Connor was behind her; she hadn't heard him approach. He plucked the photograph out of her hands and replaced it on the table.

"What happened to him?" Dea asked.

He looked faintly annoyed. "Dead," he answered, as if it were obvious.

Dea thought of the screams that had chased her out of Connor's nightmare, and felt suddenly cold. "I'm sorry."

"*I'm* sorry," Connor said, and then sighed, looking away from her. "I just don't really like to talk about it."

"Okay," she said. "I understand."

Then he was easy again, all smiles. Sometimes that annoyed her about him—he was like water jumping over stones, all surface, too quick for her. He slung an arm around her shoulders. "Ready to get your ass kicked at bumper cars?"

"Dream on," she said.

NINE

Connor and Dea met up with Gollum just outside the festival entrance. Gollum had been at the festival for an hour with her younger brothers, Richie and Mack, and had already won a small stuffed ghoul. Both Richie and Mack had had their faces painted: Richie, who was small and serious and had Gollum's triangular face, was a cat; Mack, who was older and bigger and a goofball, was a skeleton.

The carnival grounds were packed with people. Mud squelched underneath Dea's sneakers. The Ferris wheel loomed in the sky like the domed back of a monster. It was loud. The ancient rides creaked and groaned under the weight of their passengers. Periodically, screams erupted, a constant rhythm that took on the quality of waves heard from a distance. The air smelled like smoke and meat and spun sugar. Connor kept a hand on Dea's lower back whenever the crowds got especially thick.

She wondered if her mom had returned home yet, then pushed the thought out of her mind. Deep down, she knew that if her mom insisted on moving, Dea would have no choice but to go with her. But Miriam *wouldn't* insist. Not when she knew how miserable it would make Dea.

Would she?

They ate hot dogs at a paint-splattered picnic table, enjoying the November sun, while Mack and Richie ran circles in the damp grass with kids costumed like vampires and demons, and Gollum explained her theories on the metaphorical significance of the Ferris wheel.

"It's all about the futility of ambition," she said, stabbing the air with a plastic straw. "You try as hard as you can to get to the top, but you don't realize that striving will just topple you and bring you right down to the bottom."

"So let me get this straight: you *don't* want to ride the Ferris wheel?" Connor struggled to keep a straight face.

Gollum sniffed. "I don't ride metaphors," she said. "Too unstable."

They played three rounds of zombie hunter, shooting fine sprays of water into wooden figurines fitted with targets on their stomachs. Connor won the first round. Mack beat him in the second. Dea was on her way to victory in the third, but Connor reached out and started tickling her.

"No fair." She laughed, breathless, as he raised his arms and declared himself the victor. "You cheated."

"I strategized," he corrected her. For a second they were close—so close she could see his individual lashes and streaks of green threaded through the brown of his eyes and the soft planes of his cheekbones. So close she was sure he would kiss her—there, in front of everyone.

"He's got a point, Donahue," Gollum said, and the moment passed. Connor reached out and knuckled Dea's head, like she was his kid sister.

Happy. She was happy. She forgot about Connor's nightmare-visions, and her mom banging on her door saying *pack your stuff*, and the lies about her father. She forgot about anything except arcade games and the taste of sugar, the smell of corn dogs in the air, and Gollum chasing after Mack to keep him from rampaging Godzilla-style through the candy stall, and Connor's hand on her back. She wanted to extend the day, blow it up like a glass bubble that would keep them enclosed forever. Only now did she understand how lonely she'd been for years. It was like washing up on a shore and then realizing how close you'd been to drowning. She wanted to grip her happiness hard, like it was something solid, like if she didn't it would go away.

But time passed. The sun withered on the ground. It got colder. The crowd changed: parents hustled their children out to the parking lot, and Richie got cranky, and started crying when he didn't win at a darts game.

"That's my cue," Gollum said, hauling Richie onto one hip. She was surprisingly strong for someone so thin. Dea guessed it came from working on a farm. "I'm going to head back before we get to emotional Armageddon. Say bye, Richie. Say bye, Mack."

Mack shadowboxed Connor in response. Richie buried his face in Gollum's shoulder and let out another wail. With an eye roll, Gollum disappeared into the crowd.

Leaving Dea and Connor together. Alone.

On a date. Dea quickly forced away the thought.

A group of guys wearing football jackets from a rival high school, obviously drunk, wove through the crowd, jostling one another, competing over who could be loudest. Two girls with thick black eyeliner and boobs practically to their chins smoked cigarettes by the fence, and waited to get hit on.

The sun reached up a final arm before drowning behind the horizon. While Connor went to buy more tickets, Dea waited just outside the small bumper car rink, watching the random collision of vehicles, thinking about Toby escaping and how she might never have met Connor if he hadn't. Thinking life was like that: random collisions.

"Hey."

Dea turned around and was shocked to see Morgan Devoe and Hailey Madison, who had never spoken to her once, who had never acknowledged her at all except to throw empty cans of soda at her head from the window of Tucker Wallace's truck. Hailey was chewing on a straw, watching Dea curiously, like she was an ancient artifact whose use Hailey was trying to determine.

"What do you want?" Dea said. She wasn't stupid. She knew they didn't want to chat, and she wanted them to leave before Connor came back.

Morgan Devoe was supposedly the prettiest girl in school.

Dea had never understood it. She had a wide face, blank as a dinner plate, and the dull eyes of a pig pumped full of tranquilizers. She always looked bored.

"You should be careful," Morgan said, which wasn't what Dea had expected her to say. She leaned up against the fence next to Dea. She smelled like butterscotch and menthol cigarettes and alcohol. She was holding a cup. Dea wondered what was in it.

"What?" Dea said.

"Connor," Hailey said, like it was obvious, which was how Hailey said everything.

"What about Connor?" Dea said. She felt like she'd stepped into a rehearsed act. Dea was the only one who didn't know her lines.

Morgan leaned closer. She was drunker than she'd first seemed. She put a sweaty hand on Dea's arm. "Aren't you worried he might go crazy again? Slit your throat when you're not paying attention?"

"What—what are you talking about?" Dea said.

Morgan gaped at her. "You don't know?" she said. She made a face at Hailey.

"She don't know," Hailey drawled, and giggled, working her straw between her teeth.

"*Everybody* knows." Morgan turned back to Dea. She smiled big, so Dea could see the gum in her mouth. "He killed his mom. His brother, too. Beat his mom's brains out, then shot his brother in the head the day before Christmas. He was, like, seven."

"That's not true." Dea wrenched her arm away from Morgan's

grip. "That's—that's insane."

"Cooked up some bullshit story about some men who busted in and did it. It doesn't make sense though, does it?" Morgan's teeth were very white. "Nothing was stolen. What kind of robbery is that?"

Dea's stomach tightened. She was suddenly too hot. And nauseous.

"He was too young to go to trial," Heather said. Her nails were painted hot pink, and had tiny decals of Playboy bunnies on them. "But everybody knows he did it. Some woman's even writing a book about it. Bet she'll call you soon, 'specially when she finds out Connor's your boyfriend. She's calling *everybody*."

"Connor's not my boyfriend," Dea said automatically, and then wished she hadn't. It made her sound ashamed of him. She remembered the message she'd heard on Connor's answering machine the first day she'd gone over to his house. Someone calling from a university . . . a school for criminal justice . . .

"Will Briggs says Connor was jealous of the baby. Just lost it one day and . . . *bam*."

"Shut up." Dea squeezed her eyes shut and opened them again. The girls were still there; still staring at her, swallowing back their fat, stupid smiles, sucking in their cheeks, waiting to burst out laughing the second she turned around. And she was on the verge of tears. She wouldn't cry in front of them. "It's not true. You're making it all up."

"We're just looking out for you, Odea," Morgan said, fake-nice. And before Dea could stop her or move or react, she'd licked a thumb and reached out and swiped Dea's cheek with her saliva. "That's for good luck," she said, leaning close, breathing hot on Dea's face. "You're going to need it."

Then they were gone—asses bumping right to left, the smell of booze trailing them—and Morgan's spit was drying on Odea's cheek, and Dea was fighting the urge to cry. She wiped her face with a sleeve and took three deep breaths.

"I'm back." Connor was fighting his way through the crowd, holding a fistful of tickets in the air. He faltered when he saw her face. "You okay?"

"Yeah. Yeah, I'm okay." It was stupid to let Morgan and Hailey get to her. They'd probably made the whole thing up. Connor hadn't killed anyone. Of course he hadn't. But she kept thinking of the faceless men and their black-hole mouths and the screaming. "Just not sure I'm up for bumper cars after all."

"Chickening out, huh? I'll take it easy on you. I promise." Connor reached out and touched her shoulder with two fingers, like he was afraid she'd break. "You sure you're okay?"

"I'm sure," she said. She had a sudden memory of Connor's face, narrow and angry, appearing at the window. His mom stringing up ornaments behind him. Was there a baby crying somewhere in the apartment? How often did Connor dream about his family dying?

"Okay, no bumper cars," Connor said. "But you can't punk out on the Ferris wheel. Especially now that we know it's a metaphor. You promised," he added, before she could protest.

"All right," she said. But evening had come and the magic of the day had been shattered.

Maybe, she thought, a move wasn't such a bad idea. She could get a clean start.

Then she realized that a teeny tiny part of her believed what

Morgan and Hailey had told her—that Connor had murdered his family. She felt an immediate rush of guilt. Connor was the nicest guy she'd ever met.

He was more than nice. He was amazing.

The Ferris wheel was old and the seats were narrow. Connor's thighs pressed against Dea's when they sat down; their elbows bumped when he looped his arms over the guardrail. She hadn't been on a Ferris wheel in ages and was surprised by the sudden lifting in her chest, the swooping sense of happiness and fear, as the seat began to rise, stopping every six feet while the operators collected tickets and admitted more passengers onto the ride.

Up and up, until Dea's swinging feet looked like a giant's, as if she could squash the small smudgy people on the ground. Until the whole scene looked like a child's toy, and she imagined Morgan and Hailey were just toys, too, little plastic models instead of people.

They were stopped at the very top of the Ferris wheel. The view made her breathless. Connor swung his feet, making the whole seat sway. He turned to face her. "You scared?"

"No," she said, which was true. Funny how leaving the ground could change everything, make the whole world feel remote and small and insignificant. No wonder birds made the best harbingers. Even in dreams, they couldn't be contained.

"I'm glad I met you, Dea." He was smiling. In the darkness, up here, she couldn't see the color of his eyes. "You're . . ."

"What?" They were close again. He had twisted around to face her.

"I don't know. Different." Something changed in his face—a

nuance she couldn't have described, a definite switch.

"Connor," she said suddenly, and she had not been planning to ask but she did, before she could stop herself. "What happened to your mom and little brother?"

He stopped swinging his feet. He stared at her. All the lightness in his face fell away—it was like watching a plaster model disintegrate.

And it was only then, when he turned away, that she realized with a sinking feeling that he'd been about to kiss her.

"Why are you asking me that?" He wouldn't look at her. His hands tightened on the safety bar.

He'd been about to kiss her. They'd crested the highest point of the circle and were descending now, into the bones of the scaffolding, under the shadow of other couples. "I just . . . I don't know. I was curious."

"Did Patinsky get to you, too?" As they skimmed over the ground again, the noise of the carnival rushed at them like a physical force. "She's writing a book, you know. She says she just wants the truth. But she doesn't. No one does. No one gives a shit." Connor's face passed temporarily into the light. "Did she tell you how I went psycho when I was a kid and bashed my mom's head in with a lamp? How I splattered her brains across the pillow?"

They were rising again and Dea's stomach was lurching. The shrieks from below were transforming into the screams from Connor's dream. "Connor—"

"No, no. Don't tell me. Let me guess. Then I took my dad's gun and put a bullet in my brother's brain. Just held it up to his little head. *Bam.* Who else could have done it, right? Who else knew where the gun was kept?"

"Connor." Dea's throat was so tight she could barely get out his name. "I'm sorry. I shouldn't have asked. I shouldn't have said anything." He still wouldn't look at her. "Nobody . . . nobody *got* to me. I mean, I haven't spoken to anyone about you. I wouldn't."

"Fuck you," he said, but instead of sounding angry, he just sounded tired.

They sat in silence. Although their thighs were still touching, Dea felt as if he were a thousand miles away. She fumbled desperately for something to say.

"I'm leaving," was what came out. "Moving again. My mom told me this morning." He didn't say anything. They glided over the highest point of the Ferris wheel. Somewhere, out in the darkness, her mom was probably sweeping up the cat food, refolding her clothing. "I don't want to go. I'm sick of it—all the moving. How I never have a choice. But mostly I don't want to go because of you." She hadn't been sure she'd be brave enough to say the last words, so she said them all in a rush, pushing them out on one long breath. "I . . . like you. A lot."

For a minute, he didn't say anything. The ride stalled suddenly; they sat swinging over empty air.

He rubbed his forehead, like it hurt. "I don't want you to go either," he said. Just like that, the curtain between them had opened again. She felt a surge of relief so strong it was like joy. She put a hand on his arm.

"About what I said—what I asked—I'm so sorry—I never believed—"

"I was seven," he said abruptly, cutting her off. As they

plummeted again, his face was swallowed in darkness. "My dad was away. He was away a lot back then. Business. It was just me and my mom and my brother for Christmas." His words came haltingly, as if this wasn't a story he had told very often. But he must have—in court, in therapy, maybe even on the news. "Jacob was only one year old. He'd been the worst baby. He had colic. Do you know what that is?" He didn't wait for her to shake her head. "He cried all the time. All the time. It drove my dad berserk. Mom, too. But then at six months he just . . . stopped crying. It was like he was all cried out. Then he was always smiling."

She held her breath, afraid she might say or do the wrong thing again.

"It was Christmas Eve." His voice had gotten so quiet she had to lean in to hear him. Now their shoulders were touching, too. "I went to bed early. I was so excited. You know how kids are about Christmas." His hands were balled into fists in his lap. "It was the shot that woke me. The first shot didn't kill her. It wasn't meant to kill her."

Dea shivered.

"There were men—I heard voices. Everything was so confusing. I heard my mom say *please* and *no*. I was so scared I couldn't move. Couldn't even hide. I was so scared I peed. I hadn't peed the bed since I was two." He glanced at her just for a second, as if to verify she wasn't going to make fun of him. "Then I heard . . . a crack. We found out later that it was her skull. He took the lamp from the bedside table and just hammered her head in. Jacob was still screaming." He closed his eyes. "I could have saved him."

Dea found her hand in his lap. Connor squeezed it, hard.

"You could have died," she said.

He opened his eyes again. He interlaced his fingers with hers, and stared down at their hands. "They shot Jake in the middle of the forehead. Execution-style." His voice hitched. "Do you know how small a one-year-old baby is? So small. With hands like little flowers." He looked away and she saw his jaw working back and forth. She knew he was trying not to cry. "The cops said afterward that Jacob wasn't really a target. They probably shot him just to shut him up, you know? So they'd have time to escape."

Dea thought of the two faceless men she'd seen in Connor's nightmare.

"I'm so sorry, Connor." The words sounded stupid, even to her—insubstantial, narrow. *Sorry* was what you said when you accidentally bumped into someone in the supermarket, or forgot to do your homework. Where were the words for tragedies like this one?

"Thanks." He coughed. They were on their last rotation now, coasting slowly through the air, stopping again every few seconds as passengers disembarked. The carnival felt like it was a million miles away. Silence expanded between them. She thought he was done talking, but then he said, "I saw them. Just before they left, I saw them. I crawled to the door. They had to go past my room to get to the front door, you know. I was practically shitting myself, I was so scared. But I cracked open my door, just an inch, so I would see them as they passed."

"But the cops never caught them?" Dea asked.

He shook his head. "I—I couldn't see their faces." His voice was strangled, as if the words were choking him.

The ride was over. They touched ground, and two teenage kids with faces full of pimples stepped forward to disengage the safety bar. Dea was unsteady when she stood. She was suddenly disoriented by the whirring of arcade games and the smells of popcorn and hot dogs, the rapid-fire shouts, like jungle calls.

Connor didn't let go of her hand. Something had changed between them, but she didn't know whether it was a good or bad thing.

It started to rain just as they got back to his car. He put on the heat and she sat with the hot blast of air stirring the hair from her neck, tickling her throat, wishing there was something more she could say or do. She was tired, and frightened; she didn't want to go home. Now she knew they couldn't move—she couldn't leave Connor. Somehow, he had become hers to care about and worry about and protect.

Halfway back to Fielding, the rain got so bad it sliced the headlights into thousands of fragments, pummeled the roof and windows, and turned the windshield into a solid sheet of water. The wind knocked the car back and forth across the road, and she could feel the wheels hydroplaning on the road. That's how storms came in Indiana: quickly, without any warning.

It was too dangerous to keep driving. They could barely see the semis on the road until the trucks were on top of them, whooshing past them in a gush of wind, leaning on their horns. Connor found a McDonald's off the highway and parked the car in a dark spot between streetlamps. Before Dea could stop him, he'd pushed out into the rain. He sprinted toward the entrance, arms up over his head, water kicking beneath his shoes. When he returned, he was carrying his jacket like a baby in his arms.

As soon as he opened the door, Dea smelled fat and meat and delicious fried things, a smell that always reminded her of childhood. She hadn't realized how long it had been since they'd eaten. She was starving.

"For you, madam." He unfolded his jacket and revealed a paper bag nestled inside of it, just barely spotted with water. But his T-shirt was soaked. The fabric was plastered to his skin, so she could see the lines of his shoulder blades and muscles. He'd bought her a double cheeseburger—he'd remembered they were her favorite—and a Coke. They split the french fries, their hands bumping every so often when they both reached into the bag. Connor's shirt was damp, and the smell of laundry detergent and clean cotton intermingled with the lingering fast food smells. It was comforting. Like being in a fort while the rest of the world melted.

"Thanks for listening tonight," he said. "I'm sorry about how I . . . well, I'm just sorry."

"I'm sorry, too." She'd just finished the last of the fries. She was full and sleepy and happy. "I shouldn't have brought it up."

"I'm glad you did." Connor looked down at his lap. "It felt kind of good to talk about it. I've thought about telling you before. At the same time . . . I don't know. I liked that you didn't know." He turned to her. "It's been my whole life. I've carried it with me everywhere. Do you know what I mean?"

"Yes," she said. That was the problem, she thought: no matter where she and her mom went, no matter how far they ran, they carried their old selves with them, their broken-down bodies and jerky hearts, the need to walk, the dreams that clung to them like shadows.

"Hey, Dea?" Connor was smiling, just barely.

"Yeah?"

He leaned closer. He found her hand. "I like you, too."

A shooting pain went through her—what would happen if her mom insisted she leave? What could she do? Where would she live?—but she pushed the thoughts away.

"Check it out." Connor leaned over her, so for a moment his chest was an inch from her mouth and she thought about kissing the spot between his collar bones. Then the seat whirred backward, bringing her with it, so she was staring up at the roof. He put his seat back, too, so they were lying side by side, separated only by the console. The rain was a constant thrum, like the beating of a gigantic heart.

They lay there for a long time, fingers interlinked on the console, with the heat blowing and the world pouring down around them. At a certain point, Dea realized that Connor had fallen asleep. She wanted to wake him but by then she, too, was teetering, somewhere on the balance between wakefulness and sleep. She let go, instead, and let the darkness close over her.

T E N

She was in without trying, relieved to find herself not in Chicago but in some other patchwork landscape—a combination, she realized, of Indiana flatlands and an industrial yard, grass running into pavement, and warehouses turning the horizon smudgy with smoke. Connor was standing with a half dozen other boys in the center of a field, playing a version of Red Rover, except their hands were chained together and they were all wearing prison jumpsuits, vivid orange against the dull gray sky.

But even as she stood there, trying to convince herself to leave, to let Connor be, the concrete began eating up the grass, spreading like an inky stain from one end of the field to the other, and the boys froze and darkened and elongated, becoming telephone poles and streetlamps. The warehouses splintered and stretched, punching up to the sky like enormous fists. Snow began to fall, and wind whipped down the now-familiar Chicago street.

The dream was sharper than it had ever been, every detail realized, every angle precise and well-constructed. The deli with the blinking Christmas lights and the Lotto sign was fully stocked now, although there was no one behind the register. In the distance, someone was singing "Silent Night."

Connor was remembering better, more clearly. His conversation with Dea had brought back the details. She knew, too, that she was experiencing the dream so vividly because they were lying so close. There was no veil between them, no psychic interference.

A car rolled slowly down the middle of the street, beaming thick cones of light out into the whirl of snow. Already, she could feel it—a prickling unease, like being watched from a distance. And she knew the dream was changing imperceptibly, growing colder and darker. The men with no faces were coming. Above her, Connor's apartment was dark.

She went around to the back of the building. A chain-link fence separated the alley from an area for parking and garbage disposal. She hopped it easily, her feet crunching in the snow when she landed. She'd never been in a dream this real. It made her even more alert, and even more afraid.

Could you die in a dream? Really die?

She had never asked.

Stitched up the back of Connor's building was a set of wooden stairs, similar to the one that had run up and down the back of the apartment she and her mom had rented in Chicago. She began to climb. The snow muffled the sound of her foot-steps. The railing was icy, so she kept her hands in her pockets.

On the fourth floor, Connor's floor, it was dark. The light was missing its bulb. A trash bag had been dumped just outside the door, its slick black surface already pooling with snow. She eased open the screen door and tried the handle. Locked. She would need a key.

She had never messed too much with the fluid nature of dreams, except to make harbingers when she needed to find an exit. That was the whole point of walking—noninterference. But she knew that dreams flowed. They reacted to minor shifts like water breaking around a rock. That was part of why it was important not to change anything, her mom always told her.

Picture a rock dropped into a well, she'd said. *Picture all those ripples spreading outward. If the rock is big enough, you can start a flood.*

Dea squatted and sketched the rough outline of a key in the snow with a finger. She was terrible at drawing—it looked more like a knife. Anyway, nothing happened.

She spotted a wire hanger distending one portion of the trash bag. She tore a small hole in the bag, working with her fingers to enlarge it. It was so quiet and still, she could practi-cally hear the snow fall. Every sound she made was thunderous, as if it were echoing across the whole city, across the whole dream. She worked the wire hanger out of the bag, releasing a small cascade of trash in the snow: an empty hair dye car-ton, the shattered globe of a discarded Christmas ornament, a wadded-up paper towel.

She straightened out a portion of the hanger and worked it into the lock. At last, the dream responded. There was an invisible ripple, a change, like passing from air into water, and suddenly she was holding not a hanger, but a key. It turned easily in the lock. She hesitated for only a second before she eased the door open, and stepped into the darkness of Connor's old apartment.

Her sneakers squeaked on the linoleum floor, and she stood still, holding her breath, listening for sounds of movement. Nothing. A dim light up ahead illuminated the rough shape of a kitchen: countertops and cabinets. Dea marveled at the details. There was a plate, several cookies, and a glass of milk on the kitchen table—Dea realized they must be for Santa Claus and felt her heart constrict. It was amazing what the mind could recall and re-create—even things the dreamer could never remember when awake. It was like dreaming was a secret doorway into places forgotten or deliberately buried. On her left was a large living room and the source of the light: a decorated Christmas tree. The small lights glimmered in the branches, casting strange patterns on the ceilings and wall. To her right were several doors, two of them closed, one of them open just a crack. She inched slowly toward the open door, holding her breath, terrified that at any second Connor might appear—or, even worse, she'd hear the wet mouth-breathing of the faceless men somewhere in the darkness behind her. But nothing happened. She spotted the corner of a desk and a twin bed draped with dark green sheets. Connor's room, then.

She knew that what she was doing was wrong. She was taking a huge chance. Never be seen. That was the most important rule of dream-walking. But it was as if the dream was a heartbeat, pulsing through her, drawing her forward. She moved quickly down the hall, deeper into the house, deeper into the dream.

The next door led to a bathroom. That left one closed door, and one final bedroom. Connor's mom's room. Where his baby brother had slept. Where the murders had happened. She placed a hand on the doorknob, then hesitated. Maybe it was better not to know. What if she entered and saw Connor's mom's face already splattered across the pillow, his poor baby brother lying in a pool of blood?

What if she entered and saw Connor, standing over his brother's crib with a gun?

What if he had lied after all?

She dismissed that thought quickly. She didn't—she wouldn't—believe it. And still the dream seemed to draw her forward and deeper, as if she were a ship riding a strong current. She eased open the door, cold with terror.

Then she was inside the room and the fear was gone, making her feel loose and shaky. Connor's mom was sleeping on her back, lips partly open, snoring quietly. Connor's brother was curled like a small fern in a patch of moonlight in a crib near the foot of the bed. They hadn't died, not tonight, not in this dream. She knew it didn't change anything in real life, but it seemed like a miracle: in some place, in some version of reality, imagined or wished, they were alive.

She should go. She knew she should go—slip out of the dream, unobserved, no harm done. But she was moved by the sudden impulse to know what Connor's mom looked like, whether Connor and his mom shared the same chin, whether he was written, somehow, in her face. She inched forward, toward the bed.

Connor's mom's chest swelled and fell under the sheets. Her dark hair was scattered across the pillow. She was smiling very slightly in her sleep—a dream within a dream.

"What the hell?"

Dea spun around. Connor was standing in the doorway, rigid, staring—seventeen-year-old Connor, his normal self, not the six-year-old he had been when his mom had died. This was dream-logic, the push-pull between reality and projection, memory and wish.

She felt a wild seesaw of panic.

Never be seen.

"What—what are you doing here?" He took a step forward. His mom stirred.

"It's a dream," she whispered. *You must never, ever be seen.* This was wrong, all wrong. She felt the dream stretching, bending around her, as if it might come down.

"No." Connor came closer. But she found no comfort in his presence. His eyes were hard, horrified. "You're *here.*" He grabbed her arms, gripping her so tightly it hurt. "Why are you here?"

"Let me go." she said. Connor's mother moaned. His brother still slept quietly in his crib, his face obscured by a long stripe of shadow. Then Dea realized it wasn't shadow. It was blood—blood seeping from his head, pouring onto the ground, sliding across the room toward them like inky dark fingers. Connor's mom was bleeding, too. Her eyes were open and she was staring sightlessly at the ceiling, moaning over and over. Her head was split in two.

Dea was suddenly so terrified, she wanted to cry. "Please let me go."

"You shouldn't have come here, Dea." Connor sounded regretful. His face was changing, too—melting, almost, his features distorted like candle wax by heat. "Now they know where to find you."

Dea froze. "Who?" she whispered, even though she knew—she sensed it in the air, in the frigid room, in the blood pooling around her shoes.

Connor's eyes had turned black. He opened his mouth, but instead of answering, his mouth expanded, yawning open like a tunnel, and the rest of his face simply blew apart. Dea stumbled backward. He was no longer Connor but one of those things—faceless, deformed, his breathing wet and ragged.

"We've been looking for you," the thing said, and its voice was like the howl of wind through a canyon.

Then everything exploded. The room, the walls, the floor—there was a tremendous blast and Dea was falling, screaming, as the building around her turned to black dust and then evaporated. The nightmare was eating everything, turning it to rot. The monsters had consumed Connor. They would consume her, too.

She hit the snow hard and slipped. She rolled back onto her feet and began to run, crying, ignoring the pain in her ankle and wrist where she had fallen on them wrong. The snow was so heavy it was hard to move, but she plunged recklessly forward, not daring to look back. The thing was right behind her. She could hear it panting, and feel the wet blast of its death-sweet breath on her neck.

Around her, the dream was coming down. Whole buildings collapsed in an instant, thundering to the street. Scaffolding crashed through windshields; metal ricocheted into storefront windows and the air vibrated with the sound of wailing alarms.

Connor was trying to wake up.

She needed to find a way out.

The *thing* was closer now. She felt its long, wet fingers graze her back, like the touch of someone's tongue, and she screamed. A string of stoplights came down—crash, crash, crash—sparking in the snow. She dodged a fallen streetlamp, her heart screaming in her throat, her legs burning, tears freezing on her cheeks.

From somewhere far away she thought she heard her mom calling her name. *Mommy*, she wanted to scream. *Help me*. But she couldn't scream at all. She could hardly breathe. Her lungs felt like they'd been flattened, and she could barely draw in enough air to keep running.

An exit. She needed an exit. But every doorway crumbled before she could reach it. The whole city was turning into cascades of dust and dark sand. She had no time to make a harbinger. She veered toward the sidewalk, and toward a small dark archway between buildings that looked as if it might be a way out. But she tripped on the curb, half-concealed by the snow, and went skidding, facedown, on the icy sidewalk. She tasted blood in her mouth. Already the archway was crumbling, bricks thudding to the ground, as if the whole street were being rocked by a massive earthquake.

Then the thing had its hand around her ankle. She lashed out and landed a kick in its chest. It stumbled backward and she pushed herself back to her feet. When she risked a glance behind her, she saw the *thing* was no longer alone. There was a second one now, with a face like a hole and long, black fingers; it had materialized out of nowhere.

Help me, help me, help me, she screamed silently. The air was thick with dust and plaster and her ears were ringing. The city was being torn apart: it screamed like a living thing; it groaned and cried out.

She turned the corner and found herself in a narrow street flanked by warehouses and blocked, at one end, by a massive pile of rubble. A dead end. She turned around to backtrack, but the monsters burst around the corner. The buildings on either side of her began to shiver and shake.

Even though the men had no faces, Dea could tell they were smiling.

She swiveled around again, desperate, her breath slicing through her chest. Her mom's voice was still singing in her head. And then, just as the buildings around her started to crumble, tumbling soft piles of old brick and sheetrock into the street, sending plumes of snow shooting back toward the sky, as the men reached out their liquid fingers to her and unhinged their jaws, roaring, as if to swallow her whole—as she felt their wet breath on her throat and neck, their eager, tasting tongues, black as rot—a narrow opening was revealed, just for a second, as one of the warehouses shifted on its foundation. She threw herself sideways toward the thin slice of darkness, and heard a scream as if the whole world was tearing.

She woke up, gasping. Connor woke up at the same time. His face was damp with sweat. The rain was much lighter now, and the car was far too hot.

"You," was the first thing he said. Then: "What the hell? What the hell was that?"

She couldn't speak. She knew if she tried to talk, she would start to cry. Her ankle and wrist still ached, a phantom pain carried over from the dream world. She wanted her mom. She wanted her mom to run her fingers through the wild tangle of her hair and tell her it would be okay.

"You were there." His eyes were wild and wide, just like they had been in the dream. She was suddenly frightened of him. "I wasn't just dreaming you. *You were there.*" He grabbed her arms, as he had done in his dream bedroom, before the blood started pooling, before the monsters came. Fear made her stomach feel loose; she had to get out of the car, away from Connor, away from what had happened.

"Let me go," she whispered. Connor's face was swallowed by shadows, and Dea half expected that at any second, his skin might collapse, falling away like the ground around a sinkhole.

"Not until you explain," Connor said. His expression was guarded, now, tight with suspicion. "What . . . what *are* you?"

She didn't answer. Her chest was so heavy with terror and grief, she couldn't speak, could barely breathe. As soon as Connor released her, she shoved open the door and ran. She heard him call her name, but she didn't stop. Miniature lakes had formed in the pitted surface of the parking lot, and her shoes and jeans got soaked. Each time she put weight on her left ankle, a shiver of pain went up her spine, as if the dream were reaching across dimensions, making sure she couldn't escape.

Connor's headlights came on behind her, throwing a thick slab of light onto the oily sheen of the lot, little eddies swirling with trash. She made it to the restaurant doors as he was pulling his car up to the curb.

"Get back in the car, Dea," he called.

She pushed into the McDonald's, pausing to see if Connor

114

would come after her. Even through the glass, she could hear him calling to her. She kept going, her feet squeaking on the linoleum, the bright electric lights blinding after the darkness of the dream. The normalcy was destabilizing. It felt like she'd jumped scenes in a movie. A trucker with sweat stains on his back was filling up a large cup with soda; two teenagers, dressed in identical red polo shirts and visor caps, were parked behind the McDonald's counter; a woman was wiping her toddler's face with a damp napkin while the kid writhed. The air smelled like grease and cleaning solution and wet clothing.

She didn't know whether Connor would come after her but she ducked into the women's bathroom, just in case, and locked herself into a stall. She flipped down the toilet lid and sat, breathing deep, fighting the urge to cry or puke.

What are you? Connor had asked. She didn't know. She'd never known.

She should never have gotten close to him; she wasn't meant to have friends.

After a while, she ventured out of the bathroom. Connor's car was gone. He'd left. She was half-relieved, half-upset. She was stranded, now, at some rest stop an hour from home. She fished out her cell phone and powered it on. Connor had texted her four times and left two voice mails, but she deleted all of his messages without opening them.

The only other number she had stored in her phone was Gollum's. Gollum didn't drive, and Dea didn't feel like answering her questions, anyway. And calling her mom was out of the question, too.

She bought a soda, drank it slowly, and felt a little better.

She learned from one of the kids behind the counter at McDonald's that the number 37 bus stopped outside of Kirksville before heading northeast past Bloomington and toward Indianapolis. From Kirksville, she could walk home.

The bus smelled like old food and bubblegum. There were only a few other passengers, and the dim overhead lights cast their eyes in dark shadow. She kept her eyes down, not wanting to remember the men from Connor's dream and the black pools of their faces.

It was after one a.m. by the time she got home, going the long way across Daniel Robbins's fields instead of heading up Route 9, even though it was so dark she had to use her phone as a makeshift flashlight, and she could hear rats rustling in the corn. She didn't want to have to pass Connor's house. At least it had stopped raining, although the air still had a heavy, wet feel, like a damp palm pressing down on her from all sides. Every time she heard the whisper of movement behind her, she whipped around, swinging her phone, casting a jerky beam of light on the trampled-down corn and thick ruts of mud in the field, her throat seizing, thinking of the faceless men. But there was never anyone behind her, just the black, glittering eyes of animals that scampered away from the light.

Once she reached her porch, she realized she shouldn't have worried about Connor. His house was totally dark. She felt a brief pull of resentment. He must be sleeping. Even though she'd run away from him, she was momentarily annoyed that he hadn't tried to look for her. But he knew, now, what she was—and she couldn't forget his look of horror. *What are you?*

Tomorrow, she would pack her suitcase and apologize to her

mom, and they would load the car and head off. Just like they'd always done. She would miss Gollum. But Gollum would be okay. Gollum would get over it.

Connor would, too.

The door was locked, and all the lights were off. Her mom hadn't waited up, which was unusual. Dea knew Miriam must have been worried. Maybe she was proving a point, after their fight this morning.

She moved carefully toward the stairs. Toby came trotting out from the kitchen and wound himself around her legs. Her shoes crunched and she realized he must have tracked some of the food she'd spilled out into the hallway. Weird that her mom hadn't cleaned it up. But this, too, was probably a point. Dea would sweep it up tomorrow.

Upstairs, Dea snuck as quietly as she could past her mom's bedroom; the door was open just a crack. A bit of moonlight was trying to wrestle its way out of the clouds and Dea's bedroom was painted in broad, dark brushstrokes, like a careless illustration. She saw that her mom hadn't cleaned up here, either. Dea knew she was in for a serious lecture when she woke up, but she didn't care.

She wanted to get away from Fielding—away from Connor and his dreams.

She stripped off her wet clothes and got into bed naked, too tired to root around for her sleep pants. A moment later, Toby jumped up into bed beside her and got comfortable on her feet. She slowly began to feel warm. Then she was asleep, and feeling nothing.

ELEVEN

The first thing Dea noticed when she woke up was that it was raining again, a hard rain, the kind that washed away every color.

The second thing: something was wrong.

It was almost noon. Toby was gone from the bed. She'd slept through the clocks and their early morning chatter. Her mom hadn't come upstairs to wake her. The house was silent. No squeaking footsteps, no water running, no quiet burble of the coffeepot downstairs.

She regretted, now, the mess she'd made yesterday. She tripped over a pair of jeans on her way to the door and nearly cracked her head on the wall. She steadied herself and moved into the hall. Empty houses always reminded Dea of holding shells to her ear, listening to the distant white roar of an ocean she would never see. She had that feeling now—of emptiness, of distance.

"Mom?" she called out. Her throat was tight. No answer. She fought down a wave of panic. Her mom could be out buying packing tape, or getting the oil changed, or loading up on beef jerky and Cheez-Its for the road. Anything.

Then she opened her mother's door and the world somersaulted and she thought she might puke. Everything was exactly as Dea had left it the day before. If anything, it looked messier than Dea had left it—the drawers of the bureau overturned, piles of clothing and tangled bits of cheap jewelry littered across the carpet, the faint smell of cosmetic powder and perfume hanging over everything like a haze. The sheets were still balled up on the floor, the mattress bare.

Dea had to hold onto the wall. Her mom hadn't been home last night. Had she left? Had she had enough of Dea, picked up and taken off somewhere?

There was a dull pain in her head, the throbbing of a single word repeated over and over: *no, no, no, no.* She ran downstairs and hurtled into the living room, pressing her face to the window.

The car was still in the driveway. That gave Dea some relief. So her mom couldn't have gone far. She didn't remember whether she'd seen the VW the night before, when she came home.

Then a new anxiety began to pluck at her: her mom was most definitely gone. So if she hadn't left on her own, in the car, what did that mean? Something terrible could have happened. Dea tried to remember whether the front door had been locked the night before; she thought so, but she couldn't be sure. Miriam might have been abducted. She might have been killed. Some psycho might have snuck into the house. People did things like that, crazy people, just came inside and snatched you or battered your head in with an ax.

It had happened to Connor's family. It could have happened to hers. Dea had a sudden image of Connor's mother, moaning, while her brain leaked onto her pillow. Her stomach rolled into her throat. She had to stay calm.

She had to call the police.

Her phone was upstairs. She'd dumped her bag at the foot of her bed the night before. She fished her phone out of her bag and moved to the bed, to sit down. A piece of glass was wedged in the soft underside of her foot.

She noticed, for the first time, that shards of glass carpeted the area in front of her closet. She put the phone down and moved carefully into a crouch. Was this evidence of a struggle? But why would there have been a struggle in Dea's room? And where had the glass come from?

She swung open the closet door. Her secret mirrors. They'd *exploded*. Not shattered, not broken—exploded. The frames were empty, bare, as if something inside the mirror had reached up a fist and punched its way out, sending a spray of glass into her room.

She remembered what her mother had said the first time Dea saw her dismantle a bathroom mirror, fiddling with the screws, dismounting the swinging door, wrapping the whole thing in layers of black cloth before bringing it out to the trash.

"That's how the monsters keep watch," she'd said, dropping her voice. "That's how they see out."

Dea closed her eyes and opened them again. She wasn't thinking straight. Monsters didn't come through mirrors. They didn't pass through water, either, as her mom had always said, and they weren't afraid of clocks and doorways. There was no such thing as monsters—not in real life.

Her foot was bleeding. She hobbled to the bathroom, where the contents of the medicine cabinet were still scattered across the floor. She sat on the toilet and fished the glass out from her foot with a pair of tweezers, struggling to control her shaking hands. Then she bandaged her foot, went back to her room for her cell phone, and punched in 9-1-1.

The phone rang for what seemed like forever. Wasn't the point of a first responder supposed to be the response? Dea almost hung up and tried again, but at last someone picked up.

"9-1-1." The woman's voice was monotone. "What's your emergency?"

Dea tried to speak but only whimpered. She cleared her throat. "My mom . . ." Jesus. What should she say? Her mom was gone? She'd been abducted? Dea didn't know that yet.

The monsters took my mother. The thought came to her, unbidden, and she pushed it away.

"What about your mom?" Dea could hear the woman tapping away at her computer.

"She disappeared," Dea said. Her voice was steadier now.

Tap, tap, tap. "How long has she been gone?"

"I'm not sure." Dea had left the house a little before noon

the day before; her mom had come home some time afterward, and then vanished sometime before one a.m., when Dea had returned. She might have been missing for twelve hours or almost twenty-four. "I mean, I don't know exactly." She was about to explain when she heard the doorbell ring. She was so startled, she nearly dropped the phone. Connor. It must be.

She went halfway down the stairs, where she had a view of the front porch through the thick windowpanes on either side of the door. Not Connor. Two police officers. In the driveway, she saw a local squad car, lights revolving, slices of red and white reflecting in the puddled surface of the road.

"When was the last time you saw your mother?" the woman was saying.

"That's all right," she said. "They're here already."

"Who?"

"Your guys," Dea said. "The police."

"No, ma'am, I haven't—"

But Dea was so distracted, so relieved, that she hung up without listening. The police would help. That was their job.

"Odea Donahue?" one of the cops said, when she opened the door, pronouncing her name the way that people from Fielding always did, as if it was a foreign food that they found distasteful. He looked vaguely familiar. In his midforties, probably, big in the chest and shoulders with a stomach paunch that rolled over his belt. His eyes were very pale blue. The second cop—at least, Dea assumed he was a cop, although he wasn't in uniform—was a few years younger, thin, and wearing a yellow poncho and shiny leather shoes.

"Thank God," she said. It was cold, and the rain was coming

down so hard it sent a fine spray upward when it hit the porch. She crossed her arms and backed up so they could enter the hall. "I didn't think you'd come so quickly."

The two cops exchanged a look. "Can we come in?" the first one said, and Dea nodded. There was a moment of awkward quiet after Dea closed the door. Since there was no mat for them to wipe their feet on, the cop just stood there, dripping on the floor, arms extended stiffly away from his body, like a human umbrella.

"I'm Officer Briggs." This from the cop who looked familiar. Dea felt a jolt. Briggs. This was Will Briggs's dad, who'd supposedly cracked a guitar over his son's head. Connor's uncle. Briggs gestured next to his partner. "And this is Special Agent Connelly."

Special agent. It sounded like something from a movie. Dea assumed Connelly must be a high-ranking detective, someone who tracked down missing persons for a living. She kept her hands wrapped around her waist, squeezing.

"We were hoping to speak to your mother," Connelly said. His tone was casual. He might as well have been saying *We were hoping to borrow a vacuum cleaner.* "Is she home?"

Dea's heart sank. They were wasting time. Her mom was gone, and the police hadn't even been properly informed. "She didn't tell you?"

Connelly frowned. "What do you mean?"

"The dispatcher," Dea said, fighting the growing desire to scream. "The woman I spoke to just now. I *told* her. Something must have happened—she would never just leave me."

"Hold on, hold on." Connelly moved as though he was

123

thinking about putting a hand on Dea's shoulder, but he didn't. "Your mom's gone?"

"She's missing," Dea corrected him. *Gone* made it sound as if it was something Dea's mom had chosen. Connelly and Briggs exchanged a look. "Didn't they tell you *anything*?"

Connelly rubbed his eyes, as if Dea was being a big pain in the ass.

Briggs spoke up. "No one called us out here, Odea," he said. "We came on our own."

Dea stared. "What . . . what do you mean?" she said. "If nobody sent you, why are you here?"

Briggs and Connelly exchanged another look. Dea hated it when adults did that, as if she couldn't see that they were telegraphing some secret message. She was extremely aware of the clocks ticking in the quiet—seconds, minutes running by. Shouldn't they be looking for clues, or organizing search parties or something?

"I'll call it in," Connelly said in a low voice—again, as if Dea wouldn't hear, even though she was standing less than four feet away. He unclipped a police radio and stepped outside again, closing the door behind him. Dea felt a little better. At least he was *doing* something.

"Okay, Odea," Briggs said, forced-cheerful, over-loud. "Can we sit down and chat for a minute?"

"Shouldn't you be looking for my mom?" Dea blurted out.

"If we're going to find your mom, I'll need to ask you a few questions," he said, in an I-know-best kind of voice. Dea could tell he was trying hard to be nice, probably so she wouldn't freak out. She tried to imagine him taking a guitar to Will's head and

124

couldn't. She tried to find a resemblance to Connor and couldn't do that, either.

"All right," she said. She gestured to the living room. Toby jumped off the couch and darted under an armchair. No one had ever been inside the house except for Dea and her mom. Briggs eased himself down onto the sofa, trying to seem casual, smiling like this was a social visit. But Dea wasn't fooled. She watched his eyes tick over the whole room, taking in everything—the clocks, the bare mantelpiece where the photograph of Dea's fake dad had been, the mishmash of furniture from different eras.

Dea didn't feel like sitting down but Officer Briggs looked as though he expected her to, so she did, trying to control the buzzing anxiety crawling through her legs and arms, like a thousand insects.

"All right, let's start at the beginning," Briggs said. "When's the last time you saw your mother?"

"Yesterday." Dea looked down at her hands. "We had a fight." She felt the urge to cry and took a deep breath, willing herself to stay calm. She wasn't going to have a breakdown in front of a stranger.

"Did your mom seem . . . different at all to you? Jumpy? Nervous about something?"

Dea shook her head. "No." Then she corrected: "She . . . she wanted to move again. That's what the fight was about. I told her I wouldn't." If Dea hadn't been so stubborn—if she'd agreed to pack up and go, like her mother wanted—her mom might still be home, and okay. It was all her fault.

Briggs was jotting down notes. For a long minute, they sat in silence. Dea felt every second that passed in her chest and teeth and stomach. Finally, she couldn't take it anymore. "We shouldn't be sitting here," she said. "We should be out looking. She could be hurt. She could be in danger. Why are we just *sitting* here?"

Briggs put away his notebook. "Let's stay calm, okay?"

But Dea couldn't stay calm. Fear and frustration clawed up her chest. Her fault. "She could be dead. You're supposed to be helping. You're supposed to be *finding* her."

The front door slammed again, and Dea jumped. Connelly reappeared, shaking more rain onto the carpet. He didn't look at Dea, just spoke directly to Briggs. "Okay," he said. "The troopers will keep an eye out at toll points." His eyes clicked to Dea. "Does your mom have a different vehicle, other than the one parked outside?"

"No," Dea said. They were acting like her mom had just picked up and left. She dug her nails into the flesh of her hands and pressed, wishing that, like a dream, she could just find a way *out*.

"Okay, good, good." Connelly was nodding. "What about some place she likes to go? Like a country house? A little hideaway?"

"*Hideaway*?" Dea looked from Connelly to Briggs and back. "Are you . . . is this a joke? My mom didn't *go* anywhere. She didn't *leave* me. Something *happened*. Don't you get that?"

"Odea"—Briggs leaned forward, putting his hands on his elbows—"I know this must be hard for you. But your mom is in a lot of trouble. That's why we came here today. Not to find her. To arrest her."

Silence. Ticking silence. Dea counted her heartbeats. One,

two, three. Pause. *Fourfivesix*. "What . . . what are you talking about?"

"I'm sorry you have to learn about it this way," Briggs said. He really did sound sorry. She wondered if he'd told Connor he was sorry, after Connor's mom's head was splattered halfway across the bedroom. "Your mother's a smart woman. I'm sure you know that. There've been a dozen fraud investigations against her in as many years. Arizona, Florida, Illinois. Identity theft, security fraud, some petty thieving. Agent Connelly's department reached out to me after she got up to her old tricks here in Fielding."

"What do you mean, *Agent Connelly's department*?" Dea said. Her voice sounded distant, foreign, like it was being piped back to her through a cave. She turned to Connelly. "You're not a cop?"

Connelly shook his head. "I'm with the Feds," he said simply.

Dea closed her eyes. Opened them again. But the two men were still there—both of them watching her with twin expressions of pity.

"She's always skipped town before we could make anything stick," Connelly said. Dea hated the way he said *she*, avoiding Miriam's name, as if she wasn't a real person. "Looks like she's done it again." He was still standing, leaning against the doorframe, arms crossed. Still dripping on the carpet.

Dea's thoughts were disjointed. She was seeing everything in short flashes, as if the reel in her brain kept getting cut.

Connelly's boots were crusted with mud. Her mom would be mad about that—about the mud. Then she remembered her mom was gone.

"You're wrong," Dea managed to say. "That doesn't make any sense."

But even as she said it, she remembered all the times her mother had woken her in the grayness of a new dawn, whispering "It's time to go, Dea"; packing up the car before the sun wrestled free of the horizon; long hours, towns melting blurrily by the windows, her mother silent, anxious. And the other stuff: fake names, jobs that never went anywhere, money that came from nowhere, money stuffed in cardboard shoeboxes and hidden in the dashboard.

She wondered if the cops knew about the money.

"It took us a long time to pin anything on her," Connelly said. "But this time we're sure."

"I'm sorry," Briggs said again, as if that helped. As if it *mattered*.

Dea thought of the brochures spread across the kitchen table, and the urgent way her mom had woken her the day before. *We're leaving.* She must have known the police were closing in. Dea's mouth tasted like bile. Her thoughts ricocheted back and forth between anger and denial. It wasn't possible. It made sense. She wouldn't have. She must have.

All these years, when Miriam had filled Dea's head with stories about monsters and mirrors and locks on the door, she was just full of shit. She was running from the law, plain and simple.

And yet . . .

The mirrors had shattered upstairs. Small, scrappy evidence, but *something*. And her mom couldn't have gone far without a car, unless she'd ditched it in favor of the bus. But even if what the cops said was true—her mom had been stealing, using identities

128

that weren't hers—Dea couldn't, wouldn't, believe that Miriam would have left Dea behind.

Dea pictured her mother turning to her, winking, as they barreled down another nameless highway. *Thick as thieves.*

"I know this is asking a lot," Briggs was saying, in a soothing voice, like he was trying to coax Dea back onto a bike after she'd fallen down. Dea wondered whether Connelly was supposed to be the bad cop. Or the bad *Fed*. Or whatever. Neither of them looked the part. Both of them looked like tired dads. She still hated them. "But if there's anything you can think of at all that might help us find your mom—any detail, anything she mentioned in the past few days—any place she particularly likes to go . . . ?"

"No," Dea said abruptly.

She stood up, and then, feeling dizzy and realizing she had nowhere to go, sat down again. What would happen to her now?

"Think really hard, Odea." Briggs leaned forward. "Are you sure?"

"Yes," Dea said. She was seventeen. She had no family. Would they force her into some group home? Or put her up for adoption? No one adopted seventeen-year-olds. She needed to find her mom before the cops did. She had to. "No," she said suddenly. "I mean, I'm not sure. She mentioned something about Cleveland." She swallowed, licked her lips. She'd never been a great liar. "She said—she said there was something she needed to pick up. Before we left town." She held her breath. The lie sounded stupid, even to her.

But Connelly and Briggs shared another one of those looks.

"There's a bus leaves downtown every other hour, drops you

right in downtown Cleveland," Briggs said.

"We'll call it in," Connelly said. "See if any of the bus drivers remember someone boarding." He turned back to Dea, leaning forward to rest his elbows on his knees. "How old are you, Dea?"

"Eighteen," she lied quickly, figuring they'd be too busy to check right away. She wasn't sure, but she thought Briggs looked relieved.

"I want you to sit tight, Odea," he said. He had to use both arms to shove himself out of the sofa. He was big. Probably six foot five. That was the only thing he had in common with Connor. "If your mother calls, ask her where she is, but don't tell her we came by."

"What if she comes back?" Dea said.

"That's what we're counting on." Briggs smiled. When he did, his expression flattened and tightened, and he looked for an instant like someone who would have, could have, cracked his son on the head with a guitar. "We got someone watching from across the road."

Dea stood up. She was itching for them to get out. "What about me?" she said. "I was supposed to go to the library in Marborough today. For a school project." More lies. But she needed an excuse to get out of the house, and she was sure the cops would be watching.

"We'd prefer for you to stay here," Briggs said.

"Prefer it," she said. "But you can't make me."

"No." He looked her up and down, sizing her up, maybe trying to figure out if she was stupid or just stubborn. "No, we can't."

There was nothing more to say. Briggs told Dea they'd be in

touch very soon, which sounded less like a reassurance than a threat. She walked both cops to the door—Connelly flipped up his hood against the driving rain—and watched to make sure they drove away. There was a service truck parked in Connor's driveway, and Dea saw a man in a yellow slicker moving around a telephone pole. A bad time to be fixing wires. It was raining so hard, the whole world seemed to be dissolving.

Dea closed the door and leaned against it. She was struck again by how still and empty the house felt, like a hollow vessel; she could hear individual drops of rain patter the window. Her chest ached with the effort of trying not to cry. She thought of calling Gollum, or even driving the five hundred feet to her house.

But she needed to stay calm. She needed to focus.

Where could her mom have gone? Was it possible that what the cops had told her was true? Had her mom just . . . left? Gone on the run?

Dea knew she'd already accepted that at least one part of what Briggs and Connelly had told her was true: her mom had been stealing identities, maybe making fraudulent claims, pocketing cash where she could. Weirdly enough, the knowledge was actually a relief. The middle-of-the-night flights, the money stuffed in hidden places, the aliases and identities, jobs attained and rapidly quit—it all made sense to her now.

Struck by a sudden thought, Dea grabbed the car keys and, without bothering to put on a jacket, hurtled out into the rain. The storm was even worse than it had been the night before. The sky was a queasy green color, and the whole world looked unnatural, wrong. She was soaked by the time she made it fifteen feet to the car. She sat for a moment, shivering, and fumbled with stiff fingers to start the car, thumbing on the heat.

Was she being watched, even now? Would she be followed?

She scanned the yard and the garden. She didn't see anyone. She ducked down and worked a hand under the passenger seat, feeling for the large tear in the fabric, where her mom had slit open the cushion. Reaching upward, pushing her fist past a web of stuffing, she felt it: a thick Christmas stocking, stuffed full of cash. As she expected, it hadn't been moved.

She knew there was over two thousand dollars crammed into that stocking. Her mom had told her so. So why would Miriam go on the run without it? It didn't make sense.

She threw the car into gear and backed slowly out of the driveway, her wheels sloshing water up into the grass. The telephone repair guy was still moving around in the rain, fidgeting at the base of the pole, but he straightened up to watch her as she drove past. Almost immediately, he got in his truck and pulled onto the road behind her.

Of course. Briggs had said someone was keeping an eye on the house. They'd suited up a cop to look like a repairman and sicced him on her. There was probably another cop, too, camping out in Connor's house, reporting everything back to base. Dea felt a sharp pang. That meant Connor knew what was going on. Knew that her mom was a thief, knew that she'd disappeared, knew that Dea was all alone.

At the corner of Main Street she made a left automatically. The service truck turned onto Route 9 behind her. Every time she swiveled her head, it was there. Not too close, not too far. Her palms were sweating. She felt like a criminal, even though she hadn't done anything wrong.

She was halfway to Marborough before she realized she was heading toward the library. Well. Why not? She'd told Officer Briggs that's where she was going, and it was as good a place as any to sit and think. Besides, it shared a parking lot with the post office branch where her mother had kept a PO box—this, too, filled with cash. Dea had a spare key—she'd found a locksmith who had cut her a break and copied it, even though it was clearly marked *Do Not Duplicate*—and once or twice when she was flat broke she'd lifted a twenty-dollar bill from her mom's stash, figuring her mom would never notice.

She would go there and see whether that money, too, was intact.

Then she would know for sure whether her mom had run away, or—or something else.

Something even worse.

The library parking lot was a lake. Her tires created miniature wakes when she pulled in. There were hardly any other cars in the lot. Smart people were staying inside today. Dea shut the engine off and waited, her breath condensing on the windshield. Sure enough, the service truck that wasn't a service truck was still behind her. The cop didn't turn into the library; he parked at the curb on the opposite side of the street, as if that were less obvious.

Dea got out, ducked her head, and ran for the front doors.

The library was quiet and unexpectedly cold, and the smell of must was everywhere. Dea felt like she was walking into a sealed vault. Once the heavy doors swung shut behind her, she couldn't hear the rain anymore. Behind the front counter, a woman with dyed red hair was doing something at a computer; she barely glanced up at Dea when she passed. A guy wearing a filthy camouflage jacket was napping on one of the research tables, head down on an open book; Dea judged from his clothes that he was homeless. She felt another sharp pang. Was she homeless now? She would rather be homeless than go into foster care—she knew that.

She moved through the stacks toward the back of the library, where beanbag chairs were arranged in a semicircle in a small, sunken area that reminded Dea of an amphitheater. It was technically the children's area, but since moving to Fielding Dea had spent hours parked in a chair here when the library was slow, reading any book that grabbed her attention, imagining being in someone else's body, in someone else's life.

For a moment, seeing the lumpy chairs and a stack of picture books splayed across the worn carpet, where some kid must have left them, she had the overwhelming urge to curl up and go to sleep. But she kept going, toward the back door, which opened out onto a narrow spit of gravel that divided the library from the post office.

She darted through the rain again, hands up, as if she could fend off the assault from above. It wasn't until she tried the door handle and found it locked that she remembered that it was Sunday and the post office was closed. She cupped her face to the glass, blinking rain away. Dark. She banged on the door anyway, and rattled the door handle. Irrationally, she felt she *had* to get in. It was the only way she would know for sure; and if she didn't know, she would die.

She aimed a kick at the door, half hoping the glass would

shatter. It didn't, of course. Suddenly, the urge to cry—which she had been keeping back, swallowing down—became too much. It crystallized in the back of her throat, and became a word.

"Mom," she called out, into the empty air, into the rain. She had the sudden sense of being watched, an alarm pricking up all over her skin. Goose flesh. "Mom? Mom!"

Calling into the grayness, into the haze of rain, as if the moisture were a curtain and it might suddenly part to reveal her mother, smiling, walking toward her with open arms.

Nothing. Nothing but the rain spitting on the gravel. Dea was crying, now, without realizing it. "Mom!" She took the door handles and rattled them again, desperate, not thinking straight. "Mom. Where are you?"

There was a shift in the darkness behind the post office door. Suddenly a woman materialized behind the glass—big, frowning, her face distorted by the rain. Dea stepped backward, swiping her nose with a wrist, as the woman unlocked the door.

"What in the devil are you doing here?" she said. She was wearing sneakers, jeans, and a sweatshirt printed with the faded graphic of a kitten; still, she managed to look threatening. "We're closed."

Dea fumbled for an excuse. "Please." She cleared her throat. She could see the bank of post office boxes behind the woman's bulk, glinting dully. "My mom—my mom was supposed to mail me something. A message." Her throat was so dry, she could hardly swallow. "I just need to look—just for thirty seconds. A minute, tops. Please."

The woman gave Odea a long look up and down. Odea

couldn't stop herself from shivering. She had never felt so pathetic.

"Quickly," the woman said, and stepped backward. "We ain't supposed to be open."

"Thank you." Dea could have hugged her, except the woman definitely didn't seem like the type who hugged. She stepped inside, grateful to be out of the rain. Her socks were soaked, and her hair dripped down her back. The woman stayed by the door, tapping a foot, keeping her eye on Dea like she might try to steal something. "Not even supposed to be here myself," she was saying. "Left my cell phone on Friday, been hunting around for it all weekend . . ."

Dea squeaked over to her mom's post office box. Her fingers were raw and clumsy from the cold, and it took her a minute to work her key in the lock, and another second before she could summon the courage to open it. She didn't know what she wanted more: for the money to be missing, or not.

"Course now the damn thing's dead, don't know why they can't make a phone last longer than a hour, seems like they can do just about everything else nowadays . . ."

It was all there—envelopes full of cash, neatly rubber banded together. Dea felt a surge of triumph—Miriam hadn't run, after all—followed by a wave of dizziness. That meant she'd been forced or nabbed or stuffed in some psycho's trunk.

She angled her body so she was blocking the contents of the mailbox from view, then stuffed an envelope of cash in the waistband of her jeans, concealing it behind her T-shirt. That would be five hundred dollars at least, enough to get her through a few weeks on her own. *On her own.* She felt sick; she'd never before considered just how very alone she was without her mom.

"You get everything you need?" the woman asked, as Dea crossed her arms and headed back out into the storm.

"Yeah," Dea said, even though it was a lie—she had nothing, knew nothing, understood nothing. She was sure of only one thing: whether or not her mom was a liar, and a thief, and maybe even a crackpot, she hadn't gone away on her own or because she wanted to. She hadn't left Dea behind.

Back in the VW, Dea checked to see whether the cop was still waiting for her. He was, of course. She was gripped by a total-body fury. The police were supposed to help, but they wouldn't. They would do nothing.

She took a hard right out of the lot, pressing hard on the gas, without knowing where she was going—she had the sudden, vengeful urge to waste the cop's time, to lead him out into nowhere while he tooled behind her in his truck, trying to look inconspicuous. She would drive and drive and he would have to follow her until nowhere.

She took her next left at the last moment and he barely made the turn. She gunned the accelerator, speeding hard through sheets of water, the windshield wipers dancing frantically across the glass. Fuck him. She took another right and the tires skidded on the road; the wheel jerked under her hands and she overcorrected, nearly plunged into a ditch, then managed to bring the car into the right lane. She was driving crazily, dangerously, but she didn't care. The truck was still on her ass, closing the distance now, no longer worried about staying in the background.

She went faster. Water planed out from her wheels, and the sky looked like it was coming down, like something you'd see in a dream just as it started to dissolve. Thank God the roads were empty. She could hardly see twenty feet in front of her, even with the brights on: just wetness coasting across pitted dirt lanes, and wind lashing the fields into the ground. Left. Then another right. She had no idea where she was. She'd left the town of Marborough behind. There was nothing out here but muddy tracks of grass and dirt, big burnt-looking trees and some straggly evergreens, sagging toward the earth, and rain, and more rain.

Another right. She pivoted quickly in her seat, taking her eyes off the road, to check whether the cop was still following her. She didn't see him. Maybe she'd managed to leave him behind.

She turned back to the road and then it happened. She was moving through a sheet of rain; and then the rain began to change, to flow differently, to *solidify*. The water rose and joined and twisted into a shape. She slammed on the brakes, but it was too late.

The water wasn't water anymore, but two figures walking toward her. Even though they had no faces, she could tell they were smiling.

She screamed and wrenched the wheel to the right. The car jumped the gutter and plunged into the field. The wheel jerked out of her hands. She bit down on her tongue and tasted blood. Then the black arms of the trees reached out to embrace her, and she moved into the dark.

TWELVE

When Dea woke up, she was staring at the high, round Cyclops-eye of a single light fixture, fitted in a blank white ceiling. Her throat was raw, as if it had been scrubbed with a Brillo pad. The air was filled with a quiet mechanical hum, and from some distance came the echo of voices and the beeping of hidden machinery.

A hospital. Obviously, a hospital.

She tried to sit up but couldn't make it far. She was constrained by multicolored tubes running to and from her wrists, pumping blood out and liquid in. Two needles were threaded into the veins on her hand, distorting the skin slightly. She felt faint twinges of pain in her neck and shoulders when she moved. But she could move her legs and wiggle her toes. She wasn't in a body cast. She could breathe.

So: she wasn't dying, she wasn't paralyzed, she wasn't even injured, at least not that she could see.

She remembered, then, the story her mom used to tell her, of a pregnant woman lying in a hospital bed and dreaming of another pregnant woman—Dea didn't recall the details. It was some kind of fairy tale, but Dea didn't remember whether it had a happy ending.

Thinking of her mother, she felt a rush of panic. All at once, the accident came back to her: the drive through the sluicing rain, the cop in his truck, the water spinning out from beneath her wheels . . .

The monsters.

She'd seen them. Here. In the real world. It was impossible. But she knew that she hadn't been dreaming.

The hidden beeping grew more urgent, faster. Dea fumbled with the needles threaded under her skin. She needed to go home. She should have stayed home, like the cops had instructed her to do. Maybe—maybe—her mom had even come back by now. But the second she had the thought, she dismissed it. If her mom had reappeared, she'd be sitting next to Dea's bed. She'd have brought a blanket from home, and Dea's favorite slippers, and autumn leaves gathered from the yard and arranged neatly in a wreath; she'd have slung a sweatshirt over the big mirror hanging above the sink, or tried to dismount it from the wall.

She hadn't been here, which meant: still missing.

She pried out one of the needles and felt a quick stab of pain.

Blood beaded immediately on her hand, and she wiped it carelessly on the white sheet. Before she could go after the second needle, however, the door opened and a nurse came bustling in—*bustling* was the only way to describe it—looking so cheerfully and resolutely competent that Dea's heart sank.

"Well, good morning, little lady." The nurse crossed to the window and pulled aside the curtains. Dea blinked in the unexpected light. The sun was high and bright, the sky a radiant blue. She must have been out for a long time—a full day, maybe more. "Or good afternoon, I guess I should say. How're you feeling?" She didn't wait for Dea to reply, but instead took up her hand and quickly, with no wasted movements, blotted the blood from her hand with a cotton swab and replaced the IV, working the needle back and forth to get it into the vein. Dea had to look away. "Got to be careful to keep the fluids flowing. How's the pain? Three? Four?" This while fiddling with the IV bag, adjusting doses, spinning dials with her thick fingers. "That better? Good, good. You hungry at all?"

There was an untouched tray next to Dea's bed: chicken in a lumpy white sauce, some disintegrating peas and carrots, and a small carton of orange juice. Dea felt briefly disappointed there was no Jell-O. In movies, there always was. But she couldn't have eaten anyway.

"No? Well, maybe in a little while." The nurse had a square, friendly face that reminded Dea of a bulldog. Her name tag read Donna Sue, which seemed like a name she might have made up to keep her patients at ease while she was busy sticking needles in their arms and probing their asses. "You want me to turn on the TV for you?"

Dea shook her head. Donna was acting like she was going to be stuck there. "How long was I sleeping?"

"Hold." Donna Sue stuck a thermometer under Dea's tongue and counted to three, then withdrew it and checked the meter. "Temperature's normal, that's good." She made a note on Dea's chart, then looked up. Her eyes were watery blue, and her lashes so thick with mascara that little clumps of black were gathered under her eyes. "Little less than twenty-four hours. You were plain conked out. Lucky as stars, though, sweetheart. Not a broken bone in your body. No concussion either."

"So . . ." Dea swallowed. "Can I go home soon?"

Donna Sue laughed, as if Dea had made a joke. She placed a hand on Dea's foot as she moved back toward the door. "I'll tell Dr. Chaudhary you're awake," she said. "She'll be in to see you in just a few. Sit tight, okay, hon?" As if Dea could do anything else.

The nurse had left her chart near the sink. Dea was curious about what it said, but not sufficiently curious to try to maneuver out of bed still hooked to an IV. She considered disentangling herself from the needles and making a run for it. She knew that's what her mom would have done. *Get out of Dodge, slip through the cracks, blink and you'll miss us.* But she didn't see where that would get her: her mom was still missing, the cops were probably tearing her house apart, and she had nowhere to go. She could hardly show up at Gollum's and ask to be adopted. Maybe, if she was lucky, they could find her a place in their horse barn.

She felt a pulse of alarm when she remembered Toby. Would someone feed him? Was he okay?

She would speak to the doctor; she would explain that the crash was an accident, sign whatever needed to get signed, and get the hell out of there. Then she'd worry about what to do next.

She didn't wait long. There was a soft knock, more warning than request. Before Dea could respond, the door swung open. Dr. Chaudhary was young, Indian, and a soap-opera-star kind of pretty. Dea was all too aware of the thin paper gown she was wearing; the bruises on her arms; the medicinal, foul taste in her mouth.

"Odea?" Dr. Chaudhary said, glancing at Dea's chart. She spoke softly, pronouncing Odea's name in a curious singsong. Maybe she hadn't been raised in Indiana. Maybe she'd been raised in New York, or Bangladesh, or London. The idea gave Odea a curious lift of hope. Maybe she could help. "You gave us all quite a scare."

Dr. Chaudhary sat in a chair next to Dea's bed. Drawing the chart into her lap, she flipped forward to a blank page. "Why don't you tell me what you remember?"

"About the accident?" Dea asked. Dr. Chaudhary nodded. Dea remembered those faceless men made of ribbons of wet and dark, and closed her eyes, thinking of Connor instead. But that hurt almost as much. "Not a lot," she said finally. "It was raining. I must have lost control of the car."

"Mmm-hmm." The doctor nodded and scribbled something on the chart, as though Dea had made an interesting point.

"The nurse—"

"Donna."

"Yeah. Donna said I'm doing okay." Dea sat up a little straighter, trying not to look at the blood seeping through the

143

tubes in her hand, feeling a little bit like an insect in a web. "She said I didn't break anything."

"You didn't. You were very lucky."

"She said that, too." For the first time it occurred to Dea: she could have died. Was that what the monsters had intended? She dismissed the thought. She wouldn't think about them. She couldn't. Monsters weren't real. They lived in dreams and fears and nightmare-places. "When can I go home?"

Dr. Chaudhary didn't even look up. Dea couldn't imagine that what she had said justified so many notes, and wished she knew what Dr. Chaudhary was writing about her. "Home," she repeated. Finally the doctor did look up. Her eyes were the clear brown of maple syrup. "I've heard that your mother is having . . . difficulties. How does that make you feel?"

"Who told you that?" Dea said sharply, before realizing: the cops. Of course. Someone must have pulled her from the car, called 9-1-1, gotten her to the emergency room. Maybe it was the guy in the truck, or even Briggs. She didn't like to think of people putting their hands on her when she was unconscious.

"Are you frightened, Odea?" It was becoming annoying, how Dr. Chaudhary didn't answer her directly. "Are you feeling angry at the police? Are you angry about being here?"

"I'm not *angry*." Dea wished she weren't stuck in a bed; it made her feel small. Young. "Look, I just want to go home."

"We can't let you go until we're sure you're all right," Dr. Chaudhary said gently. Dea knew she was trying to be nice but didn't care.

"Nothing's broken. I don't have a fever. I'm fine. Just take my pulse or do whatever you need to do." But even as she said the words, the anxiety, the worry, yawned big in her stomach. She realized that Dr. Chaudhary hadn't examined her at all, hadn't checked her head for bruises or flashed a light in her eyes or made her stick out her tongue and say *ahhh*.

"Odea"—Dr. Chaudhary pronounced her name very carefully, as if it were made of glass and might shatter in her mouth—"it's my job to make sure that you won't try to hurt yourself again."

Dea felt the words like a full-body slap. She went hot, then cold. She should have known Dr. Chaudhary was a shrink. No wonder she was so good at dodging questions.

Dea swallowed. "I wasn't—I wasn't trying to hurt myself."

"Mmm-hmm." Dr. Chaudhary inclined her head, but obviously didn't believe her. In some ways, Dea couldn't blame her. Dea's mom had vanished, she'd been visited by the cops, and less than an hour later she'd hydroplaned her car off the road, driving batshit fast in the middle of nowhere.

And Dea couldn't explain why. If she said she'd only been trying to avoid the men with no faces, Dr. Chaudhary would probably have her locked up forever.

"Please." Panic was pulling at Dea from all sides. She felt like she was drowning in thin air—in the clean, bright room, drowning in sheets and wires. "It was an accident, I told you. I—I would never kill myself." She choked a little on the words.

Dr. Chaudhary began taking notes again. "Have you ever thought about dying, Odea?"

"I mean, I've *thought* about it . . ." Dr. Chaudhary wrote something down and Dea quickly added, "But everyone thinks about it. Don't they?"

Dr. Chaudhary looked up, sighing. "No," she said bluntly.

Dea didn't believe that. Sometimes she thought about getting splattered by a semitruck or falling out of an airplane or getting crushed by an AC unit tumbling off a roof—stupid stuff, improbable stuff, just because it was interesting to think about how thin the seconds were between alive and not. "I've never *wanted* to die," she said. It was true. No matter how lonely she had been, in whatever bleak, dust-blown place she and her mom had ended up, she had never wanted to die. Only to find a place, any place, where at last, she belonged.

"I'm very glad to hear that," Dr. Chaudhary said with finality. She stashed the pen at the top of the clipboard and jogged the sheath of papers together neatly. "We just want to keep you safe."

Dea felt a surge of hope. "So does that mean I can go home?" she said.

"No." Dr. Chaudhary smiled in a way meant to convey kindness and patience and pity all at once. "The fact is, you *did* almost die. We're going to keep you here for a few days. I'll speak to you again tomorrow."

"You can't do that." Dea struggled to sit up as Dr. Chaudhary stood and began to make her way toward the door. "You can't keep me here if I don't want to stay."

Dr. Chaudhary turned with one hand on the door. "Yes, we can," she said softly. To her credit, she sounded almost regretful.

"But—"

"Don't get agitated, Odea. Just try to get some rest, okay?" And she left the room, closing the door firmly behind her.

* * *

When Donna Sue announced a visitor, Dea hoped for a brief moment that it would be Connor. Instead, it was Gollum, dressed as always in a Windbreaker several sizes too large for her, clutching a collection of water-warped women's magazines from several months earlier. Dea bit her lip to keep from crying. She'd never been so happy to see anyone in her life.

"In case you got bored," Gollum said, setting the magazines down on Dea's bedside table. "Or were curious about the best lipstick colors for last spring."

"How did you know I was here?" Dea asked, her throat raw.

"Are you kidding?" Gollum sat down in the chair Dr. Chaudhary had vacated and drew her knees to her chest. Her sneakers were green. Dea knew she was doing her best to seem easy, casual. "No one's talking about anything else."

Dea groaned. That meant Connor had heard, of course. Even if she did make it out of the hospital—even if her mom did return—she didn't see how she could ever face anyone in Fielding again. They would *have* to move.

Gollum fiddled with the bottom of her Windbreaker, where the hem was torn. "You want to talk about what happened?"

Dea sat up a little. "You don't believe I tried to kill myself, do you? *Gollum?*" she pressed, when Gollum didn't immediately answer.

"No, no," Gollum said quickly. Her face was red, which made her hair look practically white.

"Good," Dea said firmly. "Because it was an accident."

Gollum made a face as if she were trying to swallow a hot pepper. She clearly wanted to ask more questions—Dea was sure Gollum had heard that her mom had disappeared—but let it drop. "So how long do you have to be here?" she asked.

"Don't know." Even thinking about it made her feel panicky again. "Only a few days, I hope." She took a deep breath and, before she could stop herself, blurted: "Have you talked to Connor?"

Gollum adjusted her glasses with the knuckle of one finger. "Tried to," she said. "He wasn't in school yesterday, and his phone was off." She made the hot-pepper face again. "There's some woman poking around doing research about . . . *you know.* His mom and brother and the murders and stuff. She's like a graduate student or something. Supposedly she's writing a book about it."

"Yeah," Dea said. "I heard."

"She even showed up at school. She was waiting in the parking lot after last bell. She managed to corner me but I didn't tell her anything. I felt kind of sorry for her, actually." Gollum shook her head. "She seemed pretty desperate. I think she really thinks she's going to figure it out."

"When the cops couldn't?" Dea said.

"Cops are idiots," Gollum said matter-of-factly, and Dea wasn't going to disagree. "And listen . . ." Gollum looked suddenly uncomfortable. She shifted in her chair, which gave a little squeak. "She has your name. Kate Patinsky. She knows about you."

Dea's heart began to speed up. "Knows what about me?"

Gollum didn't look at her. "That you and Connor are . . . close."

Were, Dea almost corrected her. But saying that would make it real, and she couldn't.

148

"Anyway," Gollum said. "I'm pretty sure he's avoiding her or something. I'll keep trying. I know he must be worried about you."

Dea closed her eyes, remembering his look of horror, the way he'd said *what are you?* She had the urge to cry again, so she kept her mouth shut.

Gollum stood up. "I should go," she said. "My dad had to drive me in the pickup. He's waiting in the parking lot." Gollum, Dea knew, had flunked her driver's test three times in a row, despite her claim that she'd been driving tractors for years on her family's farm. "I'll come back tomorrow, okay?"

"Sure," Dea said, still fighting the feeling she was going to break down at any second. "I'd like that."

Unexpectedly, Gollum reached down and gave Dea a hug. They'd hardly ever hugged, Dea realized. Although Gollum was thin, she was surprisingly strong, and her hair smelled like mint.

"Everything's going to be okay," Gollum whispered, and that did it: tears stung Dea's eyes before she could stop them. When Gollum pulled away, Dea swiped quickly at her face with a palm.

"Gollum!" Dea called Gollum back before she could slip into the hall. "My cat, Toby. He doesn't have anyone to feed him . . ."

Gollum grinned—the first time she'd smiled since entering the room. "Already took him home," she said. "The chickens aren't too happy about it."

She was gone before Dea could even say thank you.

The cops came in the evening. Briggs and Mr. Bigshot Connelly looked comically out of place in the small, bright room, like overinflated action figures.

"If you're here to talk about my mom, I have nothing to say," Dea said quickly. She was getting better at maneuvering with the IV in her arm, and she managed to roll over, so she was facing the window.

"We just came to check in, see how you were getting on." That was Briggs. Dea knew the cops had probably saved her life, but she felt nothing but resentment: they'd had her followed, they'd forced her to go tearing across Indiana like a maniac in the rain. If it weren't for them, she might never have turned on County Route 2. She might never have seen the monsters.

"I'm fine," she said, which was so obviously a lie. "Did you find my mom yet?"

There was a short pause. "Not yet."

That gave her some satisfaction. "You won't find her, you know. Not where you're looking."

This time, the pause was weightier. "What do you mean?" Briggs said carefully.

"It means she didn't run away. She would never." Dea drew her legs toward her chest. She missed her mom so hard in that second, she ached all over. "You're wasting your time. You should be looking for the person who took her." She thought of the surface of glass littering her room at home. She thought of Toby. She wanted to cry. "Now please leave me alone."

"Listen, Odea." Briggs was staring at her hard now, as if he could frighten her into giving something away. "We did our homework. You're not eighteen until June. If you know something that will help us find her, it's in your best interest to tell us. Otherwise we'll have to put you into the system. And nobody wants that."

150

"And if she comes home and you arrest her, I'll go into the system anyway, won't I?" Dea said. Briggs didn't answer. *"Please,"* she repeated. "Leave." She hated herself for saying *please* to them when she should have just ordered them from her room. She was halfway scared of them, just because of their badges. She pressed the nurse call button to make a point, and a light started beeping and flashing in the hall outside her door. Briggs heaved a big sigh, playing the role of Disappointed Dad.

"We'll be back," he said before leaving.

The nurse came—not Donna Sue, but another one, young, with smudgy eye makeup and an attitude—and asked her what she wanted.

"I forgot," Dea said, which earned her an eye roll. The nurse withdrew, closing the door forcefully. At least they weren't locking her in. If the doctors really thought she was crazy, they'd probably confiscate her shoelaces and strap her down and make sure she wasn't trying to hang herself with her bed linens in the middle of the night. Dea's shoes were stacked neatly in the narrow cupboard near her bed, shoelaces and all.

Dinner was soup and gloppy mac 'n' cheese and came with a single plastic spoon—she wasn't sure whether the doctors were deliberately keeping knives away from her. She hadn't intended to eat but she did anyway, ravenously, realizing that she was starving.

She hadn't meant to sleep, either, but there was nothing else to do. The nurses flowed in and out, bringing new medication— pills to help the pain, pills to keep her calm, pills to help the pills to help the pain—and then she was falling through the warm, soft surface of her bed, and there was nothing but dark.

THIRTEEN

She woke up in the middle of the night disoriented. For one second she had no idea where she was or how she had arrived there, and her mind spun frantically through all of the places she had lived, trying to latch onto a familiar feeling, an impression of home. Then in an instant her senses sharpened, and she was aware of the constant beeping and the shuffling of footsteps outside her door, and she remembered where she was. Someone had drawn her blinds, but moonlight filtered in between them, striping the linoleum floor.

She was hot and her throat was dry. It was the air in the hospital—too dry, exhaled by too many people, cycled through too many vents. She kicked off her sheets and sat up, her heart slamming hard, her head fuzzy, wondering why she had woken. Something was off—she had a tingling sense of unease, as if someone was standing behind her, breathing on her neck. As if someone was watching her.

Something dark skated across the mirror. Dea's throat squeezed. A shadow—a trick of the moon. Nothing more.

She swung her legs to the floor and stood up, carefully disentangling the tubes of her IV. Her body felt strange, as if she were made out of different component parts, some hopelessly light, some iron-heavy. She had to steady herself against one wall while the rush of blood to her vision passed. Then she made her way toward the sink, wheeling the IV stand next to her, as she'd practiced doing yesterday when she had to use the bathroom.

She was shocked by her own reflection. Her hair was greasy and matted in places. Her eyes were deep hollows in the dark, and her face was drawn and tight and white as a flame. She looked like something that should be dead. She had the stupidest thought: she was glad Connor hadn't come.

She drew water from the sink and drank it out of a plastic cup about the size of a thimble, refilling it several times before her throat began to relax. She was still uncomfortably hot, and she bent over to splash water on her face with the hand that wasn't chained to the IV, gasping a little from the cold, enjoying it. When she straightened up again, for a second she once again thought she saw a shadow move across the mirror—was someone behind her?—but when she turned around she saw nothing but the bed and the rumpled sheets and the looming silhouettes of machinery.

She turned back to the mirror.

A scream worked its way from her chest to her throat and lodged there.

The mirror was *moving*. It was rippling, like the surface of a lake disturbed by the motion of an animal below it. Her face was breaking apart, dispersing, on miniature wakes. And then, before she could shake the scream loose from her throat, before sound could crystallize on her tongue, her mother's face appeared: the big blue eyes, the dark hair, even wilder than it usually was. The bags like bruises under her eyes, the etching of smile lines at the corners of her mouth. She looked thin and tired and *real*.

Real. This was real.

Dea felt the floor swaying underneath her and had to grip the sink to stay on her feet. She hadn't realized, until then, how terrified she'd been that she would never see her mom's face again.

"Mom?" she whispered.

Miriam put a finger to her lips, shaking her head. Her eyes clicked to the left, in the direction of the hallway; Dea understood her mother was warning her against speaking too loudly. But Dea didn't care. Her mother was here and not-here. Her mother was behind the mirror, *in* it.

She wasn't dreaming.

"Where are you?" Unconsciously, she leaned forward and placed a hand on the mirror, as though she'd be able to feel her mother's face. But there was nothing but smooth glass beneath her palm.

Miriam looked temporarily irritated, as if Dea had failed to produce the answer to a very simple math question. She leaned in and brought her mouth to the glass, exhaling. Then she brought a finger to the glass and quickly scratched out a few words in the condensation that patterned her side of the mirror, writing backward so that Dea could read it.

Where do you think?

Almost as soon as Dea read the words, they evaporated.

"Are you coming home?" Dea asked, feeling a rush of panic. She was separated from her mother by a thin pane of glass and by whole worlds. This was crazy. Maybe she did belong in a loony bin.

Dea's mother shook her head no. There was a pucker between her eyebrows, a deep worry line that Dea had called, when she was little, *the dumpling.* She was sure she had confused the word *dimple* for *dumpling* but the nickname had stuck. She wanted to laugh. She wanted to cry. Her mother's dumpling was out in full force.

Miriam repeated her trick—exhaling, drawing words backward in the condensation. *There isn't much time.*

"Much time for what?" Dea said. Footsteps were squeaking down the hallway, and Dea stiffened. But they passed.

Her mother ignored the question. She swiped away the words with a fist and immediately breathed new vapor onto the glass and began scratching with a finger again.

The jagged lines of her writing, like piles of sticks, appeared quickly.

They know where you are.

Dea went cold. "Who?" she said. But her mom had suddenly gone very still, alert. She was no longer looking at Dea; her head

155

was turned slightly, like an animal listening for the approach of a predator. Dea leaned in and breathed on the glass. *Who?* she wrote, reversing the letters, as her mother had done for her.

But Miriam had turned away completely. For a second, Dea saw only the wild tangle of her mother's hair. Dea pounded once on the glass with a fist. "Mom," she whispered. And then, a little louder, *"Mom."*

Miriam turned around again, and Dea stumbled backward. Her mother's face was contorted now, drawn tight and white with terror. Her eyes were like two black pits. She was screaming soundlessly, her mouth working around words Dea couldn't hear. Dea was sweating, crying, reaching for her mother's hand beyond the glass.

Miriam shifted. For a quick second, Dea saw the faceless men behind her, ragged mouths open in a silent roar.

Then Miriam's face was back, pressed almost directly to the mirror. This time, Dea understood what she was saying.

Duck.

Dea's mother drew back a fist. The monsters leapt and Miriam swung toward the glass. Dea just had time to launch herself to the ground. The IV stand clattered on top of her. When the mirror shattered it made a sound like a vast thunderbolt. Then a tinkling, fine as rain, as all the glass came down.

FOURTEEN

She was moved into a room with no TV, no mirrors, no hard edges of any kind. The room was gray and smooth and feature-less, like a pebble worn down over time. Her door was locked by a nurse from the outside, and she had a single window, barred with steel, that looked out onto a short stretch of pavement and a brick wall: the windowless back of another portion of the hos-pital. Her food came with plastic forks and plastic spoons, and it was always inedible. All of her possessions were removed, carefully bagged, and secured in a locker. Only the nurses had the key.

Dr. Chaudhary came to check in on her more often, sometimes

as much as three times in a single afternoon. She no longer looked so pretty. She looked old, and very worried.

The one nice thing about being in the Crazy Ward, as Dea started thinking about it, was that she could avoid the police. No one was allowed to visit unless Dea gave her permission. When one of the nurses announced that a woman named Kate Patinsky had tried to gain access to Dea's room, Dea specified that the only people allowed to see her were Gollum, Connor, and her mother. Putting the last two on the list made her feel better, though she knew they wouldn't show up.

Dea was bored and exhausted all the time—whatever meds they were giving her were strong, and, because she hadn't walked a dream in days, she was weak. For two days she passed in and out of sleep. There was nothing else to do, and she didn't want to think about her mom or the monsters behind the mirror, and what it all meant.

On the third day, she woke up to an unfamiliar sound. A shadow flickered past her window, disrupting the thin daylight. She thought of her mother's hand, passing over a lightshade. She blinked. It was a bird: a bird hovering just beyond the bars that crisscrossed the heavy-duty glass. It was a lurid red, vivid against the weak gray light, and Dea felt a sharp ache as she watched it flutter, flutter, and then swoop away. The bird had brought with it some recollection, a memory of a memory of a word. She struggled to hold onto it even as her brain began to blur again, loosen at the edges . . . as she began to slip.

Harbinger. The word was *harbinger*.

Harbingers led the way out of dreams.

Her mother was trapped in a dream of monsters.

Dea struggled to sit up. Her body didn't feel like her own. It took a long time to get to the bathroom. Her arm was bandaged, spotted with old blood. She didn't feel it. She didn't feel anything.

She ran the water, bent over the toilet, stuck her fingers down her throat, and threw up.

It helped, but only a little.

Later, when the nurse came in with her afternoon dose of medication, Dea kept the pills folded neatly in her palm as she clapped a hand to her mouth and made an exaggerated point of swallowing.

"Good girl," the nurse said. This one was older, Latina, and wore a cross around her neck. Dea thought if you spent enough time in the Crazy Ward, you'd need to pray for something.

When the dinner tray came, she pushed the pills she hadn't swallowed to the very bottom of the applesauce. After only a few hours, she already felt better, more alert. She was careful to yawn and look dazed, though, when the night nurse came— this one young, skinny, and frightened-looking, with a rabbit's protruding front teeth—so she wouldn't get pumped full of sleeping pills.

She couldn't if she had any prayer of getting out of there.

On the fourth day, she answered Dr. Chaudhary's questions humbly, eyes down. Yes, she had been trying to kill herself that day in the car. Yes, she had deliberately shattered the mirror, thinking she could use the shards of glass to hurt herself. But she wanted to live now. She was ready to heal.

Later that afternoon, Gollum came to visit again, and Dea was allowed to leave her room and go greet her. The hallway

159

was full of identical rooms, some of them continuously locked, others closed only at lights-out. Through the narrow windows she could see other patients moving around or curled up in the fetal position on their beds. A guy with feather-white lashes and bleached hair suctioned his face to the window as she moved past, rapped four times against the window, as if he wanted to be let out. She touched two fingers to his fist and moved on.

The hallway dead-ended in a reception area. Gollum was waiting for her there, not even bothering this time to try to seem casual.

"Hey," she said, making no move to hug Dea. "I can't stay long."

I don't blame you, Dea nearly said. But she knew that was mean-spirited.

They sat side by side on plastic chairs bolted to the floor. Beyond the reception desk, mechanical swinging doors led off into other, less secure, portions of the hospital. They could only be opened with a code.

"Are you all right?" Gollum asked in a low voice.

"Been better," Dea said, trying to make it a joke. Gollum didn't smile. She looked younger than usual today in an old Harry Potter sweatshirt.

She reached out as though to touch the bandages on Dea's arm. Then she withdrew her hand. "What'd you do to yourself, Dea?"

"I didn't—" Dea shook her head. She knew there was no point in trying to explain. "I'm not crazy, Gollum. Okay? But it's too complicated to get into."

"I don't think you're crazy."

"Good. Because I'm not."

They sat in silence for a minute. In the corner, a TV was playing some grocery store game show, and one of the other patients was sitting in front of it, chin down, asleep.

"I talked to Connor," Gollum said in a rush, as if she had to force the words out. Dea's stomach flipped completely inside out. "He told me to tell you he's thinking of you. He . . . he misses you, Dea."

"Oh, yeah? Then why hasn't he come to see me?" Dea didn't mean to sound so bitter.

Gollum's expression turned guarded. "He's having a tough time," she said carefully. "Besides, he thought you wouldn't want to see him." She nudged Dea with an elbow. "What happened between you guys, anyway?"

Dea just shook her head.

Gollum sighed and stood up. "I got to go. My dad—"

"That's okay," Dea said quickly. "I get it." But when one of the nurses buzzed Gollum back into the hall, she was filled with an ache of loneliness so strong, it felt like her insides had been hollowed out.

There was nothing to do in the Crazy Ward—nothing to do but sit, and watch, and listen. She was a plant: unnoticeable and unnoticed, absorbing information through her skin. Over the course of a few hours, other patients drifted in and out of the waiting room. One girl was so thin her head, by comparison, looked like an enormous balloon about to pop; a fine fuzz of hair grew over her arms and even over the jutting peaks of her collarbones. Another girl—Kaitlyn, according to the nurse who eventually called her back to her room for a bath—shuffled back and forth across the worn carpet in her slippers, her head tilted to one side, as if listening to an inaudible symphony. Then there was Roddy, a grown man with the smooth, hairless face of a baby, who plunked right down next to Dea and explained that he had once been secret service for the president.

In the late afternoon two more visitors arrived to the ward, identifiable because they were dressed normally instead of in the paper gowns or soft cotton pajamas the patients wore. The anorexic stood up to greet them. They disappeared together into her room. An hour later, Dea watched the visitors—mother and sister, she thought—reemerge. A member of the cleaning crew released them back into the general wing; the janitor barely glanced at them before punching in the key code. She didn't even ask for their guest IDs. She didn't have to; they were wearing street clothing, which meant *okay to pass go.*

At six o'clock there was a long lull, a shift change, when the day nurses were released into the world and the night nurses came on—a quick half an hour when the hallway was mostly empty, when the day nurses had fled back to their cars and homes and boyfriends and kids, when the night nurses were getting ready in the break room, slugging back awful coffee, reviewing charts, complaining about the long night to come. All the night nurses were old. Or maybe they weren't old, and only looked it. That must be the effect of years on the Crazy Ward, and long, dark hours filled with unnatural light, the stink of bleach, and the cries of people whose brains had turned traitor.

Dea didn't judge. She knew, better than anyone, that reality was a tricky thing: shifting, tissue-thin, difficult to grasp.

In the evening, she repeated her magic trick, keeping her

palm cupped around her pills even as she pretended to swallow. Those pills went under her mattress. For a long time after lights-out, she lay awake, listening to the murmurs and footsteps, the dull thud of something hard banging rhythmically against a closed door. Whenever she closed her eyes, she pictured her mother's face, her mouth torn open in a scream, and the men with their ragged mouths of darkness behind her. She pictured rainstorms made of glass, and snow that fell silently and smelled like human ash.

Every time she moved to the window, hoping to see a break in the darkness, a chink of light, she saw nothing but a narrow wedge of black between the steep gabled sides of the hospital roof. She began to worry that dawn would never come.

It did, of course. The sun clawed apart the dark. Light bled down the hospital walls. The nurses changed shift again. Carts squeaked down the hall. The air smelled like burnt eggs and old yogurt. Toilets flushed and showers ran. Slowly, the ward woke up.

This was reality: the day came, whether you wanted it or not.

She would have only one chance to escape. If she screwed up, she'd probably be strapped to her bed, like she'd heard a nurse say they did to Roddy at night and when he went into one of his rages. But she couldn't wait any longer. She needed to get out. She needed to find Connor.

And then she needed to get into his dreams.

Nina, the Latina nurse, returned a little after noon, wheeling Dea's lunch tray. "How're you doin', baby? You hungry for something good?" Nina said that to all the patients. Dea could hear her singsonging it down the hall and had always assumed it was a rhetorical question, since the food in the Crazy Wing was even worse than regular hospital food. But she dutifully pronged a few grayish spears of asparagus, massed like elongated slugs at the edge of her plate. She needed the strength. She hadn't walked much in days, and she could feel it: she was weak, dizzy, nauseous. She could barely choke down her lunch.

Nina beamed at her. "I wish everybody on the floor was as good as you, sweetheart." She was sweating a little, even though the ward was always chilled to an exact sixty-nine degrees. Dea felt as if the whole hospital was just a giant refrigerator, and she and the other patients were vegetables, shivering silently inside of it. "Make my job a whole lot easier."

"Thanks," Dea said. She took a deep breath. Now or never. "Nina? I need to ask you a favor. A big favor."

Nina didn't stop smiling, but her posture changed almost imperceptibly. She was alert now, watching. She'd been in Crazyville a long time. She knew how quickly things could shift. "What's that, honey?"

"It's my best friend's birthday today," Dea said, looking down at her lap, because this lie was the hardest. Not because she was being deceitful, but because before Connor, before Gollum, she'd never had best friends—she'd hardly had *any* friends. And now she didn't know where she stood with either of them.

She just had to pray that Connor would help her. He was the only one who could. Gollum was out of the question. She couldn't drive, and didn't even own a cell phone.

"I was hoping . . . well, she's my best friend, you know? And I haven't spoken to her at all. I was hoping I could maybe just send her a quick text . . . ?" She looked up, holding her breath.

Nina was still smiling, so wide Dea could see the lipstick on her teeth. "There's a phone in the hall, honey. Why don't you ring her up there?"

There *was* a phone in the hall: an ancient rotary phone, sitting on the counter by the welcome desk—stupidly named, since there was nothing welcoming about Crazyville. The patients were allowed to make a single call a day. Roddy sometimes spent an hour or more on the phone, the cord twisted around a fat finger, ranting about the government or EPA regulations or bioengineered corn. Dea had been vaguely jealous that he had someone to call, until Eva, the anorexic, had told her that he never dialed any numbers—just picked up and started speaking.

"She never answers," Dea said. "Besides, her number's stored in my phone. Please," she added. "I haven't talked to her—I haven't been able to see her. She'll never forgive me." Dea thought of her mother, breathing words silently onto the glass, and blinked back sudden tears. "Please. I have to get through to her."

Nina hesitated. Her lashes left black dust on her cheekbones whenever she blinked. "All right, honey," she said. "One text. Let's be quick about it."

Dea was too afraid to say thank you—afraid she might sound too grateful, too eager, and give herself away. When Nina bent over to work a key in the old padlock, Dea waited several feet away, worried that if she came any closer Nina might hear her drumming heart, *feel* her nervousness, and suspect something. But she didn't.

"Go ahead," Nina said. In the small space, Dea's belongings looked pathetic, like the possessions of a bag lady on the street: her battered leather bag, which she hadn't even remembered taking into the car, piled on top of a stack of rumpled clothing—all of it sheathed in plastic. Nina had backed up several feet, so she could give Dea privacy and still make sure she didn't grab a hidden knife or razor blade. Dea reached for the bag and pulled out her phone, panicking a little when she saw the screen was dark. She'd been in the hospital for nearly a week—her battery was most likely dead. But when she pressed the power button, the screen flickered to life. Someone must have powered the phone down before stashing it.

As Dea pulled up Connor's number, Nina prattled on about the things she'd seen on the ward: drugs concealed in the lining of jeans; needles folded between the pages of a Bible; diet pills rattling in the belly of a teddy bear.

Dea's fingers were shaking as she typed out her text.

Please come. Today. BRING CLOTHES.

I'll explain everything.

Then, for good measure: **I'm not crazy.**

She hit send.

"One time, you wouldn't believe it, someone brought a lighter hidden in a shoe. Tried to burn the whole place down." She laughed.

"I'm done now." Dea replaced the phone in her bag and stood up. She wanted desperately to keep the phone on her, but she had nowhere to conceal it and couldn't risk getting in trouble. She showed Nina her hands, to prove she hadn't taken anything.

"Good girl." Nina swung the locker closed and locked it. "You send a message to your friend?"

"Yes." Dea felt like she was choking on the word. It was one o'clock. Now there was nothing to do but wait.

FIFTEEN

Two o'clock came and went, then three. She wished, now, that she had taken her cell phone, found some way of concealing it in her flimsy cotton pajamas. She wished she knew whether Connor had written her back. If he hadn't, or if he didn't come . . .

That was the biggest question. Whether he would come. Whether by now, despite what Gollum had told her, he'd decided she was a freak, suicidal, the crazy child of a crazy-ass mother. She could only imagine the stories he must have heard from his uncle, what people must be saying about her in school.

School. She'd never thought she might actually *wish* to be back in school.

She washed her face and brushed her teeth again, just to have something to do. There were no mirrors in this part of the hospital—she was glad of that, though she would have liked to see her mother again—and she hadn't seen her own reflection in days. She braided her damp hair by feel. Three thirty. She went into the hall and saw Eva, the anorexic, sitting with yet another visitor—her dad?—in the plastic chairs of the waiting room. Eva was the most popular girl on the ward, apparently.

She returned to her room and stretched out on the bed. Closed her eyes and tried to nap, but she was too agitated.

Four o'clock. She was guessing, estimating the time by the activity of the nurses doing their rounds and the quality of the light filtering through her window. If Connor didn't come, she'd have to figure out a new way to escape. She examined the locker to see if she could force it, but she had no idea how to pick a lock and nothing to pick it with, anyway. The sharpest object she was allowed was a plastic fork. She couldn't just make a run for it, either. The doors at the end of the hallway were locked. Even if she could somehow finagle it, the hospital would call the cops, and the cops would have no problem finding her if she went anywhere dressed in hospital-issue pajamas.

Connor was her only hope.

Five o'clock. Almost time for the shift change, and the perfect time to make a move. She looked into the hall again. Roddy was on the phone, gesticulating, his voice rising and falling over a swell of unconnected phrases: "Water supply. . . if the FEMA got wind of this . . . the Republican National Council . . ."

Behind him, a woman worked a mop up and down the hallway. Dea could see earphones hanging around her neck.

She closed the door, and the sound of Roddy's voice was muffled. Mid-November, so the light was dying, rust-colored on the floor. She curled up on the bed. It felt like she was dying, too—bleeding out, wasting precious minutes. It had been days and days since she'd walked a dream, and Dea was weak.

It wasn't until the knocking began that Dea sat up, realizing she must have fallen asleep. The light was gone. Her room was in darkness. Suddenly the door opened. The dazzling brightness of the hallway made her blink.

"What are you doing, sitting around in the dark?" The lights clicked on, and Maria, one of the night nurses, was revealed. She didn't wait for Dea to answer. "Come on out. You got a visitor."

Dea's mouth went dry. She stood up, unsteady on her feet, hot all over. There was Connor: standing in the hall, looking rumpled and soft, like he'd rushed there from somewhere else. She almost didn't believe it. She blinked several times, as if he were a mirage and might vanish as she approached. But he was still there. Then she noticed that his arms were empty—he hadn't brought her any clothes. Or maybe they'd been confiscated already. Her stomach sank.

"Don't take too long, now," Maria said. "Visiting's done in half an hour." She backed out of the room, leaving the door open. Yet another rule.

Conner and Dea were alone. They stood for a moment in awkward silence.

"You came," Dea said.

Just as Connor cleared his throat and said, "I got your text."

"Shh." Dea jerked her chin toward the hallway.

"I had to tell my dad I was going to Gollum's." Connor

lowered his voice so he was barely speaking above a whisper. "You said you would explain."

Dea's heart was beating so fast, she felt like she might faint. "I will. I promise." In the hall, a nurse passed, limping slightly, as if her whole body ached. She shot a quick glance into Dea's room but kept moving. "I'm in trouble."

"I can see that," Connor said.

"But I'm not—I'm not crazy." Dea's voice broke. She cleared her throat. "Please. I need your help. Get me out of here, I'll tell you everything."

Connor stared at her for one long moment, as if trying to judge whether she could be trusted. "I brought some stuff for you," he said finally. He unzipped his sweatshirt. Underneath it, he was wearing a second sweatshirt, this one so small its sleeves stopped four or five inches above his wrist bones. It was pink. "My stepmom's," he said quickly, when Dea stared. He reached into his sweatshirt pocket and pulled out a pair of leggings. "These, too. I didn't think you'd want me wearing them." It was the first time he'd cracked a smile. "And a T-shirt. I'm wearing two."

"You're a genius," Dea said.

Connor shrugged. "Don't forget, I was a psycho when I was little," he said, serious again. "I killed my family, remember? I know how these places work."

Dea wondered whether the woman, Kate Patinsky, was still harassing him—it occurred to her that people at school must be saying bad things about Connor too. But there was no time to ask him now. He backed into the little bathroom and, because there was no door, Dea turned away so he could change. Then it was Dea's turn. Connor had left the leggings, the pink sweat-shirt, and a T-shirt with a faded Coca-Cola graphic folded neatly in the sink. The clothing was all a bit too large, but Dea didn't care. It felt delicious to be wearing real clothes, even clothes that were borrowed.

The fact that she had no shoes was a problem. It would look bad—even after she left the Crazy Ward, it would raise eyebrows. And the hospital complex was big. There was no way she could make it to the parking lot without passing doctors, and nurses, maybe even some of the same people who'd admitted and treated her. She needed to blend in as much as possible. But she was running out of time. Once the night nurses finished chatting and sucking down coffee, it would be dinner time. Then the halls would be full of nurses wheeling trays and bearing pills and Connor would have to leave, and Dea would lose her chance.

"So what's the big plan?" Connor said. He had turned again to face her. She had forgotten how much she liked the angles of his face, and his eyes, warm and bright. "You can't just walk out of here."

"Visitors do it all the time," Dea said. "They get punched out by the cleaning crew, no questions asked."

He looked her up and down, frowning. "Stay here," he said, as if she had any other choice. She couldn't even leave the bathroom; if she did, she'd be visible from the hallway to anyone who passed. And she couldn't be seen in street clothes. So instead she sat on the toilet lid, sucking in deep breaths. Her heart was worse than it had been in years. She pressed a palm flat across her chest, thought *calm down, calm down, calm down*, but it didn't help. When she stood up again, blackness clouded her vision.

Connor reappeared, holding a pair of cheap-looking black heels, scuffed at the toes. Dea couldn't believe it. "How?" was all she could ask.

"My stepmom works in an office," he said. "She always keeps extra shoes under the desk. For dates with my dad or business meetings and stuff." He shrugged. "The nurse working the welcome desk must be on break. But the shoes were there."

"It's shift change." Dea pulled on the heels. She couldn't even feel guilty about stealing. "She's probably in the staff room gossiping with everyone else."

The shoes were too small, and looked ridiculous with her outfit. But she didn't care. She took a few tentative steps around the bathroom, wobbling a little. She hoped they wouldn't have to run.

"What now?" Connor was watching her with an expression she couldn't decipher.

Dea took a deep breath. "Now we walk out."

"Just like that?"

The back of her neck was sweating. "I hope so."

"What about the nurses?" he said. "What about the doctors?"

"You tell me," she said. "You're supposed to be scouting."

"I'll take that as an order," he said. He vanished again, presumably to duck out into the hall, and reappeared a second later. His face was practically gray. Dea realized he was risking a lot—risking *big* trouble—just to help her. She was sure his family had warned him against her. Gollum had implied he was practically on lockdown. For all he knew, Dea was actually crazy, and would try to impale herself with a butter knife as soon as they were out of the ward. Or impale him. "Coast's clear," he said. "Except for someone mopping. And there's a girl sitting out by registration."

"A girl?" Dea's heart sank. She hadn't even considered the idea that one of the other patients might be killing time in the waiting area.

"Super skinny," Connor said.

Eva. Dea knew hardly anything about her—they'd spoken only once, when Eva had unexpectedly volunteered the information about Roddy's fake phone calls. She had no idea whether Eva would be inclined to give her away or not. On the one hand, she didn't think Eva could possibly have anything *against* her. On the other hand, people were petty on the ward. She heard the chatter all the time from the nurses. Roddy wasn't speaking to Andrew, because Andrew supposedly got more pudding with his dinner. Melissa had accused Kaitlyn of stealing her favorite socks. And on and on.

She had to risk it.

"Let's go." She tugged up her hood and cinched it tight, shaking her hair forward so it mostly concealed her face. She edged out of the bathroom behind Connor, uncomfortably aware of the loud clicking of her heels against the linoleum. She heard a burst of laughter from down the hall, in the direction of the staff room, and Nina hooting, "Girl, you're *crazy*. You oughta be locked up, too."

Connor glanced at her and she nodded. Her throat was so tight she could barely swallow.

They moved out into the stark-bright hall. Dea's whole body

was alert, stiff with fear. The guy with the bleached hair was standing at his door again, peering out the small window into the hall. As they moved past him, he suddenly reared his head back and slammed it once again the glass. Thud.

"Stop it," Dea whispered desperately. He did it again. Thud. Connor had frozen. Thud, thud. "Stop it, please." She wasn't even sure if he could hear her. She knew that once he got started, he wouldn't stop until the nurses came with more medication. Already, the voices in the break room had gone silent. "Please. It's okay." She pressed her palm to the glass, as if she could reach through it and force him to be still.

It worked. He jerked his head back and stayed there, his eyes clicking from her palm up to her face again. Dea felt a bead of sweat trickle down her back. Seconds stretched into infinity. At last, he smiled and touched his finger to her palm, through the glass.

"Bye-bye," she whispered. She watched him mouth the words back: "Bye-bye."

The nurses' voices started up again.

Ten more feet and they'd be at the swinging doors. Dea felt like she was moving through a dream, like every step she took she was actually getting farther from escape. But then they were there: standing just inside the doors that led to freedom, next to the waiting room with its crappy green carpet and the collection of plastic chairs. Eva wasn't even watching TV. She was just sitting there. Dea kept her head down, hoping her face was mostly concealed. The janitor was still wearing headphones, working a wet cloth over the reception desk.

"Excuse me." Connor was doing his best to sound casual but

Dea heard the strangled quality of his voice. "Excuse me." He had to tap the janitor to get her to look up. She did, finally. "Can you let us out, please?"

She lifted a headphone away from her ear and shook her head, like *I didn't hear you.* From the corner of her eye, she could see Eva watching them—rigid, suspicious.

"Out," Connor repeated.

The janitor moved for the door.

"Wait," Eva called out.

Dea's chest seized up. She willed the janitor to punch in the code, to let them through, to ignore Eva. But now the woman's hand was hovering, hummingbird-like, in front of the keypad. Dea felt herself turning against her will.

"Dea." Connor's voice was a low whisper, strangled. But it was too late. She had met Eva's eyes. They were staring at each other across the short distance.

Eva's eyes looked like the carvings on statues Dea had seen in certain history books, as if they had been gouged out of her skin with an instrument. Dea had stopped breathing. Now Eva would raise the alarm. Now the nurses would come pouring out of the break room, rushing down the hall to see what the fuss was about, and Dea would be hauled back to her room and strapped down to her bed for all eternity.

"I like your sweatshirt," Eva said. She had a husky voice, low as a boy's. For a quick second, Dea was sure she saw Eva smile.

"The code," Connor said. *"Por favor."*

The janitor didn't look at Dea again. She punched in the code—a quick string of numbers and letters—and the doors clicked open. Suddenly, in a panic, Dea forgot how to move.

Voices crested behind her, ricocheting off the walls—a burst of laughter, a subtle shift in the pattern of conversation. The nurses were coming to do rounds.

Connor took Dea's hand and pulled her forward, into the hall. Dea took a quick, gasping breath, as if she'd just surfaced after being too long underwater. The doors closed behind her with a soft *whoomf*, and she heard the lock slide home.

Connor kept hold of her hand, and she didn't once turn around.

SIXTEEN

They walked as fast as they could without seeming as if they were hurrying. Two doctors passed them without so much as glancing up from their charts. So far, so good. Dea scanned the hall, the clusters of nurses in their identical scrubs, all of them indistinguishable in her panic. Would they recognize her? Had these been the same nurses who had stuck her in the Crazy Ward in the first place?

They took the first stairwell they could find, moving quickly, in silence, to the ground floor. Dea was hoping the stairs would lead them to an emergency exit but instead they found themselves in yet another hallway. It reminded her of the maze she'd walked with her mother years ago in Florida, the high white walls and halls that dead-ended or abruptly switched directions, signs indicating an exit that never materialized. Everything looked the same: blue doors and speckled linoleum floors and bad pastel art.

But finally the hall dumped them into a lobby, and then they were through the revolving doors and out into the dark.

The cold was shocking. The wind cut right through her sweatshirt and wrapped a hand around her lungs. The sky was clear. The glare of the hospital complex couldn't quite obscure a smattering of stars. Dea wrapped her arms around her chest, inhaling clean, sharp air, watching her breath condense in clouds. It felt like a long, long time since she had been outside. She still half expected an explosion of shouting to begin at any minute, hands to materialize from the dark and grab her.

But they made it to Connor's car without trouble. He'd parked at the edge of the parking lot, in a dark wedge of space between streetlamps. As always, the car smelled like gum and old wood shavings, and once they were inside—with the rest of the world locked out, pressed and flattened behind walls of glass—it finally hit Dea that they had done it. She was out. She should have felt triumphant but she was overcome with exhaustion. Her whole body was numb with cold. They had studied shock in Health Ed, and she was pretty sure that her uncontrollable shivering, plus the way her thoughts kept bouncing off each other like deranged rubber balls, meant she had it.

Connor punched on the heat, and wordlessly passed her a blanket from the backseat.

"All right," he said. "Talk."

"Not here." She heard the wail of an approaching siren and tensed; but it was only an ambulance, pulling into the ER.

"Dea . . ." His hands tightened on the wheel. For a second, she was terrified he would order her out of the car.

"I promise, I'll explain everything. I swear. But we're not safe here."

He exhaled—a long, heavy breath. "Where do you want to go?"

She shook her head. She was out and free and she had nowhere to go. She couldn't go to Gollum's—it was the first place the cops would look, and besides, Gollum was already covering for Connor. She had no money. No ID. No living relatives that she knew of. She wished, now, that she'd risked pocketing her cell phone and some cash from her purse. At least if she had money, she could get a motel room or buy a plane ticket somewhere.

She thought of the envelope full of rolls of twenty- and fifty-dollar bills, stuffed into the soft interior lining of the passenger seat in the VW.

"My car," she said. "I need to get into my car."

Connor stared at her. "Your car is totaled, Dea." She was surprised that he sounded angry. "You nearly killed yourself. Remember?"

"I wasn't trying to—" She broke off. There was no point in trying to explain what had happened; it would have to wait until they were somewhere safe. Somewhere else. Instead she said, "I really wrecked it? Bad?"

"You drove straight into a tree," Connor said, as if she were an idiot. "They had to pull you out. The hood folded up like an

179

accordion—that's what my uncle said. It's probably scrap by now. Demo'd." She looked at him blankly and he said. "Demolished."

She thought of two thousand dollars, shredded underneath the metal teeth of a giant machine. She needed that money.

"We have to check," she said. "We have to make sure. Maybe they haven't . . . demo'd it yet." Seized by sudden inspiration, she said, "It's evidence, isn't it? It's evidence of a crime."

"What are you talking about?" Connor said.

"That was my mom's car. And the police think she's on the run. So they might keep the car, right?" The more she talked, the more it sounded possible. "Maybe—maybe they think the car is a clue. Or—or like proof that she was doing bad stuff. She probably *stole* that car." Dea knew for a fact that she hadn't, but she needed to make Connor say yes; she needed to convince him to keep helping her.

"I'm not going anywhere until you tell me what's going on." He yanked the key out of the ignition, cutting off the engine.

Dea took a long breath. "Okay, look. There's money in that car. I need it. I have nowhere to go. If I get caught, I'll get thrown back in there." She jerked her head toward the hospital, looming toward the sky like a vast white wave tunneling toward them. "Everyone thinks I'm crazy, but I'm not. They think my mom ran away, but she didn't. You're the only one who can help me. Will you help me?"

For a long time, he just looked at her. Then he turned the ignition back on and put the car in drive.

Dea had crashed somewhere on the border of Marborough and the flat run of land on the western side of it. There was only one tow company she knew of: Sanderson's, which was actually in Pellston. Mark Sanderson was in Dea's grade, and rumor had it he sometimes lent out cars to his friends for drag racing. If your car went to Sanderson's, there was no telling what it would look like when it came out.

They drove to Pellston in silence, with black space hurtling past them. Connor had obviously given up trying to get Dea to talk. There were things she almost asked him—not even about Kate Patinsky and whether she was still bugging Connor's family for information, or what people were saying about Dea at school—but normal, everyday things. It would make her feel real, like the same old Dea, and not like somebody just returned from a spaceship.

She couldn't believe that only a couple of months earlier she'd taken Connor on a tour, pointed out the mini-mart and the mega-mart, complained that nothing ever happened and that Fielding must be the most boring town in America. She would give anything to go back to being bored.

Dea had driven past Sanderson's Tow and Impound lot plenty of times but never paid it much attention. It was bigger than she'd remembered, a large lot encircled with a high fence and illuminated with large floodlights. In contrast to the surrounding darkness, it looked like the set of a movie, and the rows and rows of cars, lit up from above, were like carefully arranged toys.

The gate at the entrance was closed. A laminated sign instructed them to buzz. Connor did. A second later, a skinny guy with a shaved head and tattoos crawling up his neck all the way to his jaw materialized and unlatched the gate, which was encircled with a padlock. He waved them in. He had the glitter-bright eyes and sunken face of a junkie. Still, she saw a resemblance to Mark. So: maybe his older brother.

Connor pulled up to the office, a tin-sided booth no bigger than a janitor's closet. Inside of it, a guy with a wide sprawl of a nose was leaning on a desk, watching something on a minuscule TV. He, too, had Mark's face but much fatter, as though someone had taken an air pump to his head.

"So what's the plan?" she said. But Connor was already getting out of the car. She climbed out after him, ignoring the temporary wave of dizziness that overtook her.

"What are you doing?" he whispered, glaring at her. They were standing on either side of the hood, facing off. "Get back in the car."

The tattooed guy had shut the gate behind them. He shook a cigarette out of a pack and stood smoking, watching them from a distance.

"What does it look like I'm doing?" Dea spoke softly, so Mark's brother wouldn't hear. "I'm coming with you."

"Let me handle it," Connor said. He started walking toward the office.

She hesitated. She'd been assuming she could just weave her way among the cars, looking for the VW. Still she would need fifteen minutes at least—more, given how weak she felt—and Mark's brother wasn't taking his eyes off her. But she was sick of sitting around and waiting; she'd been sitting around, waiting, for days.

So she followed Connor, limping a little. As soon as she got some cash, she was going to buy a real pair of shoes. She was going to need to walk a dream soon, too. Her heart was twitching like a dying insect.

She caught Connor as he reached the office. He shot her a dirty look but didn't say anything. It was too late to order her into the car, anyway. Mr. Sanderson was already leaning forward.

"Yeah?" was the first thing he said.

Dea realized that she and Connor hadn't agreed on a cover story. But without hesitation, Connor started talking. "I been working on my dad's car," he said. His voice had changed. It sounded gruffer. More Fielding-like. As if he'd just come from drinking beers and fiddling with a transmission. "He's got an old VW. An original. Busted to hell, though, and we need some new parts. I heard you might have parts."

Sanderson's jaw was working back and forth over a piece of gum. His eyes moved from Connor to Dea, and she was glad that she had her hood up. Reflected in the smudgy glass window, she barely looked like herself—just a sickly-pale girl with stringy hair and big dark hollows for eyes. She highly doubted Sanderson knew who she was, but just in case.

"We towed a VW about a week ago or so, yeah." Sanderson turned his eyes back to Connor. He spoke slowly, as if each word was an effort. Dea imagined that if she could hear his inner thoughts, they'd sound just like radio static, or the buzz of a fly in an empty room. "Got pretty banged up. Don't know how much good it'll be for parts. Might be better for scrap. What're you looking for? You working the engine or body?"

Connor dodged the question. "Can I see it?"

Sanderson shook his head. He picked up a paper cup and spit into it, a thick brown liquid, like tar. Dea realized he wasn't chewing gum, but tobacco. "Don't have it here," he said, and her stomach sank. "Cops got it in impound behind the station. We won't see it till they're done. Could be weeks. You want me to call you when it's ready to go for scrap?"

"Sure," Connor said. He scrawled down a name and phone number—both fake, Dea noticed—on a piece of paper, then fed it through the gap under the grille. "Thanks a lot."

They reversed out of the lot, and Mark's brother swung the gate closed and locked them out. All the time, he was watching them as if he knew something. She was glad to be back in the car.

"Well, that's that," Connor said, as soon as they were on the road.

"What do you mean?" Dea said. "Sanderson said my car's still in impound. So that's a good thing. It means it didn't get junked yet."

"A good thing?" Connor repeated. "Dea, the cops have it. That's a very bad thing."

"*Please.*" Dea's voice cracked. She knew she sounded desperate. She *was* desperate. And guilty, too—Connor should have stayed far away from her. He should have known better. "We have to try."

"Try what? The cops are looking for you, Dea."

"They're looking for me. They're not looking for *you*," Dea said. Connor went silent. She'd never known guilt to feel this way, like there was something alive inside her stomach trying to get out. She added, "Besides, the last place they'll look is at the police station. Right?"

"This is crazy," Connor said, shoving a hand through his hair, so it stood up in spikes. Dea remembered, then, the first time she'd seen him: how he'd emerged from the water, how he'd smiled at her. "I have my own shit to worry about, Dea. My own shit to deal with. And everyone knows we're—" He broke off suddenly.

"Everyone knows we're *what?*" Dea asked. There was an ache deep in her chest. How was it possible for things to change so quickly, for time to squeeze down like a giant thumb, for everything to go so wrong? In dreams, everything was reversible. There was no time, and so nothing was done that couldn't be undone.

She wished real life were like that, too.

"Nothing," Connor said, shaking his head. "Everyone knows we're friends, that's all." Funny how she used to love hearing him say the word *friends*. Now it sounded flat to her, like soda left uncapped. "My *uncle* knows. As soon as the hospital gets in touch with him, he'll know I helped you run."

"That just means we have to hurry," Dea said. "You promised to help me," she added softly.

They were coming up on Fielding again. Dea could see the ExxonMobil and mini-mart, casting beams of light toward the sky—like earthbound stars, drowning in the dark. A single red light was blinking at the intersection. If Connor turned left, they would reach Route 9, his house, her house. Her old house. She had never known how much she loved it until now: the old rooms, most of them unused, the vast comfortable sprawl of the place with all their pretty rented belongings.

Right was Route 22, which went past the police station— and from there, west out of Aragansett County and eventually all the way out to California.

Connor slowed the car to a crawl and then to a stop. For a second, they sat bathed in intermittent red light.

"Damn it," he said, and wrenched the wheel to the right.

Dea could have kissed him.

SEVENTEEN

A half mile before they arrived at the police station complex, when Dea could already see a halo of light hovering above the sprawling one-story building, Connor pulled over, bumping the car onto the side of the road.

"Get in the back," he said.

"What? Why?"

He exhaled heavily. "You know this is idiotic, right? Because it is. Idiotic. I'm not going to get in trouble for harboring a fugitive or whatever the hell you are, and I'm not going to let you go to jail, either. I'm not even supposed to be here, okay? I'm supposed to be at Gollum's, helping her birth a frigging calf."

"Really?" Dea couldn't help but say.

"It was her idea," Connor said exasperatedly. "So my dad would be too grossed out to check. The point is, you do what I say now. So get in the back, and when I say get down, get down. Got it?"

Dea knew it was no use arguing with him. A small dark crease had appeared between his eyebrows, like it always did when he was going to be stubborn about something. Besides, he had a point. So she climbed out and moved around to the backseat, which was cluttered with random clothing and sporting equipment, old textbooks and a backpack, dirt-encrusted hiking boots, and empty soda bottles, as if all of the runoff from Connor's life flowed and accumulated here.

She cleared a space among the piles of clothing. She felt better back here, protected, concealed by the dark and surrounded by so many forgotten objects. She drew the blanket over her shoulders, folded it around herself like a cloak, like it might give her superhero powers.

They were nearing the police station now.

"Get down," Connor said, his voice tight. Dea flattened herself against the backseat, her face pressed to an old sweater, inhaling wool fibers and the faint taste of cologne. A second later, she heard sirens shriek by. There must be an accident somewhere. Or—her stomach clenched—the cops had been called out to the hospital, to track her down, to bring her back.

She'd been expecting Connor to turn into the lot, but he kept going straight. She was desperate to sit up but knew Connor would yell at her, so she stayed where she was. Her cheek was starting to itch where it was pressed up to the wool.

"What do you see?" she finally said.

"I'm making a loop." Connor was whispering, as if they might be overheard otherwise. "Checking out the impound lot. Entrances and exits. I want to know what we're dealing with."

She couldn't stand it anymore. She sat up cautiously. She could feel the cold vibrating through the glass. Connor glanced at her in the rearview mirror but said nothing. They had passed the main entrance to the station, anyway. Connor hooked a right, and then another right down a service road.

"That must be the lot," he said, narrating as if she couldn't see for herself. He was nervous. This lot was much smaller than Sanderson's but similarly fortified, encircled by a tall fence topped with chicken wire. "Guard hut." Connor's fingers were so tight on the steering wheel that even from the backseat, Dea could see the white indentations of his knuckles. "Two cops."

She had almost forgotten that Connor hated the police. He thought they were idiots and had never forgiven them for failing to find his mom and brother's killer.

Except for my uncle, he'd said. *He's all right.* Briggs had been living in Chicago when Connor's family was killed. Connor had told Dea his uncle wasn't supposed to have worked his mom's case—he was too close to it, according to his superiors—but had insisted, vowing to learn the truth for his brother's sake. Because of his uncle's influence, Connor had ultimately been absolved, at least formally. There just wasn't enough evidence to pin the murder on him, even if there was no evidence to pin it on anyone else, either. He'd told her all this on the drive back from the Fright Festival, when they'd had to pull over because of the rain, and she'd been desperate to ask whether it was true what people said about Will Briggs and his dad and the guitar—she didn't see how someone good could do something so terrible.

She thought of her mother, and all the midnight running away, and the frauds. Maybe people were more complicated than she thought.

Connor exhaled heavily. "No way in," Connor said. One of the cops, starkly visible in the brightly lit interior of the hut, had a paperback bent across his knee—a crossword puzzle book?—but the other one, with the face of a hound dog left too long without its owner, watched them as they drove past. Dea hunched down in her seat, though she knew she couldn't possibly be seen.

Then she spotted it: at the very edge of the lot, a ruined sculpture of metal, broken lines of steel and singed rubber. Her heart caught in her throat. Connor had prepared her for this but still, she couldn't believe it: the car, her mom's car, was folded nearly in half. Its doors gaped open; she imagined they no longer closed correctly. Or maybe the cops had needed to wrench the doors from their hinges to get her out. Two tires were completely blown out, so the car listed like a ship in shallow water. She hadn't realized until now how lucky she was to be alive. She felt the sudden, wild impulse to cry, to call her mom up, to tell her she was sorry. Her mom loved that car.

"There it is." Her voice, amazingly, was steady. She stubbed a finger into the glass, even though Connor kept his eyes on the road. "I see it. It's right there. Next to the jeep." There were fewer than two dozen cars in the impound lot, scattered seemingly at random, many of them still papered with bright orange parking tickets or fitted with a metal boot, like a monster's giant teeth, around one wheel.

"Did you hear me, Dea? I said there's no way in. They have guards posted for a reason."

The lot was fenced on three sides and backed up on the station: a long, low building, jointed in several places where it had undergone expansion, so the effect was of a lumpy gray caterpillar tacked to earth. On the far side of the lot, next to the Dumpsters, three cops were standing, smoking, in the narrow wedge of light carved out by a propped-open service door. She saw the flare of cigarettes, like the distant glow of fireflies.

"Through the station," Dea said. Connor was hooking another right, circling back around toward the front.

His eyes went to hers in the rearview mirror. "What?"

She looked away. She didn't like the mirror, and didn't like thinking of what she had last seen reflected in it. "There's a way into the lot through the station. I saw cops on smoke break." He said nothing. "You could get in. You could ask to see your uncle."

"Even if he hasn't heard you pulled a disappearing act by now," Connor said pointedly, "I've never once come to see him at work. Don't you think he'll be suspicious?"

"Make up a story. Tell him you were with Gollum and got a weird message from me. Tell him you went to the hospital and I wasn't there. Or don't tell him anything. All you need to do is get in. Find a back door. Grab the money and get out. I would do it myself, if I could."

Connor was quiet for a moment. They had turned off the service road and were bumping around toward the main entrance again, traveling down a spit of a dirt lane barely wider than the chassis. "Where's the money?" he said quietly.

"In the passenger seat," she said. "There's a hole under the seat cushion, and a stocking inside of it. It should be there. It was the last time I checked, anyway."

Dea once again stretched out on the backseat, as Connor angled the car into the lot. She felt suddenly exposed. Every few feet, as they passed under a streetlamp, a bright disk of light swept over her. She eased down into the narrow space between seats, where it was shadowed, where she would be almost entirely concealed from view.

Connor parked and turned off the engine. Voices vibrated thinly through the windows. How many cops worked the county? Ten? Twenty? More? How many of them knew—or thought they knew—about Dea and her mom?

"Stay here." Connor spoke quietly, without turning his head. "I'm locking the car. Don't open up for anyone."

"Okay," she whispered back. She was seized by a momentary terror—she didn't want him to go and leave her alone in the dark. But it was the only way.

He was gone.

Her legs soon began to cramp, but she was afraid to move. There seemed to be a constant flow in and out of the station, a rhythm of voices and doors and conversations abruptly interrupted or swallowed by distance. She tried to picture where Connor was and what he was doing—he must be in the building now, maybe even heading to see his uncle, scouting the building and its various exits on the way—but she was too nervous to be very imaginative, and a vision of Connor sitting in a plain white room behind two-way glass kept intruding.

Or maybe—the idea came to her so starkly, in a flash, she went breathless—maybe he would sell her out. He might regret helping her.

She dismissed the idea as soon as it came to her, but the worry stayed with her. Her breath crystallized and dispersed, but sweat moved down her spine and pooled under her arms. She fantasized briefly about showers, running water, soap-scented steam rising from a bath. Her mother had always drawn the best baths, the surface knit with bubbles as thick as clots of cream, heavenly smelling.

She imagined she might wake up and find this had all been a dream.

No. A nightmare.

More minutes passed. She was sick with hunger, anxiety, and exhaustion. It felt like she had left the hospital days ago, though it had only been a matter of hours. She couldn't remember whether she'd eaten any lunch. Her right foot was falling asleep. She tried to adjust her position, and caught a textbook with her elbow, wincing as it thunked to the floor, and several papers, water-warped and ringed with coffee marks, fluttered bird-like after it. But no one heard; no one came. Her thighs were shaking now. She eased backward, shifting her weight off her legs, so she could sit down.

Where the hell was Connor? She had no sense of how long it had been. Ten minutes? Twenty? How long would she wait? She could spend the night here, if she had to. But if Connor had been caught, she'd need to move eventually. She wished he'd left the keys. She couldn't possibly stroll out of the car, dressed the way she was dressed, and hope to make it even a minute without attracting someone's attention.

There was another volley of voices outside, a rapid-fire back-and-forth she couldn't understand, and then suddenly the driver's side door opened.

It was Connor. Even though he had his back to her, she could tell that he was shaking a little from the effort of keeping it together.

"Did you . . . .?" she whispered.

"Shhh," he said. He turned on the engine. Then: "Yes." A second later, an envelope thudded at her feet. She pulled it into her lap. All there. Two thousand dollars, maybe a little more.

"Did you have any trouble?" she asked. She was dying to sit up, to stretch out her legs, but she didn't want to move, not until they'd packed miles between the car and the station.

Connor didn't answer. She thought he must not have heard.

"Connor?" she prompted.

He sighed. When he spoke, he suddenly sounded much, much older.

"It's your turn to talk," he said.

EIGHTEEN

Connor picked a direction and started driving. When Dea judged it was safe, she wiggled out of her hiding space, her legs dull and heavy, feeling a little bit like something jostled out of a drain. She was glad, in a way, that Connor didn't stop so she could take shotgun. It was easier to talk from the backseat, easier when she didn't have to look at him and wonder what he was thinking.

She told him everything: how she had learned to walk dreams, how her mother had taught her, how she got sick when she didn't walk for a while. She told him some of the basic rules, how birds were harbingers and dreamers unconsciously responded to intruders and worlds fell apart when the dream was ending. How if you weren't careful, you might become trapped.

She told him she believed that's what had happened to her mom: she had become trapped, somehow, in one of Connor's nightmares.

It was the only explanation that made any kind of sense. Dea's mom was *with* Connor's monsters. That meant she'd found a way into his dreams.

But Dea wasn't ready to tell Connor about the monsters. Not yet. She wasn't ready to tell him that her mother had warned her away from mirrors and water and that she suspected, now, that those substances served as doorways between the two worlds. That because Dea had allowed Connor's monsters to spot her, they had followed her, pursued her to a country road in the real world.

After she ran out of story, he was quiet for a bit. The only sound was the gentle shush of the highway under the tires. It was completely dark—she couldn't tell where the road ended and the fields began, and didn't even know where they were headed—except for intermittent and unexpected bursts of civilization, a sudden cluster of lights off in the distance, or a billboard rearing out of the dark, featuring some plastic-looking girl with fat lips and fake boobs perching on six-inch heels, or an advertisement for a family-planning clinic. It wasn't until she saw a sign for PRIVATE EYES: OHIO'S PRETTIEST GIRLS that she even realized they'd headed east and had made it across the border. They passed a billboard, stripped bare, on which someone had graffitied: *Jesus Saves*. The words flared briefly in Connor's headlights, as if they were burning. Dea felt a squeeze of sadness. She wished it were true. She wished it were as simple as that.

"I knew it," he said at last. "You were *there*. I knew I wasn't just dreaming you. It felt different. . . ." He went silent again. Dea didn't want to say anything. She was so relieved that he didn't sound angry—or worse, disgusted—she was afraid to ruin it by making a sound. "And you've always . . . been this way? You've always walked?"

She nodded, then remembered he couldn't see her. "Yeah."

"So what changed? Why did everything go to shit all of a sudden?"

You, she almost said. As soon as she thought it, she knew it was true. Things had gone to hell because when she met Connor, her whole world had lit up, and she wanted to be close to him, to know his secrets, to know every dark, twisty corner of his mind.

Because she was in love with him. She knew that was true, too—all at once, with total clarity. She was in love with him because of the almost-dimple in his chin and the way he could make everyone, even strangers, laugh; she loved him because of how soft his T-shirts were and the fact that he pronounced her name as if it were a lyric in a song he knew by heart. Because he was loyal and funny and smart and had gone through hell and hadn't been broken, hadn't turned hateful and mean.

And now she was going to have to ask him to go through hell again, and he would have every right to hate her.

She said, "I broke the rules."

They were coming up on a town—Wapachee Falls, according to the sign. Dea had never heard of it, but she'd never heard of any of the towns they'd passed so far. From the highway, Dea could make out a blur of gas stations and motels, a sudden blaze of neon signage against the night.

She was surprised when Connor turned the car off the road.

"What are you doing?" she said.

"I'm tired," he said. "Hungry, too."

She looked at the dashboard clock and realized they'd been driving for almost three hours. It was after eleven. She was exhausted, and weak, and hungry. But she was worried about stopping.

"Do you think it's safe?" she said.

"There must be five hundred motels between here and Fielding," he said. "It's safe. At least for tonight."

"For tonight?" Dea repeated. "Don't you have to go home?"

"God, Dea." Connor sounded tired, but not angry. There was even a hint of a smile in his voice. "You really are an idiot sometimes, do you know that?"

But he didn't say it meanly, and she let it drop. She was just glad she didn't have to say good-bye yet.

Wapachee Falls was even smaller than downtown Fielding, but it consisted entirely of chains: McDonald's, Burger King, Taco Bell. Motel 6, Holiday Inn, Quality Inn, Super 8. BP and Texaco. There wasn't a single business that catered to locals: just places where nameless strangers could pass out, pass the time, pass through. It was perfect.

At the Burger King drive-through she moved into the front seat. Connor ordered them double of everything, and Dea paid with a twenty she found rubber-banded at the back of the envelope, behind the fifties. For a minute they could have been anyone, going anywhere, two kids with the munchies and a craving for fries.

They ate in the parking lot, the bags pooling with grease resting on their thighs. Dea was so hungry, she barely tasted the food, burning her fingers and tongue. She'd been on hospital food for more than a week. She licked the salt and grease off her fingers and swallowed her burger in three bites. By the time she stopped eating, her stomach was cramping and she was nauseous. But it was better than being hungry. She had money. She was with Connor. Best of all: she'd told the truth, and he was still talking to her.

They scouted the motels next, looking for the darkest, dingiest, and least likely-looking place. They settled on a no-name motel on the very end of the commercial strip, painted a bleak shade of gray that looked more suited to an internment camp. Half the letters on the neon sign were burnt out, so it read simply: VAC CY.

"This looks like a place where people go to die," Dea said.

Connor angled the car into a parking space as far from the street as possible, where it would be roughly concealed behind an industrial-size Dumpster. "This looks like a place where people leave you alone," he said. He jerked his chin toward one of the few illuminated windows.

Through a narrow gap in the curtains, Dea caught a quick glimpse of naked skin—a man and woman together. She looked quickly away, her face burning. It hadn't fully occurred to Dea until she and Connor were walking together, through the slicing air, that she would be sharing a room with Connor. Maybe even a bed. Even though this was by necessity and not by choice, she was both excited and terrified. She thought of the moment on the Ferris wheel and wondered whether he might try to kiss her again.

But no. Their relationship had changed. She'd ruined everything. He hadn't looked at her that way again—it had probably been temporary insanity.

For the briefest second, she thought of the vision she'd seen in the gap between the curtains and wondered what it would be like. With Connor.

The lobby was painted the same dingy gray as the exterior. It was hardly larger than Dea's hospital room had been, and it stank of burned coffee. There were holes in the carpet. A guy, maybe twenty or twenty-one, his face an explosion of pimples and scars, was sitting behind the desk, hunched over his phone. He barely looked up when Connor and Dea entered.

"What's up?" he said.

"We need a room." Connor was trying to sound assertive, but Dea could tell he was nervous. Dea leaned on the counter, partly because she was trying to look casual, partly because she was still troubled by dizziness that overtook her in waves, rolling the floor out from underneath her, tugging at her knees and telling her to fall.

The guy squinted at Connor. "How old are you?"

"Old enough," Connor said. Dea hoped that was true. She had no idea how old you had to be.

The guy sighed, like they were being a big pain in the ass. "IDs?"

Connor hesitated. The last thing they wanted to do was give over their IDs—besides, Dea didn't have one.

Dea jumped in, "Look, we just want to get in and get out. All cash. No trouble." She'd seen her mom do this hundreds of times. *No trouble, please, will you make an exception? Just for us, just this once.* And a fifty would pass hands, palm to sweaty palm, and that would be that. Dea had tucked the envelope of cash into the waistband of her leggings, under her sweatshirt. She removed it now, making sure that the guy behind the desk was looking. He was. His expression shifted, turned eager, calculating.

"Cash?" he said. He licked his lips, which were very thin. Dea nodded. "It's gonna be sixty bucks for the night," he said quickly. Dea was sure he was lying, doubling the price at least, but she didn't care. "Plus a twenty-buck deposit," he added, when he saw Dea thumbing through her money. "Because of no ID." He was a terrible liar.

Connor started to object but Dea just shook her head. She laid a hundred-dollar bill on the counter.

"I don't have change," the guy said. Another lie. His face was the color of ketchup. Even his pimples seemed inflamed.

"Just give us the key," Connor said, losing patience.

"Seventeen." The guy slid a small metal key across the counter. "Make a left out the door and go all the way to the end. You'll have lots of privacy," he added, with a smile Dea didn't like.

She grabbed the key. "Thanks."

Outside, Dea wobbled a little in her too-small heels and Connor put a hand on her back, then quickly released her. Their breath seized and vanished in the air. Beyond the lights of all the fast food chains and motels, Dea could make out a light sprinkling of stars, like a dusting of sugar.

They had to walk past the room where they'd seen the man

and woman together. The curtain was now totally shut, but as they approached, Dea heard a headboard knocking against the wall and the sound of a woman moaning. She could feel her whole body blush.

"Very theatrical," was all Connor said. Dea wondered whether he had a large basis for comparison and then felt stupid for being so petty. It was none of her business.

Shockingly, the room was all right. Clean, at least. The TV didn't work and the shower curtain was speckled with mold, but the beds were made with fresh sheets and the smell of cigarette smoke had been mostly obliterated under the acrid tang of bleach and something thick and floral, like the kind of scent people sprayed in public bathrooms. There were two double beds. Dea was relieved and also a teeny, tiny bit disappointed.

Connor sat on the bed nearest the door. He leaned his elbows on his knees. His eyes were bloodshot. Dea wanted to go to him and smooth down his hair. But she stayed where she was, against the door, suddenly paralyzed by awkwardness and the awareness that she hadn't showered and she looked ridiculous and she was alone in a locked room with Connor, the boy she loved.

"Now what?" Connor said. "I'm just supposed to . . . sleep?"

Dea nodded. She had told him in the car that she needed back into his dreams, although she hadn't told him the whole truth: she didn't know how much longer she could make it without walking.

Now, he kicked off his Vans, one at a time, and stretched backward on the bed with his arms folded behind his neck. But he didn't close his eyes, and he didn't turn off the lights. She'd never tried to walk a dream with the knowledge—participation, even—of the dreamer. She wondered whether it would change things.

Dea forced herself to move away from the door. She felt awkwardly tall, standing in her heels while he was lying down. She went to the second bed and sat. The mattress was flimsy and sagged under her weight. "Do you think your parents will be worried about you?"

Connor shrugged. "My dad will figure it out. My stepmom doesn't care. She doesn't like me." He said it matter-of-factly. "I think she really believes I did it, you know." His eyes ticked to hers. "To my mom and little brother. Sometimes she looks at me like I might be two seconds away from grabbing a hatchet."

She felt guilty that she had ever envied Connor, and assumed his family to be perfect. She had never known her father, but she had also never suffered a loss. And her mom was her best friend. Crazy and infuriating, yes. A massive liar, check. And trapped in a dream. Still—Dea's best friend.

"What about school tomorrow?" It was either Tuesday or Wednesday; Dea knew that. "You'll get in trouble."

Connor turned to face her. The bare fluorescent bulb above the bed cut his face into hard geometric shapes. "Damn." For the first time all night, he was smiling, just a little. "You've got your days crossed, don't you?"

"What do you mean?" Dea was sure—sure—it wasn't a weekend. She'd kept track in the hospital as best she could, and she couldn't be that far off.

"It's break," Connor said. "Tomorrow's Thanksgiving."

She had completely forgotten. She'd been pulling herself through the hours one by one, like a snail tracking slowly across asphalt, taking it inch by inch.

"I'm sorry," she said. She really was.

"For what?"

She looked away. It was nice of him to pretend she didn't have to apologize, which made her feel even guiltier. "For dragging you into this. For getting you in trouble." She was, too. Sorrier than she could ever say. "I'm sorry you're missing Thanksgiving."

"That's all right." Connor shrugged. "I never liked Thanksgiving, anyway. Too much turkey."

This made her smile. For a second, he sounded like the old Connor—the one who could hardly ever keep a straight face, who made her laugh until she snorted her soda. "Well . . . thanks. For everything." She stood up. Her body ached with exhaustion. At the same time, she wasn't ready to lie down. She wasn't quite ready to venture into Connor's dreams—she was afraid of what she would find and also what she might not find. Miriam had to be where the men with no faces were, which meant she had to be in Connor's nightmare. Or did she? What if Dea was wrong? She, too, was delaying. "I'm going to shower," she said. "Try to relax."

"Relax," he repeated. His face got serious again. "So you can walk in my head. *In* me."

She nodded. There was nothing to say—no words of comfort she could give him.

In the bathroom, she avoided looking at the mirror directly, and quickly hooked a towel over the bare bulbs mounted above it. She felt better once her reflection was concealed.

She took an extra-hot shower, scrubbing with the flimsy

rectangle of soap that had been provided, as if she could wash away the past few weeks and everything that had happened. She re-dressed in the leggings and sweatshirt, silently vowing to go shopping as soon as she could. She should do something with her hair, too—dye it or chop it. She experienced a moment of superficial regret: she'd spent her life hating her hair but it was still hers.

She left the towel hanging over the mirror and returned to the bedroom. At first she thought Connor was asleep already. The lights were off, and he had the covers pulled up to his chest. But when she started to climb into her own bed, he spoke up.

"I won't be able to fall asleep if you're just going to be, like, staring at me."

The sheets were very cold. A radiator was spitting ineffectually in the corner, but the wind still came through underneath the door, and vibrated the windowpanes. "I'm not going to stare at you," she said. "I'm going to close my eyes."

"Still." He was quiet for a minute. Then: "Come here."

She was sure she'd misheard. "What?"

"You said it would be easier if you had an object. A doorway object. Or if we were touching." He had rolled over so his back was to her. In the fine line of moonlight coming through a gap in the curtains, his shoulders were just outlined in silver.

"Easier," she said carefully. She had told him about doorway objects in the car, and how they could substitute for closeness. "But—but I don't need to."

"I want you to," he said, and she felt the impact of the words—*I want you to*—everywhere, all through her body, as if she were swimming, as if she were absorbing them through her skin. "I'm letting you into my *dreams*, Dea. It's weird that you're halfway across the room. Besides, I'm cold."

She couldn't think of any other excuses. She stood up. Her body, dressed in strange clothing, walking through the dark of an unfamiliar room toward a boy's bed, felt alien. Her heart was opening and closing, opening and closing, like a hand grasping for something just out of reach.

She slipped into bed beside him. She was acutely, painfully, ridiculously aware of his body next to hers, of the rise and fall of his breathing and the smell of his skin. His bare shoulders and chest. The dark shadow of his hair against the white pillow. She was afraid to move or even breathe. She lay on her back, staring at the patterns of moonlight on the ceiling, and the occasional illumination of passing headlights. Their feet were only a few inches apart.

After a minute, he rolled over onto his back too, so their shoulders were touching. She felt his hand skim her thigh and she stopped breathing. A mistake, she was sure.

"Your hair's soaking," he said quietly. "Aren't you cold?"

"I'm all right." She wanted to say: she was burning. Her whole body was on fire, was alive at the awareness of Connor so close. She could tell he was looking at her. Part of her wanted to turn her head and another part of her was too afraid. Their lips would be practically touching. What if he wanted to kiss her?

What if he didn't?

They lay there for a while, breathing hard, fast, as though they were running. She felt like she was drowning in the dark and the quiet, in the anticipation. She wanted to say something. She wanted a shift, a change. She wanted *something* to happen, just to bleed out the tension in the room.

"Roll over," Connor said at last. His lips were next to her ear. She could feel the warmth of his breath.

"Which way?"

He put a hand on her waist—solid, gentle—and rolled her over, so that her back was against his chest. She wanted to die. She wanted to be reborn in the space beneath his hand.

Spooning. The expression came to her—she'd heard about spooning, read about it. It was all wrong, she decided, while Connor's chest swelled against her back with his breathing, and his exhale tickled her neck. *Spooning* was something hard and metallic. *Spooning* was organized, like a silverware drawer. This was warm and soft and fluid. This was a cup of milk before bedtime, sunshine pouring like liquid down a wall, soft model clay, imprinted with a finger.

She felt calmer, warmer, happier than she had in weeks. She was drifting, breaking apart on soft, insistent waves of darkness. She fought against the sensation of sleep, tunneling her down into dreamlessness. She needed to focus.

"Connor?" she whispered.

He didn't answer, and she knew he had fallen asleep. It was time.

I'm sorry, she mouthed silently. She closed her eyes. She felt the velvet pressure of Connor's mind almost immediately, a momentary resistance; then, just as quickly, the resistance yielded. She broke through the surface. It was like throwing a stone into the water and watching a reflected image ripple away.

The blackness dispersed.

She was in.

NINETEEN

It was different, much different, walking Connor's dream now that she had permission to be there. It was far easier. He seemed almost to be working with her, as if he could sense the direction of her thoughts, her needs and impulses, and was trying to give her as much help as possible. Doors opened at her touch. Glowing exit signs appeared to light the way out of the long white corridor in which she now found herself—a hospital corridor, she thought, except that on both sides of the hall were not rooms but enormous fish tanks, most of them empty. There was no resistance—no overstructure, no maze of concrete rubble to navigate. It was as though he'd been expecting her—which, of course, he had.

"Chicago," she said out loud, into the empty hallway, even as she began to jog toward the glowing exit sign. Her voice echoed back to her. "Bring me back to Chicago."

She felt the dream shifting, the way that sand shifted underfoot on a beach. Connor was listening. Connor understood. The moment she burst out of the glass doors she was there, on Connor's old street.

This time, there was no snow. It was blazingly sunny, and hot. Summertime. In the distance, she heard the faint tinny music of an ice cream truck. A woman was watering flowers on her porch; as Dea watched, they grew enormous, into shading vines that clawed up the front door and started reaching for the windows. Down the street, a nurse was wheeling a girl with a swollen balloon-head on a stretcher. This was dream stuff, mixed-up imagery and time frames, a jumble of past and present.

She started walking, then quickly drew back, sucking in a breath, into the shadow of a nearby alcove.

Connor. She recognized him immediately, though he was much younger—maybe eleven or twelve; a time when, in real life, his mother was already dead. He was still tall, but all elbows and knees and awkward angles, and his hair was longer, nearly hitting his jaw. He was wheeling a bike, walking next to a few kids—friends?—all of them sweating in the heat. He didn't stop at his house, but instead swung a leg onto his bike and pushed off down the street. As soon as he was gone, his friends evaporated like liquid in the heat.

She cast a quick, instinctive glance up toward Connor's apartment as she passed and stifled a small cry. In the window, Connor's mother was standing naked, her waist encircled by the arms of an enormous cockroach. The insect was the size of a man, and Dea felt her whole body go tight with fear and disgust. She looked away quickly and hurried down the street, trying not to think too hard about what it meant.

Her mother was here—somewhere in this world of concrete and heat, of buildings that shifted in the flat light, grew new planes and angles or rubbed away into nothing as Connor's mind shifted or failed to sustain them. But where? The monsters knew, she was sure of it. They had her imprisoned, or they were tracking her. Dea sensed, intuitively, that it was because of the monsters that her mother had been sucked into this dream-space in the first place. But that was no help. The men with no faces were tracking her, too—that much was obvious. She had to find her mother without being seen, without being sniffed out. That meant disturbing nothing, working quickly, staying concealed.

Several blocks from Connor's apartment, the city began to lose its shape. Buildings opened to the sky. Telephone poles tapered to tips no wider than a pencil. Cars were mere suggestions, sculptures of metal and rubber. This far away from the center of the dream, from its focal point, laws of sound and motion became fluid and flexible.

She was uneasy. She had the sense both of being observed and of total solitude. Every few minutes, she turned around, convinced she would find the monsters grinning raggedly at her. But there were only empty streets, increasingly undefined and undetailed, as though she were entering a drawing sketched by a toddler. Even the streets were changing, turning to a dark ink, sticky and difficult to step through.

"Mom?" She tested her voice and then paused, still, alert.

Nothing. She called "Mom" a little louder and heard her own voice echo back, rolling off the planes of the empty city. She kept going, wondering whether at a certain point Connor's dream would simply run out, would turn to the darkness of unconscious space and force her to turn around. Or maybe it would go on forever, just getting less and less convincing, until she was walking through a smudgy gray space where buildings were shells and the landscape existed only in silhouette.

Above her, the sky began to *shrink*—narrowing like water into a fine stream just before it pours down a drain. Simultaneously she realized she was no longer walking but *climbing*. The ground was now steeply pitched, and, furthermore, covered with a fine, blowing layer of sand—so much so that after a few feet she could hardly keep her balance and fell forward, gasping, driving her hands out to brace her fall.

She banged her knee, hard, even as her hands closed on something metal: the rung of a ladder. Twisting around, fighting a surge of dizziness, she saw that the road had somehow led her not out but *up*: up a sheer-sided tunnel embedded with a metal ladder. Sand continued to rain down on her shoulders and neck from above.

There was nowhere to go but up. She found a foothold and began climbing the ladder toward the small circular opening of sky above her. It was hot—lava-blast hot—and wet, like being inside a living body. She reached the end of the ladder, where the cascade of sand was even more constant, and hauled herself free of the tunnel. Her arms were shaking as she staggered to her feet.

She was in a desert. In front of her, in the direction of the low-hanging sun, stretching to the horizon, was sand, and more sand—soft ocean swells of it, baking in the heat. When she turned around, she saw that the pit from which she'd emerged wasn't unique. There were thousands of holes, some gaping wide, some no larger than a human mouth, stretching toward the horizon. And even as she watched, she saw the sand shifting slightly, almost breathing, as new holes bubbled up and others collapsed.

"What the hell?" she said out loud. Her voice sounded small. When she peered over the lip of the pit from which she'd emerged, she could still see in the very distance—so small it was like looking through the wrong end of a telescope—the trembling silhouette of Connor's Chicago skyline.

So what was this desert and all these pits? A new dream? No. She knew what it felt like when dreams changed. This was different. It was almost as if she'd climbed *out* of Connor's dream.

But then where the hell was she?

With a growing sense of anxiety, she edged toward a different pit, testing her weight on the sand before she committed, worried that a hole might open up beneath her feet. Endlessly far below her, she could see the interior of an unfamiliar living room buried in its depths. At the bottom of the next pit was a scene of war, flashing momentarily into view before turning, abruptly, into a suburban barbecue.

The thought flashed: other dreams. Each of these pits—the endless quantity of them—contained dreams.

Just as quickly, though, she forced the idea from her mind. This *must* be Connor's dream, all of it. The alternative didn't make any sense.

Still, just to be safe, she took off her sweatshirt and tied it to the top rung of the ladder she'd climbed, leaving a bit of pink fabric visible in the sand. And as she set out across the desert, she couldn't shake the feeling she was leaving Connor behind, and leaving behind her way out, too.

But she had seen a set of footsteps leading across the golden hills, dark as shadow, stalking off toward the unknown. A woman's footsteps, she judged, from the size of them.

That meant her mother might have come this way.

The sand made it hard to walk, and soon she was sweating. She was dressed in the same leggings and T-shirt she was wearing in real life—an aspect of walking she had never fully understood, as if she carried an unshakable image of her own body with her, and couldn't get rid of it. She moved parallel to the line of footsteps, keeping them in her sight—though increasingly, she wished she had stayed in the city and not ventured out this far. It felt like she'd been walking for hours already. Birds circled overhead, black spots against the clouded sky, and she was at first comforted by them. Harbingers. Then one swooped closer and she recognized its stringy neck, red as exposed muscle, and ugly, old-man face. A vulture. It seemed like a bad omen.

And suddenly she was furious. Furious that this was her life, her legacy, her curse. Furious that her mom had dragged her into this, had even given birth to her, when she was meant to spend her life fumbling through other people's dreams, *feeding* on them.

"Mom!" she yelled. Nothing. Just the silent drift of the birds across the sky. Her mouth felt gritty with sand and dust. "Where are you?" She felt reckless and careless. She would almost welcome it if the monsters appeared and gave chase. At least it would mean she was getting closer.

As though in response, a soft wind rose, shifting the sands. Very faintly, she heard sounds of laughter.

Her anger was gone as quickly as it had come. She hurried forward, scrambling up a steep slope of golden sand, using her hands for purchase, and cursing as the ground shifted underneath her weight. The sounds of laughter and voices swelled; she heard the faint timpani jangle of music, too. At the top of the hill she stopped, panting a little, feeling her dream-lungs contract in her dream-body—all of it real, far too real.

Beneath her, cupped in a dip of land, was a long line of weathered caravans, like the old-fashioned kind she'd seen in history books about the settling of the American West—but wheelless. A fire was going in the sand, sending up a smoke that looked practically orange against the vivid sky, and dozens of people were laughing and milling around the makeshift camp, dressed in loose clothing. There were no horses, and for a moment Dea stood there, swiping at the sweat that stung her eyes, trying to make sense of how the caravans moved. Then she saw a bunch of enormous birds, some of them still yoked for service, feeding at a narrow trough, and realized that the caravans didn't roll. They flew.

She was so stunned she forgot to conceal herself. One woman caught Dea's eye and cried out. All at once, the whole group—at least thirty of them, Dea estimated—fell silent, turning in her direction, shading their eyes from the sun.

A bead of sweat moved like a finger down Dea's spine. Finally, she couldn't stand the silence. She cleared her throat.

"I'm looking for my mother," she said.

One of the members of the caravan came closer. Everyone else remained frozen, watching Dea. His skin was dark from sun, his bare arms roped with muscles, his black hair nearly to his jaw. He was about her age, she thought, and something about him was familiar, and set off an electric wave of anxiety, deep in her stomach.

"Where did you come from?" he asked, stopping when they were separated by about ten feet. Dea was glad. If he'd come any closer, she might have run.

She ignored that—she didn't have an answer for him, anyway. "She was taken by the monsters," she said, and there was a small ripple of response from the assembled crowd. Dea wasn't sure, but she thought she heard a woman say *king's army*.

The boy half smiled as if she'd said something amusing. "Which monsters?" he said. "There are many different kinds here. They come in all shapes and sizes."

"The men with no faces," Dea said, concealing her fear behind impatience, and ignoring the fact that there might be more monsters, worse ones.

He shook his head, so his hair fell over one eye. "You don't find them," he said, still smiling that infuriating smile. "They find you. They'll keep after you, until you give them what they want. It's what they're trained to do."

He was staring at her so intensely, Dea wanted to look away. But she couldn't. She still had the sense that she *recognized* him from somewhere. "What do they want?"

"What do any of us want?" He crossed the distance between them casually, but all of a sudden it was done, closed, and he

215

leaned forward, and she could feel the roughness of his lips bump once against her ear as he whispered: "What belongs to them."

He pulled away and Dea gasped. His eyes were the deep gold of honeyed candy, and suddenly she *knew*.

"You," Dea said. She instinctively reached out, but stopped an inch away from touching him. "I've *seen* you before. In another dream."

As soon as she said it, though, she realized she'd seen him even more than once. There was a time in Sedona, Arizona, when she was walking the dream of her old bus driver: a freaky dream, which had ended in watching the driver drown a kitten in the kiddie pool. She'd never taken the bus again. The boy, *this* boy, had been standing just on the other side of a white picket fence.

Then there was a time just a few months ago, when she'd stolen the hair clip from Shawna McGregor and walked a dream of a lame basement party. This boy had been one of the few unfamiliar guests; she remembered that he had almost spotted her. And now he was here, in Connor's dream.

But it was impossible. People didn't dream about the same things. Was this boy a walker, too? Were all these people walkers? Were they *following* Dea?

The boy looked amused—and satisfied, Dea saw, as if he'd been waiting for Dea to figure that out. "I've been curious about you," he admitted.

"You've been following me," Dea said.

"Not exactly," he said. There was sand between her teeth, sand tangled in the long, sun-streaked strands of the boy's hair. Too real. "We're pickers. We make our living from the pits.

Whatever we find, whatever we salvage, we sell in the city."

"What city?" Dea shook her head.

"The king's city," he said. Something flickered in the boy's eyes, an expression gone too soon for Dea to name it. "The only city there is."

"Can you tell me how to find my mother or not?" Dea said. She was trying not to cry. She'd imagined somehow she would simply *feel* her mother's presence. She'd imagined she would take her mother's hand and draw her out of whatever dark place was holding her.

And then what? They'd walk out of the dream together, triumphant? Dea didn't even know how her mom had gotten *in*. Not by walking, certainly. Walking was just like dreaming, in a way—the physical body remained in the real world while the mind traveled. But Miriam had entered the dream world completely.

"You won't find her unless the king wants you to find her," he said. "You'll need to take it up with him."

Dea was on the verge of tears. She channeled the feeling into anger, forced her rage to take shape. "What are you talking about?" she said. "What king? What is this? Who—who are you?"

He shook his head again. "It's who *you* are that matters."

"Stop speaking in riddles." She was losing it. She no longer understood the rules; she didn't understand who these people were, and how Connor's dream could possibly extend so far in so much detail. "You aren't real," she said, although without conviction. "None of this is real."

"Oh no?" The boy moved barely an inch closer but Dea stopped breathing. She'd never been so close to any boy, except

Connor. But standing next to Connor was like huddling under a warm blanket: a fuzzy whole-body feeling that made her feel stupid and happy.

Standing next to this boy, whoever he was, was like putting a hand on an electrified fence: a blast of voltage that left her dizzy and disoriented. Before she could stop him, he reached out and traced his thumb along her lower lip. Her body reacted. She couldn't help it. His touch made her feel like she was standing beneath a sky full of fireworks. Like she was a firework—all light and explosion. "Are you sure?"

She wrenched away, shaken. No one else had moved. The whole group was as still as a painting, and she knew that no one would help her, either. She turned, blinking away tears, and started back in the direction she'd come.

"Wait." The boy called her back and she stopped. Maybe he regretted how he'd spoken to her. He came toward her, holding a leather flask. He stopped when they were still separated by several feet, as if he knew he'd crossed a line.

"Water," he said, extending the flask to her. For just a second, he looked very young. "You might need it."

Dea nearly didn't take it. But when he didn't move, just stood there with one arm out and a penitent expression on his face, she did. She wouldn't thank him, though.

"You better hurry," he said. "The winds are changing." Then he turned abruptly and made his way back down the hill toward the encampment.

Dea set off again, holding the flask by its neck. The boy was right about one thing: the wind had picked up and mostly eradicated her tracks. She started walking, wiping sweat from her eyes, scanning the sky for vultures. She disliked the birds, but they were still birds, and might be useful.

She was suddenly desperate to find a doorway out of the dream, to wake up next to Connor in the small motel room, with its sputtering heat and faint smell of detergent, to return to the real world with its leaky toilets and boring school days and inconveniences and dangers and familiarity.

As the panic built, grew, pushed at her chest, Dea started to run. Sand, sand in every direction. How far was she from the nearest way out? How far had she come? What if Connor had already woken, and the city had fallen and turned to more sand? The idea chilled her, even as she blinked sweat from her eyes, struggling up steep desert peaks, her breath rasping in her chest.

Impossible. This *was* Connor's dream. It must be. The alternative was too strange, too frightening: that there were dreams that existed in a kind of permanence. That there were dreams that existed with no one to dream them at all.

And that she, Dea, was in one of them.

Then—a miracle—she crested a hill and saw the dappled shadows of thousands of holes, some of them just opening, some of them disappearing as the sand shifted, moved, like a slowly flowing ocean. Even from a distance she could see her pink sweatshirt, occasionally lifting in the wind, snapping an arm as if to wave at her.

She hurried forward. But as she moved, the sand moved with her, foaming and sliding under her feet, barreling down toward the pits like a wave moving toward shore, so she could barely keep on her feet. *A landslide.* Dea grabbed hold of her sweatshirt as her legs were whipped out from underneath her. She went sliding over the edge of the pit on a coursing wave of sand, coughing dust from her lungs as her fingers found the cold metal rungs of the ladder. She clung there, feet kicking in open air, as sand continued to drum down on her head and shoulders. Far below her was the distant landscape of Connor's dream. Chicago had disappeared entirely. She was dangling above a dizzying funhouse landscape, a city made not of buildings but of enormous roller coasters and tents as large as mountains.

The sand was coming so fast now it had obliterated all the light above her.

The pit was collapsing.

Connor was waking up.

She lost her grip on the ladder and fell, or slid, or was pushed—she didn't know. There was sand in her mouth, her eyes, her ears. She clawed for open air and came up blinking, coughing, struggling to stand. But before she could get to her feet, a roller coaster fell in slow motion, a giant iron skeleton coming apart. Its collapse sent out a booming echo so loud it knocked her off balance. Now the sky was breaking apart in pieces, like a jigsaw puzzle being disassembled: sand poured through the cracks, a steady downpour of it.

She got to her feet but made it only a few staggering steps before another structure fell, before the ground trembled and bucked and sent her to her knees. Up again. A surge came toward her—a shimmering high wall of white sand—and before she could move or turn or cover her face, she was trapped. There was sand in her shirt, in her nose, sand choking her. She fought blindly against the sucking weight of thousands and thousands of tons of sand—sand shaved over centuries from dream-mountains. Then she was spit out, tossed into the fine brightness of the air. She rolled onto her back, hacking, as the sand continued to bury the dream.

Most of the dream was gone—rubbed away, leaving only a faint smear where the colored funhouse tents had been, an aureole of dust and destruction. She would never make it. Still, she took a step forward, and then another: moving mechanically, instinctively, without hope.

It hurt to breathe. She had never been so thirsty. She uncapped the water that the boy had given her, but before she could drink, the ground shifted again. She stumbled, landing on her hands and knees. The water seeped into the ground, a dark line of it, like a snake being sucked underground. She grabbed for it, trying to palm some of the wet sand into her mouth, desperate for even a drop, a taste, of water.

Instead, the sand gripped her fingers, ate at her wrists and arms, sucked her downward. She let out a short cry and then was jerked to the ground, face pressed to the hot sand, as a whirling, unseen pressure continued working at her, spiraling her downward, as if an invisible monster were sucking her slowly through a straw.

Then she realized: a door. The water had made a door.

But it was unlike any door she had ever used. She was being pulled headfirst into the ground. She shut her eyes and held her breath. She was kicking at the air, and then her legs were pulled under, too. She was caught, trapped, buried in the sand, and for a second she believed the boy had tricked her, and she would die.

Boom. Even through the muffling sand, she heard the last of

Connor's dream-city falling. *Boom.*

Just when she knew she couldn't hold her breath any longer—just when she was ready to give up, and float away—there was a small, subtle shift in the pressure around her. She gasped and tasted air. She kicked out and felt the tangle of blankets around her ankles.

She sat up, stifling a cry, as Connor came awake beside her.

TWENTY

Boom.

For a second, still disoriented and terrified, she thought the echoes had followed her into real life. Then she realized that someone was knocking on the door. Her eyes went to the clock on the bedside table: 7:35 a.m.

"Connor?" A woman's voice, unfamiliar. His stepmom? But Connor looked confused, too. "Dea?"

Connor eased out of bed, gesturing for Dea to stay put when she moved to follow him. At the window, he parted the cheap curtains with a finger and peered outside. Then he reared back quickly, as if something had bitten his nose, just as the woman started knocking again.

"I just want to talk to you. Five minutes. Ten, tops." Even through the door, Dea thought she heard a sigh. "Listen, you're not going to get rid of me, okay? I'll wait around all day. So you might as well let me in."

"Damn it," Connor muttered. His hair was sticking straight up, and sometime in the middle of the night, he'd lost a sock between the sheets. Now one of his feet was bare. Dea wanted to go to him and give him a hug. But she stayed where she was, still half-dizzy from walking.

"Who is it?" she whispered. Her throat was raw, as if she'd really inhaled sand.

But he just shook his head and moved to open the door, even as the knocking started up again. They'd locked the door twice and put the chain up the night before, and it took Connor a minute to work the door open. When he did, Dea was momentarily dazzled by a vision of pale blue sky and wintry sun. A beautiful Thanksgiving.

"Christ." The woman who stepped into the room was weirdly familiar, although Dea was sure they'd never met. She was balancing a cardboard tray of Dunkin' Donuts coffee—four cups, Dea noticed—in one hand. With the other, she unwound an enormous scarf from around her neck, carefully disentangling the fabric from a pair of dangly earrings. "You're a hard person to get ahold of, you know that?"

And then Dea knew her. She recognized the voice. Kate Patinsky, who was writing a book, who'd been trying to talk to Connor for days, who'd tried to visit Dea in the hospital. Kate was younger than Dea had expected. She'd been imagining a woman in her forties or fifties, with the long snout of a bloodhound and the kind of mean, calculating expression that Morgan Devoe and Hailey Madison had perfected long ago. But Kate looked only a few years older than Dea. She was wearing fingerless gloves and several layers: a T-shirt, an army jacket, an ivory wool peacoat sporting several coffee stains.

"Do you ever give up?" Connor hadn't moved from the door—maybe he was hoping Kate would take the hint and leave again.

"No," she said, finally unraveling the scarf and tossing it onto the foot of the unused bed. "I brought coffee," she said. The tray she put on top of the TV. She reached into her enormous purse and extracted a crumpled Dunkin' Donuts bag. "And bagels. Mind if I sit?"

"Yes," Connor said.

Kate ignored that. She took two of the coffees for herself, leaving the other two in the tray. When she caught Dea staring, she winked. "Only fair," she said. "I've been up all night."

"Why are you here?" Connor asked bluntly.

Kate sighed. "Look. I know you think I'm out for blood."

"Aren't you?" Connor asked, crossing his arms.

Kate looked up at him. Her eyes were big and warm and brown, like a cow's. "I'm out for the truth," she said. "This case has been my life. It made a huge impact on me. It's one of the reasons I wanted to study criminology in the first place. The way they treated you . . ." She broke off, shaking her head. After another moment of hesitating, Connor crossed the room and snatched up the coffees—still glaring at Kate, as if he wanted her to know that he resented her just the same. Connor passed Dea one of the coffees and the bag of bagels. The bagels were warm on her lap and the coffee was amazing: delicately flavored, swimming with cream. She almost—almost—couldn't hate Kate Patinsky anymore.

"How did you find us?" Connor asked.

Kate had settled on the unused bed and produced about seven packets of sugar from the pocket of her peacoat. She emptied them, one after the other, into her coffee. "Wasn't hard," she said. "This one"—she jerked her chin toward Dea—"makes a break for it and at the same time, *you* disappear. It doesn't take a genius to figure out you'd be together. And I figured you wouldn't drive more than three, four hours without stopping." She popped the lid back on the coffee and took a long, gratified slurp. "I called *fifty-six* motels before I found someone who said he'd seen you."

The desk clerk. Jesus. Dea seriously regretted the hundred bucks she'd given him.

"Connor," Dea said, anxiety prickling in her stomach. "If *she* found us—"

"That means you can be found," Kate interrupted her. "Exactly. I don't want to waste your time."

"What do you want?" Connor asked. His voice was hard, and he *looked* hard, too: his face chiseled out of gray light, like a stranger's.

Kate leaned forward, elbows to knees. "I told you. I want the truth." The weirdest thing was that Dea believed her. "Look, Connor, I understand why you've been avoiding me. Shit, your uncle tried to have me run out of Fielding." Something flashed in her eyes, a momentary anger that made Kate look unexpectedly older. "But I don't care about your uncle. You may think

226

I don't care about your family, that I've made myself a pest—"

"I don't think that," Connor interjected. "I *know* that."

Kate smiled faintly. "Fair. But I do care. I care about the victims." Connor flinched when she said *victims,* as if he still wasn't used to hearing his mother and brother described that way. Her voice got softer. "I care about your mom. I care about your little brother. And I care about you, too." This made Connor look up. Kate shrugged. "You were a victim. Not in the same way. But definitely a victim."

Connor's eyes were hard to read. His mouth started moving, as if he was having to chew up his words before saying them. "So . . . you don't think I did it?"

"I *know* you didn't do it." Kate paused, letting that sink in. "That's why I'm writing this book. This case should never have gone cold. Living witness, closed crime scene, likely committed by someone the victims knew. Someone screwed up big time. I want to know who, and why."

Connor looked away. "It's over," he said. "What's done is done. What's the point?"

"The *point,*" Kate said, "is that your family deserves answers. You deserve answers." She hesitated. "Don't you want to know?"

Connor turned away abruptly and moved to the window. For a second he stood there without speaking. Finally, he turned around again. "All right," he said at last. "What do you want from me?"

Kate set her coffee by her feet and spread her hands. "Just to talk," she said. "Take me through it. Tell me what you remember. Help me, Connor. I can help you, too." Her eyes flicked to Dea. "Looks like you two could use it."

In the silence that followed, Dea found herself hoping that Connor would say yes. She realized that she trusted Kate implicitly, now that she'd met her—believed in her, too, though she didn't really see how Kate could help them. Maybe just by finding out the truth, for Connor's sake. So the nightmares would stop.

The idea flashed: Did that mean the monsters would stop, too?

Outside, Dea heard the muffled sound of voices. It took a moment for her brain to bring them into focus, but then she stood up, her heart rocketing into her mouth, her body high-wired on alert.

The clerk was babbling excuses. "They paid cash, I had no idea they were in trouble, I never would've let them in. Don't tell my boss, okay?"

"My uncle," Connor said, even before he turned back to the window to confirm. He yanked the curtains closed all the way, leaning against them, as if that would keep the police from finding them. "My *uncle*," he repeated, staring at Dea with a look of pure panic. A second later, someone pounded against the door and Connor flinched.

"Connor? Connor, open up. I know you're in there."

Kate was on her feet. "You," she said in a low voice, pointing at Dea, then jerking her thumb toward the bathroom. "Window. Now."

Connor cleared his throat and spoke up, so he could be heard through the door. "One second. Jesus Christ. Stop shouting." Casually, as if running off to some godforsaken motel were totally normal. As if his uncle had woken him early on a Saturday.

"Connor, I'm serious." The door shook on its hinges.

"*Now*," Kate repeated in a whisper, snapping her fingers in Dea's direction. Dea cast one look at Connor. He nodded, mouthed *Go*. She grabbed the envelope of cash from the bedside table and stuffed it in her waistband.

The door handle rattled.

"I'm putting my boxers on. Give me a minute." Connor directed his words to the men on the other side of the door.

She didn't bother with the shoes—she could barely walk in them anyway, much less run. She slipped into the bathroom and closed the door just as the cops poured into the motel room: rapid-fire voices; walkie-talkie static; Connor's uncle's voice, loud and outraged. "What were you thinking?" he kept saying.

And the phrase, endlessly repeated, like a terrible drumbeat: "Where is she? Where is she, Connor?"

Kate was talking over everyone, trying to be heard. "It was my fault. I thought if I could get finally get Connor one-on-one . . ."

There was only one way out: a small, dirt-encrusted window just above the toilet, its frame warped from years of sweltering summertime heat. Dea leaned against the window frame. For a second, it stuck, and she experienced a moment of total fear, full-body panic, like being caught again in the stifling mouth of airless sand.

She pushed. Outside the door, the voices crested and changed melodies, triumphant and terrifying: "The shoes. Look at these shoes. She's here somewhere. Find her."

Find her.

The window released. She shoved it open, striking out the screen with a palm. It landed with a clatter. She doubted that anyone had heard, but it wouldn't matter anyway: in a few seconds, they would find her. Already, she could hear voices coalescing, massing around a single word: *bathroom.*

Find her. Bathroom.

She climbed up on the toilet and went headfirst through the window, into the cold gray air, struggling momentarily to fit her hips through the frame. She fell the last foot to the pavement, keeping her head protected, skinning her arms and elbows. She barely felt it. She was on her feet. The ground was freezing but she didn't feel that, either.

She'd emerged at the back of the motel, cluttered with Dumpsters and accumulated trash. A narrow spit of pavement ran up against bare fields, glittering coldly in the new day. Through a line of thin trees, she saw rundown houses, mobile homes, a bunch of rusted cars perched on cinderblocks. Beyond them, she knew, would be more fields, more farms, more woods and hiding places.

She ran.

TWENTY-ONE

She wouldn't get very far and she knew it. She wasn't in great shape—she never had been, because of her heart—and her feet were cut up and swollen with cold. *She* was cold. Once she stopped running, she was freezing. Her nose ran and her eyes stung. The wind felt like it was cutting her straight down the middle.

Still, she managed to evade the cops all morning. She stuck to the woods whenever she could; when she couldn't, she cut across backyards and ducked under laundry lines where towels swelled like puffed-up sails, always staying off the roads. When she was so cold she thought she might die, she found an abandoned Volvo and climbed inside to get warm for a bit, stuffing her feet into the holes in the upholstery until feeling returned to her toes.

She wasn't thinking about leaving Connor behind, or how she would reach him, or what would happen to her next. If she began worrying, she would lose hope. She focused instead on her immediate problems: she needed shoes, a jacket, and a hat, or she would die out here.

It was risky, but she decided to stop in the next town she came to: Sawyerville, probably four times the size of Fielding, a dumpy cluster of bars and big-box chain stores. Shoes first. Her toes had lost all feeling again, and she was worried that she might get frostbite and end up having to amputate with a pen-knife like she'd seen someone stranded in an avalanche do once on TV. She stopped at a Lady Foot Locker—not her first choice for style, but she was in no position to be choosy.

"What happened to your shoes?" was the first thing the sales clerk, a guy with a shiny, shellacked helmet of blond hair and the look of a choirboy, said to her.

"I was camping," she lied quickly. "They got stolen." She picked out a pair of sneakers and a whole bag of fluffy white socks. She felt a thousand times better once she was wearing shoes, like she'd graduated from freak runaway to normal human in less than five seconds. The store was bright and over-heated, and even though she needed to get moving, she was hesitant to leave.

"It's a little cold to be camping, isn't it?" he said. His eyes went buggy when she pulled out a roll of cash, but he didn't say anything.

"Not with the right equipment," she said. It was another improvised line, a lie of convenience, but then an idea struck her. They'd crossed into Ohio last night. They couldn't be very far from the border, and Ohio's Largest Corn Maze. "How far are we from DeWitt?"

He shrugged. "Ten miles. Twelve, maybe."

A woman with teased hair and lips painted baby pink was doing a very bad job of pretending she wasn't paying Dea any attention. Had Dea been recognized? "Thanks," Dea said. She half expected the woman to call out to her as she moved for the door, but the woman continued moving through the racks of athletic clothing, flipping tags, and Dea relaxed as she stepped out into the sunshine.

She found a Walmart. She was beginning to think that in America, you were never more than ten miles from a Walmart. Her mom had spent years railing against the destruction of the American landscape, comparing big-box stores to massive pimples exploding the pus of same-old, same-old all over the country. But they came in handy when you were a teenage runaway.

If she ever saw her mother again, she'd tell her.

Because of the holiday, the store was practically empty. Dea went directly to the section for sportsmen, people who were used to toughing it out. She bought a big backpack designed for hikers, a water bottle and a sleeping bag, a tent, a heavy jacket, a hat and gloves, a portable kerosene stove and a knife, hair dye and scissors, sunglasses, changes of underwear, a zip-up fleece, thermal underwear, a flashlight, and a can opener. She spent nearly four hundred dollars, but she wasn't too worried. She still had enough, more than enough, to cross the country on a

233

Greyhound or even book a flight. And there was nowhere she wanted to go, anyway. The answers were here, with Connor. With the monsters.

In the parking lot, she snapped the tags off her jacket, hat, and gloves. Once she was geared up, she could have been anyone. She was a faceless, shapeless girl, bloated with layers of winter clothing. She felt better about being on the roads now. She was floating in plain sight, just another drifter moving across the vast shiny scars of pavement. Still, she stopped at the next gas station she came to and asked to use the bathroom. She hacked off her hair before it dyeing it—ignoring the guy who started pounding five minutes in, demanding she open the door because he had to pee—fearing and hoping every time she looked in the mirror that she might see her mother looking back. Instead, she saw a girl's face, drawn and haunted, underneath a messy shock of black hair. She barely recognized herself.

She was starving. She moved through the aisles of the gas station. She bought SpaghettiOs and Coke, candy and bags of chips, feeling an unexpected burst of joy, of richness, with her money still strapped comfortably in her waistband. She was too hungry to make it far, and ducked behind a Dumpster to set up her cookstove before realizing she'd forgotten to buy a pot. She heated the can directly over the stove until the paper label began to singe and curl, then ate the SpaghettiOs with her fingers, crouching in the thin, cold air, feeling at once exposed and totally anonymous. How many people disappeared every year? How many people dropped out of sight, wandering, forever scraping out a living? Probably thousands.

When she was satisfied, she washed her fingers with water carefully poured from the bottle, then repacked her backpack and shouldered it. She stopped a guy pumping fuel in an old Chevy truck and asked for directions. She set off in the direction he indicated—toward DeWitt, and the maze.

By the time she arrived, the sun was already setting, and the maze was lit a reddish gold. From a distance it looked as though it had been cast in bronze. She estimated it was four or five o'clock, and very quiet—the kind of stillness and silence that comes only in wintertime, in places abandoned or forgotten. All across the country, people would be gathering around dining room tables heaped with golden-skinned turkey and cranberries glimmering like crimson jewels. Or maybe they were already done eating, and were sitting in darkened rooms, pants unbuttoned, complaining about that last piece of pie; watching TV, washing dishes, brewing coffee, sobering up.

She was on the other side, now: the animal side, a place of shadow and slow time, a part of the world untouched by human intervention. She might as well be a gopher, an owl, or a rat.

She paused to get out her flashlight before entering the maze. She didn't want to get caught in the dark before making camp, fumbling for supplies by touch. Though she had navigated the maze once already—she pushed aside the memory of that day, its warmth and sun, the lightness of Connor's fingers and quickness of his smile—in the dark it looked grotesque and strange. After half an hour of fruitless wandering, she began to fear the maze was changing shape around her, penning her in. But that was the point: she would be hard to find, impossible to surprise. She would be safe in the middle of the maze.

At last she made it to the center, and the small metal sign that congratulated visitors for untangling the maze and reminded them that smoking and littering were forbidden. It was totally dark. She set up camp fumblingly, painstakingly, gripping her flashlight under her chin so she could have use of both hands. She had to take off her gloves, and her fingers were soon stiff with cold. Her breath made clouds in the air. Above her, the stars looked like flakes of snow that had gotten stuck in the black tar of the sky.

She had camped with her mom a few times, when money had run low, when they were between towns—and, Dea thought, probably between cons. Despite what she now knew of her mom, she couldn't bring herself to feel angry. She couldn't even resent all of those wrenching displacements, the sudden relocations, the nights eating shitty gas station sandwiches and sleeping in the car or in a tent set up hastily on the side of a no-name road.

Dea wanted Miriam back. She would take it all—she would live it all again—if she could just have her mom back.

Her earlier feelings of freedom had been replaced by a deep loneliness, a physical ache, as if someone had carved a space between her stomach and her chest. She was all alone. There was not a sound anywhere, no signs of life or movement, except for the rustle of small animals in the dark. It could have been a thousand years in the past, or a thousand in the future, after all humans were wiped out. She might be the only person left in all the world.

She knew it must still be early, but she was tired, and she didn't want to think anymore. She crawled into her tent and shook out her sleeping bag. Eventually, she stopped shivering, and the hollow inside of her became a long pit, and she fell, and slept.

TWENTY-TWO

A day passed, and then another. Still, Connor didn't come. It was stupid to think that he would remember a throwaway conversation they'd had nearly two months earlier, and even stupider to hope that he would come and find her.

She risked dialing Connor's cell phone, from an ancient payphone she spotted a mile from the maze, sitting in front of a shuttered hair salon, which was now scrawled over with graffiti. The receiver was sticky in her hand, but she still squeezed tightly, as if she could somehow reach Connor by touch. The phone rang and rang and then clicked over to voicemail. The second time she called, a woman—Connor's stepmother, Dea assumed—picked up after the third ring.

"Hello?" she said breathlessly. Then: "Who is this? Who is this?" Her voice was shrill and it made Dea's head hurt. She hung up.

She called Gollum's house several times, hoping to reach Gollum directly, but someone else always got to the phone first, usually Richie or Mack, and, once, Gollum's father. She always hung up. Maybe she was being paranoid, but she wasn't sure who she could trust, and she didn't want to get Gollum in trouble. She was sure that if the cops knew Gollum had been in touch with Dea, they wouldn't leave her alone. One time, both Gollum and Richie picked up simultaneously, and before Dea could second-guess herself, she blurted out "corn maze" before hanging up. Immediately, she felt like an idiot. She hadn't even given Gollum time to recognize her voice. But when she dialed back, it was Gollum's dad who answered.

She wished she'd thought to take Kate Patinsky's number.

She was bored, which she hadn't expected. She hadn't realized it would be possible to be so constantly anxious and simultaneously so flat-out bored that she almost wished the thing she was afraid of would happen, just so that *something* would. She thought this must be what it felt like to go to war, to spend hours playing cards and choking on the thick dust of a foreign desert, almost wishing that a bomb would explode.

She hiked to the nearest gas station twice, not because she was low on supplies, but because it broke up the hours and gave her something to do. But the second time, she caught the guy behind the register giving her funny looks, and figured she could go back only once, maybe twice more before he started asking questions. Then she would have to move on. She'd pack up and head south.

But not yet. Just in case.

Her schedule was slowly flipping. It was better to walk the roads at night, hit a diner when she needed to get warm, slip between the faceless shifting crowds of truckers doing their cross-country hauls, and gray-faced strippers, makeup harsh under the lights, eating pancakes at three a.m. She slept most of the day, swimming through the hours, trying not to think too hard.

On her third day in the maze, Dea woke to the sound of voices. She rocketed up in her sleeping bag, fumbling for her knife, which was stupid, because she would never be able to stab anyone and she knew it. She unzipped the tent flap and eased out into the open, careful not to make any noise, blinking in the bright light. It was clear and cold, not a cloud in the sky, shadows drawn starkly, like cardboard cutouts plastered to the ground.

She heard a child squeal and a mother speak sharply. She relaxed, but just a little. She'd thought the cops had tracked her down again, but it was just a family, exploring the maze despite the cold. Still, if they found her, they'd be sure to call someone—the police, most likely—and report the girl living alone at the center of Ohio's Largest Corn Maze.

She stood up and began hastily dismantling her tent before realizing it was no use. The voices were already so close, she could make out individual words: the low, sarcastic drawl of a teenage girl, complaining that it was too cold and she was hungry; the shrieks of a younger child; the father and mother arguing about whether to go right or left. She stood, rigid and terrified, waiting to be discovered. But then the voices receded, and Dea knew the family had given up and had decided to backtrack. She stayed where she was, hardly breathing, until the roar of their car engine had faded. Then, struck by an idea, she stood and moved into the deep shadow of the maze, hugging her jacket tighter.

She was in luck: the little kid had dropped a glove, a red fleece mitten so small Dea could fit only three fingers inside of it, and still faintly warm from the child's grip. She tucked the mitten inside her jacket pocket, stupidly happy. She would walk today, as soon as possible. Her body was craving it, a compulsion she didn't want to think about too closely. She needed to keep her strength up.

She retreated into her tent, pulling the sleeping bag all the way over her head so that it blocked the light filtering through the nylon walls. She felt the mitten, beating through the fabric of her jacket like a second heart. She knew it would be many hours before the little girl's bedtime, but she had nothing else to do. She waited, her mind revolving slowly around the idea of the mitten, and the idea of the girl who'd possessed it, waiting for a break or a change. She drifted in and out of sleep. The sun passed overhead.

And eventually, she felt a change, the dark tangle of another mind rushing toward her, like the ground coming closer in a dream about falling. She leapt with her mind; she reached out to push; and after a brief wrangle, a sense of entanglement, she was in.

She hadn't walked a kid's dream in a while—not since she was a kid. Kids' dreams were erratic, often fractured, and moved too quickly to be satisfying. She was relieved that this dream was simple and relatively orderly.

Dea was standing behind a large hedge. This was the child's

defense, her attempt to prevent a stranger's intrusion. Beyond the hedge, Dea saw a group of kids tearing around a pool deck. Dark shapes were moving fleet-fast through the water—more kids, Dea assumed, until one of the shapes surfaced and she saw glistening dark skin and a set of teeth. Some kind of sea creature, then.

She felt a light touch on her elbow. She spun around, startled, and swallowed a scream.

It was the boy. The boy with honeyed eyes and a tangle of long brown hair, the one who had given her the water in Connor's dream.

In *Connor's* dream.

"Why are you following me?" Dea took an instinctive step backward, colliding with the hedge. The leaves slithered away, like a nest of snakes disturbed by a stone. "And *how*?"

"Calm down, okay?" the boy said, holding up both hands as if to reassure her he wasn't holding a weapon. He sighed. "Look, I'm trying to help."

"You can help me by leaving me alone," Dea said.

The boy raised an eyebrow. "You want to find your mother, don't you?"

Dea went cold. "What do you know about my mother?" Then: "Before, you told me I couldn't find her."

"I told you that you *wouldn't* find her, unless the king wanted you to." The boy paused, watching Dea searchingly. "She must have been taken through the mirrors. It's the fastest way into the city from your world. If you want to find her, you'll have to go in after her."

Dea felt pressure behind her eyes and realized she was about to cry. She didn't know what was real anymore—she didn't know what to believe.

"It's just a dream," she remembered her mother had whispered, the first time Dea had walked a nightmare and seen a tidal wave of mud and human bones barreling blackly toward her. "Just a dream." Now she found herself saying the same words again, out loud, as if they contained a protective spell that could help her.

"Just a dream?" the boy repeated. He looked faintly annoyed. "I'm as real as you are. We all are."

"We?" Above her, Dea saw three birds, bellies flashing red against the blue sky. Harbingers. She should leave—she'd taken what she needed, sucked in as much strength as she could. But she couldn't move. She was transfixed by the boy's eyes, like two hard candies, and by the black brushstrokes of his eyelashes. By his skin, deeply tanned, and the faint white scar above his left eyebrow. Real. The word kept drilling in her head like an alarm.

"There are more of us," the boy said, shrugging. Like it was no big deal. Like it was obvious. "Millions more, in the city. Masters and slaves and pits to hold them. Servants, pickers, barkeeps, bankers."

"That's impossible." The dream around Dea was shifting. Now the hedges webbed together, and became curtains of heavy velvet. They were standing backstage, in the stifling heat. Onstage, the little girl was flying without wings while an invisible audience applauded. "The dreams . . . collapse. Everything falls."

"Not everything." It was so dark, Dea could barely make out the angles of the boy's face, a bit of light from an unseen source touching his cheeks and chin. He smelled like leather, like campfire and smoke. "People dream, and when they wake up, their dreams collapse. That's what makes a picker's job dangerous." He smiled slightly, as if he was proud of this. "But there's more. Certain things are left. Like . . . rubble. Residue. A whole world of things is left. You saw some of it. You *walked* it. Even the desert goes on for days."

"So where did it all come from?" Dea asked bluntly. She was unreasonably angry. "Who dreamed it? And when?"

"Who dreamed *your* world?" The boy was standing so close, Dea could smell him: sun-baked leather and salt and something she couldn't identify, something deep and earthy. "Look, I have to go." Onstage, the little girl thudded to the ground. She tried to fly again, lifting her arms, bawling. Nothing. The audience began to boo and jeer. "I have to get back," the boy said, in a different tone. "You should go, too. Remember what I said about the mirrors. I'm on your side. I'll be watching for you."

The boy pressed something into Dea's palm. Dea opened her hand and saw a coil of soft leather. But just as quickly it changed, and became a moth—and then, expanding, a bird with feathers of soft velvet folds, and eyes winking like buttons. It hovered briefly above her palm, and then took off, swooping off into the dark.

"See you later," he said. Then he turned around and vanished. He moved into the dark, or became the dark, Dea didn't know which. She felt the sudden brush of wingtips; the velvet bird swooped past her cheek, and she followed it. One step, two steps, into darkness.

Then the bird vanished through a fissure between the heavy curtains, and Dea knew she'd found a doorway out. She elbowed past the curtains, choking on the sudden sensation of fabric in her mouth, pouring down her throat, and woke up sweating in her sleeping bag, the fabric stuck to her mouth, her zipper pinching the skin of her neck. She sat up, gasping, unzipping her jacket, swallowing against the phantom sensation of choking. It was still dark outside but she knew she wouldn't go back to sleep.

She crawled into the open air and stood, sucking in deep breaths, grateful for the wind. Still, she could feel a phantom fluttering pressure against her palm. She grabbed a flashlight from her backpack and started into the maze. The wind whispered and hissed through the dried corn husks. She thought of what the boy had said.

We're as real as you are . . .

Who dreamed your world?

She saw a rat, frozen, dark-eyed, in the beam of her flashlight—she yelped and it scurried off quickly, its tail slithering in the dried leaves. The rats grew big out here, in the fields, feeding off mice and the litter from passing cars. She walked more quickly, suddenly eager for the bright lights of the gas station, for the stink of gasoline and the burnt smell of all-night coffee and shriveled hot dogs rotating on spits, where she could at least feel like a person, and pretend that she was just another normal girl, stopping late-night for a bag of chips and a soda.

It was a good mile and a half to the gas station, walking next to the highway and then down a thin ribbon of concrete that passed for an exit ramp. The night clerk was the same as always, a guy a few years older than she was, who might have been good-looking except for his low-lidded eyes, like a lizard's.

He was probably stoned. She could feel him watching her as she moved through the aisles, picking up random supplies, lingering, grateful for the ritual.

"Hey," he said, when she went to pay. Her stomach knotted up. She didn't respond, hoping he would take the hint and stop talking. He didn't. "You live around here or something?"

"Where's the bathroom?" she blurted out, to avoid having to answer, though she knew where the bathroom was and had, in fact, washed her hair in the sink two days earlier. He pointed, looking vaguely disappointed.

The light in the bathroom was broken, and flickered on and off, creating a strobe effect and plunging her at intervals into long seconds of darkness. She locked the door and leaned against it. The strangled feeling had returned. She had no choice: she'd have to move. Which meant that she was officially on the run, possibly forever.

Like mother, like daughter.

She stepped to the sink and ran the faucet, cupping her hand under the water and drinking, suddenly parched. She splashed water on her face and looked up just as the lights flickered off once again. Her image in the mirror was suddenly transformed, all holes and dark planes, and she thought of standing backstage with the girl and seeing faint light reflect off the white of her teeth.

The light went on again. Now it was just Dea in the mirror, water clinging to her eyebrows and upper lip.

She must have been taken through the mirrors.

You'll have to go in after her.

She reached out, very cautiously, and touched the mirror with a finger. She didn't know what she expected, but she felt

245

nothing but smooth, cold glass. She jerked a hand away, as if she'd been burned, and then exhaled. Stupid. She was going crazy.

And yet—and yet—her mother had come to her in the mirror at the hospital.

The lights clicked off once more. Dea ran the water again and dampened a finger. Quickly, before she could reconsider, she reached up and scrawled across the mirror: *Let me in*. Almost immediately, the words began to dissolve, gravitating down across the murky reflection of her face.

And then—Dea swallowed to keep from screaming—all at once, the mirror began to dissolve, too. Her face was gone. The glass was melting, pouring, beading into the sink; and everything it touched dissolved just as quickly, as if the liquid were an acid that was swallowing objects, transforming them into shimmering, reflective pools. There was no longer any sink, or wall, or floor. There was nothing but a vast hole, full of a shifting darkness, and a path through to the other side.

Dea's ears were filled with the sound of wind. She felt an invisible pressure on her lower back. She thought of the men with no faces, and towers built from the bones of men.

She knew if she took even a step forward, the life as she knew it, real life, would change forever; it would mean she had gone insane. Or that the world had gone insane.

The wind blew harder. She thought—just for a second—she detected traces of her mother's scent.

She went forward, into the mirror that was no longer a mirror, along a path of darkness.

PART THREE

I dreamed I was a butterfly, flitting around in the sky; then I awoke.

Now I wonder: Am I a man who dreamt of being a butterfly, or am I a butterfly dreaming that I am a man?

—*Chuang Tzu*

TWENTY-THREE

She was in a tunnel filled with the smell of damp; the paving stones beneath her feet were slippery with trickling water and garbage and other substances she didn't want to think about. Up ahead, she heard voices and shouting, and, through a vaulted archway, had a glimpse of a sun-dappled street, and people passing back and forth. From a distance, they looked like bright blobs of color, streaming together into a single rainbow image.

She glanced behind her but the mirror was gone. The dream—because this was a dream, she was sure, though unlike any she had ever walked—had sealed shut behind her like skin around a wound. There was simply more tunnel, running off into the darkness, and huddled shapes she originally mistook for animals until she realized they were people—mostly men—filthy and obviously homeless, gazing at her through alcohol-hazy eyes.

"You look like one of the lucky ones," one of them rasped. She couldn't tell if it was a man or a woman.

She turned around and hurried forward, toward the street. Her footsteps echoed on the stone, and made it impossible to hear whether she was being followed. She was too afraid to turn around, worried that if she did, she would find one of the men lurching after her. But she made it to the end of the tunnel, and when she finally risked a glance behind her, saw that she was alone.

Emerging onto the street, she was immediately forced to leap backward, pressing herself against the wall of a building, as a man driving a carriage came barreling down the narrow street, holding a whip, scattering the people in front of him. She had a quick view of his face, pockmarked and cruel, and the animal yoked to the carriage—like a huge housecat with an elongated snout—and then the carriage was gone, rounding a dizzying curve in the street, and the crowd flowed back into the space left in its wake.

Dea didn't move. She closed her eyes and took several deep breaths, trying to stop the crazy pounding of her heart. But every time she opened her eyes, she was gripped by a terrible feeling of vertigo. Or maybe the reverse of vertigo: she felt she was standing at the very bottom of an enormous canyon, and was in danger not of falling down but of being crushed from above.

Because the city she'd entered was built not just out, but

up. She must have been on one of its lowest levels, although when she finally managed to take a staggering step forward, she passed over a grate through which she could see people moving below her, their necks yoked with heavy gold bands like the animal pulling the carriage had worn. Slaves.

The street was teeming with people and lined with shops and market stands, and at intervals staircases led up to another level of buildings, where even more staircases wound to another level, and another, and another—so much construction, all of it built on top of previous construction, it seemed impossible the whole city could remain standing.

High above her, so high she had to crane her neck all the way to see it, was the sky, and small dark shapes zipping through it. Birds? She couldn't tell. Looming above the rest of the city was a tower that seemed to have been hacked out of an ancient mountain, built half of rock and half of spiraling structures of glass—this, too, a construction so absurd and disproportionate it could have existed in no real place.

"*Entschuldigung,*" a man said, shoving by her. She thought the word was German; all around her people were shouting in various languages, some of which she recognized, some of which she didn't. A woman was arguing in rapid French with a vendor of mirrors—thousands of mirrors, glinting in the sun, were laid out along a table. Dea had studied French since eighth grade but understood nothing but *remboursement*, refund. As she passed, she noticed that all the mirrors reflected not the landscape in front of them, but random scenes, maybe other portions of the city.

Or maybe, she thought with a tiny shiver, portions of her

251

world. She remembered her mom had once told her: the mirrors are how they see out.

It was so crowded she had no choice but to move along in the direction of the rest of the foot traffic. It was hot and noisy and it smelled bad, but she didn't mind the clamor or the closeness: she felt secure here, lost in the crowd, unobserved and unobservable. And she was so stunned by the sheer size of the city and the great canyon walls of its growth that she even forgot to worry about her mother; she just walked, and watched, filled with wonder and awe.

Women hung from the windows of nearby buildings, calling down to passersby in the street. Kids with bronzed arms threw olive pits into the crowd and then ducked away, giggling. Dea saw stacked cages filled with strange hybrid animals: feathered reptiles, horses no bigger than housecats, duck-like creatures with the scales of a snake. She passed a store selling masks that moved and grimaced, like human flesh, and one in which pale white statues chanted and muttered through porcelain lips. Suddenly the street opened up and deposited her in a square: on a cracked stone platform at its center, a man with two heads, arranged not side by side but front to back, was auctioning off slaves, drumming up bids from the assembled crowd. Dea watched a girl, probably no more than eight, her posture distorted by the weight of the two thick bands around her neck, be led to the block, and felt suddenly sick.

The crowd surged forward, flowing down toward the slave auction, but Dea turned and fought her way against the flow of people, reaching a stairway stitched vertically between buildings. She grabbed hold of the railings like a drowning person finding a lifeline, and began to climb.

The staircase corkscrewed several times and then dumped her on another street, this one a good twenty feet above the square, and the shouting, jeering crowd, and the slave auction. It was only slightly less crowded than the street she'd come from. She could still hear shouting from the auction below, and it made not just her ears but her whole body hurt. It didn't take her long to find another staircase, this one so steep it was practically vertical, sandwiched between a shop that sold nothing but wooden puppets and a tavern from which an alcoholic stink rolled out in waves. She took the stairs, sweat moving down her neck freely now, but also dimly aware that she felt stronger here, healthier than she'd ever been.

The architecture changed as she reached the city's higher levels, as did the nature of the shops and the look of the people strolling the streets. In the city's lower levels, the buildings were built primarily of thick blocks of grimy stone, green with age and jammed together like a series of overlapping teeth. But up here, Dea saw steel and glass and other modern materials. The streets were quieter, and lined with trees and flowerbeds, and the shops sold sparkling jewelry on velvet cases, including dazzling cat-shaped brooches that paraded back and forth in the windows, flicking their diamond tails; or long dresses made of white silk that looked like bits of cloud. Stone bridges spanned the vast chasms down to the bottom of the city, and even the staircases between city levels were better built, out of winding iron or dramatic marble, with ornately scrolled banisters.

She'd climbed six street levels already; still, she was only about halfway to the final level, and the tower that twisted like a ribbon of steel and stone toward the sky. But at the top of the next stairs, two men were standing, blocking her passage. Dea drew back, swallowing a sharp cry as they turned to face her: each of them had only a single eye, large and unblinking, and a mouth full of hundreds of sharp, overlapping teeth.

For a second she just stood there, frozen, fighting the urge to turn and run.

"*Passage interdit*," one of them said at last. "*Niveaux privés.*"

"What?" It was so shocking to hear the *thing*—the man—speak well-accented French, Dea temporarily forgot to be afraid.

He switched seamlessly to English. "Restricted access," he said. "You have a pass?"

Dea shook her head. "I—I didn't know I needed one."

The men kept on staring. They couldn't help it, Dea supposed, but it made her stomach turn: their eyes were enormous, like the lenses of a telescope. "Levels nine and above are restricted access," one of them repeated. Dea wondered whether he was being deliberately unhelpful, or whether he simply didn't know very many English phrases.

"Where do I get a pass?" she asked. She couldn't explain it, but just as she felt somehow stronger here, freer, more purposeful than she ever had, she was also being drawn up and up, pulled toward the very top of the city, as if the whole landscape were exerting on her a reverse gravitational force.

The men exchanged a look. Despite the strangeness of their faces, Dea could tell that they were bewildered. "From the king," one of them said, turning back to Dea. "Where else would you get it?"

"But—" Dea started to protest. Then she heard footsteps behind her, and a voice, half-breathless, spoke up.

"She's with me."

It was the boy again: the boy from the desert, the one who'd told her to come through the mirrors.

"You're following me," she said, to conceal the fact that she was relieved to see him.

"You're welcome." He barely glanced at her, instead reaching into his shirt pocket and removing a small golden book that resembled a passport—presumably, this was the pass from the king. When he handed it to the guards, Dea sucked in a quick breath. Immediately, the pass dissolved into a hundred winged insects, glittering like gold, which arranged themselves into a complex design in midair.

"The king's crest," the boy said. Dea wasn't sure if he was speaking with her or to the guards. Today he was dressed all in black, in standard trousers and a shirt with a stiff collar. He'd even made some effort to untangle his hair. She wondered whether this was his city look.

He held out his hand again and the shape collapsed, siphoning into his outstretched palm, as the insects once again flattened themselves into a paper booklet.

"All right." The guard stepped aside. "Just keep your pass handy. You'll need to show it again."

"I know the rules," the boy said. He gestured for Dea to go first. "After you."

Here there were hardly any shops at all: just beautiful homes set behind high gates, half-concealed behind enormous trees Dea had no name for.

"*Why* are you following me?" she asked in a low voice, as soon as they'd left the guards behind, since the boy no longer denied that he was.

"I'm helping you," he corrected her. "This way." He grabbed her hand and pulled her toward yet another staircase, this one flanked by stone lions—that, Dea noticed, shifted position occasionally, or yawned, or blinked. Dea again felt that explosion, as if someone had set off a fire deep in her blood.

"Where are we going?" She removed her hand from his, deliberately, partly because she had suddenly wanted *not* to remove it—to cling to him, to beg him to stay close to her. Then she thought of Connor and felt guilty and angry with herself.

He had already started climbing. Now he stopped and turned around to face her, with that mysterious half smile that reminded her of a satisfied cat. In the sun, his eyes were honey-brown, filled with light.

"To the very top," he said. Then he kept climbing.

TWENTY-FOUR

"What is this place?" Dea waited to speak until they had left the guards behind. She was scared, which made her angry. And the boy seemed as unconcerned as ever. He even whistled occasionally, something tuneless and vaguely sad.

"Isn't it obvious by now?" He looked at her with that infuriating half smile of his. Today his eyes glimmered in the sun, practically yellow. "This is the king's city. Some people call it the first city. It's really the only city that matters. Beyond the borders are just deserts and free people."

"Like you?" Dea asked. He put his hand briefly on her back to steer her down a narrow, cobbled street, its walls crowded with an explosion of flowers and climbing vines, and she quickly sped up.

"Like me," he said.

The boy's name, Dea learned, was Aeri: a strange name where she came from, but he told her it was common enough in this world. For someone who had been following her through dreams and had managed to track her down in the enormous city, he seemed largely uninterested in her company, and answered most of her questions in as few words as possible, or with circular nonresponses that left her more frustrated, not less.

"Why are we going to the tower?"

"I told you. To get answers."

"How?"

"We'll speak to the king."

"Why?"

"He'll have answers."

Eventually she gave up, and they walked in silence. She needed to save her breath, anyway: on the city's upper levels, the streets were steeply pitched, winding toward the tower, which she now knew to be a portion of the king's palace. Here, the city became busy again—servants bustled between enormous stone mansions and homes built of rose-colored glass, although it was strangely silent, a peace disturbed only by the twittering of invisible birds and the rhythm of water flowing in various delicate fountains. Aeri explained briefly that these homes were, actually, property of the king, gifts to his favorite friends, military officers, and supporters. Some of them, he said, were actually connected via passageways to the palace's lower levels.

When she peered down over the wrought-iron railing of one

of the bridges to admire the city stretching out beneath her, the people at its very bottom looked hardly bigger than ants. From here she could see not just how deep and tall the city was, but how vast: buildings, bridges, streets, and market squares sprawled all the way to the horizon, so much space and so much life she couldn't imagine how many people it contained. How had Aeri tracked her down? How would anyone be found in a place this size? It would be like trying to pinpoint an individual grain of sand on a beach. She thought of her mother and felt a sharp ache of sadness.

She hoped Aeri was right, and the king would have answers.

Aeri had shown his pass to gain access to every subsequent level of the city after level nine, and Dea had noticed that the guards grew more numerous as they'd climbed—and more monstrous, too, with deformities that ranged from multiple sets of eyes to multiple sets of heads, mounted on the same neck like flowers budding from a single stalk. She was happy, now, that she and Aeri weren't speaking; she wasn't sure she could have formed a sentence.

When the tower was directly above them, so that it cast them in shadow, Dea could see that her original assumption—that it seemed to have been hacked out of the mountainside, and then extended and modified with glass-and-steel additions, was correct. The palace itself was much larger than the individual tower, and sprawled across the high apex of the city like a series of smaller foothills clustered around a mountain peak: walls and battlements, exterior staircases and vaulted archways, plazas and gardens. The palace was in itself the size of a small city: probably the whole population of Fielding would fit in just one of its outbuildings.

Thinking of Fielding made Dea feel dizzy all over again. How was it possible that any of this was real? And yet . . . standing here with the sun warm on her neck and Aeri's shoulder touching hers, she knew it was. Now, it was *Fielding* that seemed like a dream.

They entered the palace through a narrow passageway guarded by monsters so hideous that Dea drew back, gasping. These monsters weren't men, not even a little: they were patchwork creatures of snout and teeth and scales, so ugly Dea couldn't stand to look at them.

"It's all right." Aeri touched her lower back, and she felt a small burst of warmth there. "They won't hurt you. We're on the king's business."

"I don't understand." Dea was embarrassed to feel tears burning the back of her eyes. "Where does he get them? And what *are* they?"

Aeri shrugged. "He recruits them. Pulls them from the pits. From dreams," he clarified, when Dea only shook her head. He was doing his best to seem casual, but Dea could tell he was just as tense as she was. She could see it in his jaw, in the way he kept withdrawing the pass from his pocket as if to verify it was still there. "They work for him as guards and soldiers. In exchange he gives them power and freedom. He gives them *life*." He managed a small smile. "What else do monsters want?"

Monsters. A tiny shiver moved up Dea's spine. What did that say about the men with no faces? What did it *mean*? If all those pits in the desert were dreams, then what was this place? Could the men with no faces be recruits in the king's army as well? Had the king somehow pulled them—extracted them—from Connor's dreams? Was that why Dea's mom had insisted on precautions for so many years—because they were being pursued?

But that didn't make any sense. Why would the king care about Dea?

Aeri was right. The guards left them alone, watching them silently with glitter-black or yellow eyes or eyes the raw pink of a new wound, as they moved into a small room with glass doors. Only when the room began to shoot upward, the view rapidly swallowed by a vision of sheer stone walls, did Dea realize that they'd entered an elevator.

"Are you okay?" Aeri said, as the elevator began to slow. It was the first time he'd expressed any concern for her. He was looking at her with the strangest expression—his mouth was all twisted up, as if he wanted to tell her something but was holding the words back by physical force.

Dea nodded, not trusting herself to speak.

The stone walls released them and they floated up through the floor into a beautiful, high-ceilinged atrium. Sunlight poured through enormous skylights set in the domed roof. Through them, Dea saw massive, swooping dark shapes that were not birds, but winged and catlike creatures. The room itself was inlaid with an intricate mosaic pattern made of marble, and decorated gilded columns that appeared to be made of molten gold. As Dea stepped out of the elevator behind Aeri, she felt her knees give momentarily and worried she might fall. Hundreds of those creatures, the king's monsters, were arrayed in a circle around the room, and a long line of people snaked toward a man sitting on the raised central dais.

And yet somehow, despite the distance between them and the assembled crowd, the king's eyes went immediately to Dea. She got a sudden electric shock, as if someone had pinched the back of her neck. She didn't know what she'd been expecting, but after seeing all the monsters, she'd imagined the king must be a sort of monster himself. Instead he just looked tired. His hair was graying at the temples, his face just softening at the jawline. But he looked like anybody, like any teacher at school, like any father she might have seen in Fielding, loading his kids into an old minivan.

But of course, he wasn't. With a gesture so subtle Dea nearly missed it, he managed to convey that everyone else should be dismissed from the room. There was a burst of murmuring and protest from the crowd, quickly silenced when dozens of monsters came forward to herd everyone out through a set of double doors at the far end of the room. Dea wished desperately that all the monsters would leave, but half of them remained standing, watching her through faces half-melted, smiling with mouths studded with teeth.

She still hadn't moved. For a long time, she and the king stared at each other, and she willed herself not to faint or turn around and run.

When the king finally spoke, it was to Aeri. "All those years I was recruiting soldiers, and really I should have just sent a boy to do the work," he said. Again, Dea was surprised by his voice, which was light, faintly sarcastic, full of humor. "Go on," he said, inclining his head toward the double doors. "One of my men will see you get paid."

Dea turned to Aeri as understanding opened like a hand in her chest, leaving her gasping. "Paid?" she repeated. Aeri wouldn't meet her eyes. At least he looked embarrassed. She turned back to the King. "Paid?" she said again. Her voice was loud in the room, rolling off the marble floors, but she didn't care. Anger made her feel careless. "He told me you'd have answers for me."

The king laughed, a sound so rich and warm that Dea felt again uncertain. "You *are* the answer, Dea," he said.

Dea took a step backward. Could she escape before she was caught? It was a desperate thought, stupid. She wouldn't make it even a step before the king's monsters pounced. "How do you know my name?" she asked, wishing her voice weren't trembling.

Next to her, Aeri sighed, with a helpless gesture toward the dais, the throne, and the man who sat in it. "Dea," he said. "Meet your father."

TWENTY-FIVE

There was a long minute of silence. Dea felt her mind wink on and off, freeze and unfreeze, like malfunctioning software.

"No," she said at last.

"Yes," the king said. He stood up. He was dressed in white pants and a buttonless white shirt, like someone playing God in a school production.

"No," she said again. "Impossible. My father is . . ."

But she broke off. Her father was what? What had her mom said, besides the lies? What had she said when Dea had confronted her about that stupid photograph? *Your father is powerful. Your father is complicated.*

"What?" the king prompted her. Now he was obviously amused. "What lies did your mother tell you about me? Please, I've been desperate to know. She won't tell me."

Dea's heart started hammering again, so hard she brought a hand to her chest instinctively, as if to keep it from leaping through her skin. "My mom," she said. "Is she—?"

"She's here," he said. "And safe," he added quickly, almost exasperatedly, seeing Dea's face. "I'm not the monster she's made me out to be." When Dea said nothing, he rubbed his forehead. "She didn't tell you anything, did she?"

Dea shook her head.

The king—Dea's father—muttered something, rubbing his forehead again. And in that moment he looked so normal, so like any other father, that for the tiniest sliver of a second, Dea had the urge to run to him, to throw her arms around him, to cry and be held and listen to him say her name again: the father she'd never known, the father she'd always desperately wanted.

Then he raised his voice again. "Everyone, leave us," he said, waving a hand, and her attention was drawn back to the monsters standing in the shadows, and the memory of the men with no faces—how they'd pursued her through the darkness, panting through open mouths, tasting her.

Aeri hesitated. He leaned in as though to whisper something to Dea. She jerked away, glaring at him.

"Sorry, princess," he said. He touched his fingers to his forehead once, a kind of salute, and then he was gone. But his words had left Dea feeling dizzy again.

Princess. It was true. She was a princess of this city of chasms and levels, of all these people, of the slaves with their poor slender necks, bent under the weight of their chains, and the monsters and the flying beasts and the gutters running with sewage.

She was home.

She turned away, feeling sick, bringing a hand to her mouth. The doors banged shut behind the last retreating monster, leaving a sudden silence. How was it possible? How was any of it possible? She tasted salt before she realized she was crying. After a while, she became aware that her father was standing next to her.

"I'm sorry, Dea," he said softly. "I know this must be very hard."

She swiped at her cheeks with a sleeve, furious at herself. Furious at him. "Oh, really?" she said. "Do you?" She whirled around to face him. "I almost died, you know. You almost killed me. Is that what you wanted? Is that what you want now?"

He stared at her. "Of course not," he said. "You're my daughter, Dea. I've been searching for you your whole life."

"You haven't been searching for me. You sent them—those *things*—to do the work for you." She took a step toward him, but then stopped, too afraid to go any closer. "How did you find me?"

"You got careless," he said simply.

Of course. Dea had broken the rules. She'd started interfering, making herself visible, making herself obvious. The monsters in Connor's dream had seen her. And so her father had *used* them to track her. She was gripped with a fury that felt like cold—a blizzard of anger, freezing her insides.

"You sent the men after me," she said. Her voice, too, cracked as if it were frozen. "You pulled them from Connor's dream."

She expected him to get defensive—angry, even. Instead, he

just looked amused. "I don't know Connor," he said. "I recruit all my soldiers from the pits. The pits, as you know, aren't permanent. Dreams collapse. The monsters collapse with them. They have to be reborn, and redreamed, every time." He shrugged. "I can give them new life. Real life. A kind of permanence and power." Then his expression darkened. "They were under strict instructions not to harm you. To take you, yes. But not to harm you. Just as the soldiers who came for your mother were under instructions to deliver her safely."

Dea's stomach turned when she thought about the mirrors, and the exploded shards of glass carpeting her room. Her old room. She wasn't crazy: monsters really had come through the glass.

He shook his head. "But I don't always find my soldiers easy to control," he said. "So I decided on a . . . different tactic."

Aeri. Jesus. Dea felt like such an idiot. It was like some bad TV plot—all it took was a cute boy with dark hair, and she went trotting like a dog after him. The icy rage inside of her cracked all at once and became a flow, a river. She was lost in it.

The room was too big, too cold, all hard surfaces. Those swooping dark creatures in the sky cast shadows across the marble floor; the tile mosaic, Dea saw, was very slowly moving, shifting orientations and designs while she watched. It was dizzying. But turning toward the windows, looking down from this vast height to the tiny dark blots of tens of thousands of people, was just as bad.

She waited to speak until she was sure her voice would be steady.

"I don't understand this place," she said. "How did it get

here? How did any of it get here?"

When he spoke, the king's voice was soft. Gentle, even. "Some people say the world was made from the dream of the first god," he said. He smiled and waved a hand as if to say, *But we know better.* "The pickers like to take credit, of course. They say they brought a grain of sand out of one of the pits, and it became the desert, and from the desert grew the great city." He shrugged. "The truth is, no one knows. Do you know where your world comes from? Can you be sure it isn't somebody's dream?"

Dea didn't answer that. "What do you want from me?" she said.

He stared at her as if he hadn't understood. "Dea," he said, drawing her name out. "This is your home. This is where you belong."

"Wrong." Dea shook her head.

"I'm right." He sighed, and moved past her to the vaulted windows that extended, floor to ceiling, over the city. "Your mother took you, Dea. She stole you from me when you were just a baby. Did she ever tell you that? Did she tell you how she brought you into the other world?"

Dea said nothing. Of course her mom hadn't told her; she had, Dea realized now, never told her the truth about anything. Dea was on the verge of tears but refused to cry here, in front of this man who was supposed to be her father.

The king turned back to her. And Dea found herself looking for a resemblance, for any feature or habit or twitch she'd inherited from him. But she saw nothing—nothing but a tired man with an army of monsters. "There's a war coming," he said quietly. "I can't say what the outcome will be. I want you here, by my side. I want to know my daughter."

"And what if I say no?" Dea lifted her chin and did her best to appear unafraid. "What if I don't want to stay?"

Her father shook his head. "Despite what you may think, I'm not a monster."

"No," she cut in quickly. "You just use monsters to do your dirty work."

His smile tightened. "I'm the king, Dea. Kings need armies."

"Are you going to throw me in prison if I refuse to play along?"

"Don't be ridiculous," he said, in an exasperated tone. For a moment Dea's chest ached as she realized she was fighting with her dad, like any normal girl. But one look at the mosaic tiles, crawling over one another like square beetles, reminded her how far from normal she was. "I'm not going to keep you here against your will. If you don't want to come home, that's up to you."

"What's the catch?" Dea said, watching him closely.

"Honestly"—he threw his hands up—"there's no catch. Stay in that world, if you want—where everything is dull and everyone grows old and dies at the same rate. A world where you'll grow, where you'll get sick. Or come home, to this world, where you belong, where you're the daughter of a king. I'll let you choose."

Dea thought of Connor's face, and the sputtering of a motel room heater, and the way his body felt lying next to her in bed. The world she knew, the world that was everything she understood.

A world where she would be homeless, without family,

pursued by the police.

Still, she knew she wouldn't—she *couldn't*—stay here.

"So that's it?" she said. "I can go now, and those—those monsters won't come after me again?"

He smiled again—sadly, this time. "Those monsters," he said, "will stay in your friend Connor's nightmares. And in his memories, of course."

Dea looked at her father one last time. She tried to memorize the lines of his face, the fine bits of stubble shadowing his jaw and neck, the low-drawn look of his eyebrows. *Father.* But the word had no meaning. No matter what he said, she didn't belong here.

"I want to talk to my mother," she said.

Something flashed in his eyes—anger or grief, Dea couldn't tell. "Your mother stays here, Dea," he said warningly. "That's part of the bargain. If you go, I'll make sure you never see her again. I can keep you out, you know. Of the city. Even of the pits."

Dea felt as if a fist had plunged inside her chest and ripped away her insides: hollowed out, breathless. Of course. She'd known there would be a catch.

"I want to see her," she repeated.

"Be my guest." Dea's father turned around, gesturing to a plain wooden door almost directly behind the dais and the throne. "You'll find her in the tower. And Dea." He called her back when she'd already started for the door. "I'm not a monster, but I'm not a saint, either. Patience isn't one of my virtues. You have twenty-four hours to decide."

TWENTY-SIX

Beyond the wooden door was a small, bright room, airy and pretty—maybe some kind of study or sitting room; there were walls full of books, graceful columns that extended up to the painted ceiling, and gilded chairs arranged around an unlit fireplace. Through a skylight she could make out the tower, which must have been almost directly above her.

She heard footsteps approach and, fearing more of her father's monsters, crossed quickly to a painted door across the room, reaching for the elaborate gold handle. As soon as she touched it, it started to *move*. It began to melt, to change, to slither; it was soon a metal snake, weaving its way up her arm, coiling itself around her shoulder, its belly hard and cold as steel. She shouldn't have been surprised, but she was. She was being careless, forgetting that this was still a world built out of dreams—that things were fluid and likely to change.

"Through the door and to the left," the snake hissed. "Straight to the top of the tower." Then it slithered back down her arm, curled up, and became a door handle again.

This time, the door opened easily at her touch.

She found another set of stairs, this one broad, carpeted, and well-lit. As she climbed, she wound past more windows, all of them open, letting in a warm wind that smelled like orange peel and tobacco, unwashed bodies and frying meat, and other things she couldn't identify. She was sweating in her jacket and nearly stopped to take it off, but fear, and a burning desire to see her mother, to *understand*, compelled her on and up.

Soon, the natural world began to intrude: thick moss grew on the stairs instead of carpet, and narrow vines stretched across the walls like gnarled fingers. Flowers grew in fissures of plaster. The windowsills were crowded with bluebells and honeysuckle, flowers that had always reminded her of her mother. Morning glory crept over the ceiling, and blossoms hung like newly formed raindrops, suspended briefly before they fell.

The higher she climbed—until the city was just a shimmering, undifferentiated mass of glass and wood and gold, a manmade patchwork—the stronger the impression was of her mother's touch, until she was practically running, despite the heat and the shaking of her thighs.

At last, she reached a narrow wooden door at the top of the stairs. Locked. She began to pound with a fist. She wished she could cry but she couldn't—her throat was dry, her eyes were burning, she felt hollow, as if all her feelings had been burned out.

"Let me in." Her voice echoed back to her. It, too, was hollow—a stranger's voice. Had her father lied? Tricked her? She kept banging, and kept calling. "Please. *Please*. Let me in."

"Dea? Is that you?"

Dea stumbled backward, swallowing a sob. It was a trick. It must be. She was suddenly flooded with terror—she was more afraid than she had ever been, at any point since her mother had disappeared. She didn't want the door to open, and she couldn't stand the gummy seconds that stretched into an eternity while it did. She couldn't breathe. She wanted to cry. She wanted to run.

Then the door was open and Dea's mother was there and alive and *real*.

And yet Dea couldn't move. She couldn't go to her.

Miriam was different—so different that Dea felt shy and nauseous, all at once. Her hair was loose and she was wearing a long white dress, very plain, and very different from anything she would have worn in real life. Her feet were bare. She was wearing slender, braided vines around her wrists and arms like stacked bracelets. She looked better, much better, than she had the last time Dea had seen her. She had gained weight. Her eyes were bright. Dea understood that it was being here, in the dream city, that was feeding her. She felt a quick pulse of revulsion.

And in that moment, she knew that everything her father had told her was true.

"You found me," Miriam said softly, and the moment of revulsion passed. Everything passed but the intensity of Dea's relief, and she stumbled forward into her mother's arms.

Miriam still smelled the same—like soap and strawberries, like long summer days and shimmering asphalt and all the windows open. Like home. She let herself cry at last. She leaned into her mother's hug and took huge, sucking sobs, even though everything was okay: her mom would make everything okay.

"I knew you'd come," Miriam said, murmuring into Dea's hair, and rocking her at the same time, the way she had whenever Dea was upset as a little girl. "I was afraid you would. Oh, Dea. I've been a terrible mother. I'm so sorry. Can you ever forgive me?"

"Yes," Dea whispered. She knew she should demand answers and explanations. She knew she should be furious. But she had already forgiven her mother for everything. She was alive. She was real. That was more important than anything.

Miriam smiled. But her eyes were sad. "Come on," she said, reaching for Dea's hand. "Come inside."

"Mom." She withdrew her hand. She hadn't realized what she'd come to ask until the words were out of her mouth: "Mom, please come home."

"Honey." Miriam looked at her with those wide gray eyes, a mixture of affection and exasperation. "This *is* my home."

"No." It was the same thing her father had said and yet Dea couldn't, *wouldn't* let it be true. "Your home is with me. In Fielding. Or wherever we decide to go. California or Santa Fe. St. Louis or New Orleans. You've always wanted to go to New Orleans, haven't you?" She was babbling. She couldn't help it.

Miriam looked tired, as if she'd had a long day of work at a new job and had just remembered there were no groceries in the house, an expression that was both familiar and seemed insanely out of place here, on a stone landing in a tower high above a dream-city. "Come, Dea," she said again, and gestured for Dea to follow her.

The tower room was pretty but bare. It was encircled on three sides by large windows that looked out over the city and let in broad sweeps of golden sunlight. Creeper vines and pale white roses had begun to overspill the windowsills, climbing down into the room, cascading like water onto the stone floor. A chair was drawn close to the window. Other than that, the only furniture consisted of a faded rug, a narrow cot, and, to Dea's surprise, a large and ornately carved mirror.

Miriam caught Dea staring at it.

"Oh, well," she said. "It's no danger to me now. Besides, I like to keep an eye on you."

Dea let herself go to the pull of anger inside of her. "What *are* you?" she spat. She remembered that Connor had once spoken the same words to her, and this made her even angrier—that she was joined to this strangeness, chained to it. "No more lies," she said quickly, when Miriam opened her mouth. "I want the truth. The *whole* truth."

Miriam sighed. She crossed the room and put a hand on Dea's cheek. Dea wanted to pull away, but her mother's hand was cool and dry and familiar. "I'm a dream," Miriam said softly. "And so are you."

Then Dea did jerk away. "What the hell is that supposed to mean?"

"It means we come from here. It means we belong here, in the dream." Miriam gestured, as though to encompass the room, the city, the sunlight lapping long and thick across the floor, like a golden tongue. Her eyes were unnaturally bright.

"That's why I had to leave you, Dea. To protect you. Don't you understand?" She tried to approach Dea again but Dea stumbled backward, until she was pressed against the door. "The dream was always after us. You've seen your father now. You know how powerful he is. He wanted us back."

"Why?" Dea willed herself not to cry. "Why won't he leave us alone? Why won't he just let us go?" Her mind was cutting back and forth between different images: Aeri saying *the monsters want only what belongs to them*; the erratic rhythm of her heart, beating out the tempo of a different world; the relief of walking, like sucking in air after a long time underwater. Then something occurred to her. "You could talk to him," she said. "You could *beg* him."

"It wouldn't do any good," Miriam said. "Look. I'll show you." Miriam moved to the chair and sat down. Instantly, the vines encircling her wrists began to move. They slithered around the arms of the chair and began to squeeze, digging deeply into her flesh until it began to pucker, until her hands turned white and Miriam gasped in pain. Of course. Her father had said that her mother was safe. But she was still a prisoner. Dea couldn't believe she'd felt the urge, even for a second, to run to him.

"Punishment," Miriam said simply. "For trying to run the first time." When Dea moved toward her, Miriam shook her head. "It's all right," she said. The vines loosened all at once and withdrew, curling up around her mother's wrists and falling still again. Miriam winced, rotating her wrists. "He knows I won't try to escape again."

Dea was dizzy. She didn't trust her legs to carry her, so she sat. "Why did you do it?" she whispered. "And how?"

Miriam leaned forward. She seemed radiantly beautiful, in that moment, and also fragile—as if she might scatter into light and wind. Her mother, the queen. The mother who always made tomato soup by swirling in cream cheese, who liked to listen to jazz on rainy days and wade through old flea markets with her sleeves rolled up, as if she were in a swamp, catching frogs. Who liked American cheese sandwiches on white bread, and couldn't stand apples unless they were baked into pie.

"Remember that story I told you, about the pregnant woman who was very sick? She was dreaming. She dreamed of another woman and another baby, but healthy."

Dea nodded. She did remember: it was a fairy tale her mother had always told her. At least, she'd always assumed it was a fairy tale, although she'd never been able to find it in any books. She no longer recalled the details: just that a pregnant woman was asleep in the hospital, and she dreamed of another woman, and when she woke up she found that she had given birth to a baby with eyes the color of ice.

Like hers.

And suddenly the knowledge was there, gathering like a wave just beyond her consciousness.

Miriam's voice was barely a whisper. "That's how I did it," she said. "Before I knew what I was doing—without even thinking about what it would mean—I escaped."

"You didn't," Dea choked out. It was over; the wave crashed. A tide of nausea rolled up from Dea's stomach to her throat.

"It was too late for them, anyway," Miriam said, as though that made it better.

A dying woman. Her mom had taken the body of a dying

woman and her dying baby. That's how she had made Dea: from someone else's bones and skin.

Dea stood up. She needed air. She couldn't breathe. She stumbled to the window and leaned out, retching and coughing, tears burning her eyes. But nothing came up. The sickness was lodged inside of her.

"I had to," Miriam said. She was talking quickly now, trying to get Dea to listen, to understand. "It was our only chance at life away from here." She added more quietly: "Your father and I . . . well. We weren't happy."

"You—*what*?" All of this—everything her mother was describing, everything she'd done—because her mom wasn't *happy*?

Miriam seemed to realize she'd misspoken. "There are no seasons here," she said hurriedly. "Only the direction of the wind. Spring can come for a thousand years or not at all. What is born doesn't always die." Her mother paused, and added more quietly, "I wanted to know seasons, and order, and rules. I wanted to be . . . free. I wanted *you* to be free."

Dea took a deep breath. Below her, the city shimmered in the late afternoon sun: crowded and irregular, improbably huge, like litter spit up over an eternity by an endless ocean. She tried to understand the meaning of Miriam's words: a world both of permanence and of ever-shifting rules, subtle changes and subterfuge. It must be exhausting, like eternally navigating ever-changing currents, trying to stay afloat.

But her mother had done terrible things, and Dea *couldn't* understand that.

"You stole money," Dea said. She turned around, surprised that her voice remained steady. "You hurt people."

Miriam winced. Had she really thought Dea wouldn't find out? "I did what I had to do."

"No." Another thought occurred to Dea—scarier, even, than the knowledge of what her mother had done. "You did what you wanted to do. You did what you felt like."

Miriam frowned. But she didn't deny it, and Dea knew that she was right. She felt the way she had when, after standing on line to meet Santa Claus at the mall in Florida, they'd emerged into the parking lot fifteen minutes later to see him standing between two Dumpsters, smoking a cigarette, his beard yanked hastily to the side.

Her mom just did things. Not for any great reason, not because she had noble goals or beliefs. Just because. She'd wanted to run and so she ran. When she needed money, she'd taken it.

"I kept you safe for so many years," Miriam said. Her voice had turned desperate, wheedling, like a salesperson trying to off-load a subpar vacuum cleaner. "That's why all the rules. The mirrors and the clocks . . . time is the enemy of dreams. Dreams are allergic to order. I was hoping I could keep your father away. That's why I was always running, too. I didn't want to give him the chance to . . ." She broke off. "I know it was hard for you."

"It was awful," Dea said, but without anger. All the feeling had left her at once, had simply drained away, leaving her numb. She knew the truth now, at least. She was a monster. "It was *wrong*."

Again, Miriam frowned. "Wrong, right." She waved a hand. "People in the other world obsess about the difference. The truth is more complicated."

"The *other* world?" Dea repeated. She nearly laughed. "That's my world. Or it *was*, until today."

For a moment, Miriam was quiet. Dea turned back to the window. She watched the light sliding between the buildings, leaving long shadows in its wake. She could just make out the silhouette of distant peaks—either mountains, or more buildings.

"I'm sorry," Miriam said at last. "I did my best. And in the end, it didn't matter, did it? He found us anyway. I don't know how." There was a rustling as she stood. "Two of his soldiers came looking for you. I let them take me instead. I was hoping that once he had me back, I could convince him to leave you alone."

Dea gripped the windowsill. "It was my fault," she said, her tongue tripping a little on the words. But what did it matter anymore? She'd broken the rules, sure. But what her mother had done was far worse. "I walked my friend's dream. More than once. And then . . . I was seen. By Connor—my friend. And then the men with no faces came, and they followed me out of his dream, and everyone thought I was crazy. But I wasn't—I'm not. They followed me."

Miriam put her hands on Dea's shoulders, forcing Dea to turn and face her. Dea tried to ignore the way the vines around her mother's wrists shifted slightly. "It's not your fault," she said. "They would have found us eventually. There are as many monsters as there are people to dream them. That's why your father's so powerful. There are always more soldiers for his army. Even if they're killed, or defeated, more will come."

"But . . . but they can be defeated?" Dea said. "They can be killed?"

Miriam shrugged. "The strength of the monsters is in their numbers. Individually, they're not difficult to defeat."

"How?" Dea thought of the men and their wet, sucking breathing, the ragged dark holes where their mouths should be, and the way they reached for her with long fingers. It didn't seem possible that they could be vulnerable.

Miriam smiled faintly. "The monsters come from people's nightmares," she said. "From their fears and anxieties, from all the things they don't like to think about. That's where their power is. That's what makes them so effective in the king's army. They *feed* on fear."

"But . . ." Dea shook her head. She thought of the men with no faces: what they meant to Connor, what they represented. The way they transformed the air around them, freezing it, as if the whole world was stilled by terror. "How can I stop being afraid?"

"Pull out their teeth if they bite," Miriam said, and for a moment Dea felt as if she were looking at a stranger. "Blind them if they have a hundred eyes. Give them faces, if they have none. Then, they'll just be men."

Dea had a thousand more questions—about the monsters, about her father, about his army, and the war he had said was coming. About her monstrous birth, into the body of a dying child. About stupid stuff, like all the little scams her mom had run. But she found she couldn't ask a single one. She was so tired, she could barely think. "He says I have to decide," she said. She couldn't bring herself to say *the king*. She definitely couldn't say *my father*. "He says he'll give me twenty-four hours."

Miriam looked away, biting her lip. "He isn't—he isn't all bad," she said. "He looked for you, all these years. He wanted you back."

So what does that make you? Dea nearly asked. Instead she

just hugged herself, squeezing so she could feel her ribs. Dream-bones, dream-skin. And yet: her real self. "Am I supposed to feel grateful?"

Miriam turned her eyes to Dea then: big, gray eyes, the color of a stormy sea. The eyes Dea knew best—even better than her own. "Of course not," she said. Then, defensively: "I'm sorry, Dea. But I thought it was for the best not to tell you."

"Yeah, well, now I know." Dea's voice came out more sharply than she'd intended. She had the urge to cry and blinked rapidly. "So what am I supposed to do now?"

It was as if Miriam had been waiting for Dea to ask. Suddenly, she broke. She was crying, and Dea was horrified. It occurred to her that never, not once, had she seen her mom cry. "Listen to me, Dea. I want you to be happy. That's all I ever wanted."

Dea knew, in that moment, that her mom wouldn't ask her to stay. And she didn't want to stay—of course she didn't. But the fact that her mom wouldn't ask her to, wouldn't *beg* her to, made her feel hollow, empty, as if she'd been cored out with a knife.

"He said he won't let me see you." Dea was shaking so badly she could feel it all the way in her knees. "He said I can never come back."

"Dea." Miriam reached for Dea's face again. "I'll always be watching you. I'll *always* look after you."

Dea stepped away. She had nothing more to say. Now the hollow in her chest was a great bubble of grief, threatening to burst. "So that's it?" she said. "And I never see you again?"

"I want you here, Dea," Miriam said. Her voice cracked. "Of course I do. But I can't . . . I've been selfish. You need to make your own choices."

It was like being caught in a sudden autumn downpour: Dea felt freezing and sick and clammy. A thought occurred to her for the first time. "If I don't walk again—what will happen to me?" She would get sick, she knew. But how sick?

And how quickly?

Miriam's face clouded. Dea realized, in that moment, that Miriam didn't know. "You'll be okay," she said, but without conviction. "I'll make sure you're protected."

"Like you made sure I was protected before?" Dea said. It was petty, spiteful, but she couldn't help it.

"Go," Miriam said, giving Dea a little nudge. "If that's what you truly want, then go. It will be hard." Her eyes were welling up again. "I made a mess of things, didn't I? And you're so young. But I believe in you. You'll find a way—just like I did."

Dea had been desperate to escape this world. But now, faced with the reality of leaving, she didn't want to. *You'll find a way—just like I did.* Would she have to go on the run? Become a criminal, like her mother? Shoplift food from gas stations and deodorant from pharmacies? "No." She shook her head. "I won't go. I won't leave you. I don't want to."

"Oh, Dea." Miriam brought a palm to her eyes, as if she could press back her tears. "I'd like that. I'd like that so much. But you have to do what will make you happy. There will be sacrifices either way."

Connor. Dea thought of the way his face came together like a puzzle when he smiled. She thought of Gollum, too, her wispy-wild hair and clothes that were always the wrong size. The way the sun burned through the summer haze and the snows that came in winter, turning the world to white. Little things, and everything.

"Listen." Miriam was in control again. "You don't have to choose this minute. Go now. Think about it." When Dea hesitated, she said, "I'm still your mother, Dea."

The words were so ordinary—*I'm still your mother*—that they might have been back in Fielding, arguing over homework or whether Dea had cleaned her room. Dea wanted to throw herself into her mom's arms again. She wanted to stay with her mom forever, and she wanted to scream at her, to turn her back on Miriam and what she had done.

Instead, she said, "I love you."

"Dea." Miriam's voice broke, and when she looked up, Dea saw she was crying again. "I've been a terrible mother. But I love you so much. Never forget that. I'll be watching. I promise you."

Dea turned and started for the door, but Miriam stopped her.

"Not that way," she said. "This way will be quicker." She was suddenly in charge again, piloting Dea forward, toward the window and the climbing vines.

"What are you—?" Dea started to ask, but she didn't finish her question.

Her mother threw something out the window—petals, Dea saw, crushed by her palm into small dark folds. In the air they unfolded like origami figures, like dark wings, merging together into a floating dark shape. A door.

"What—?" Dea started to say. But then Miriam pushed, and Dea pitched forward out the open window, falling into the bright thin air and the dark mouth of a door in the sky, rising up to swallow her.

TWENTY-SEVEN

Dea came joltingly awake, shouting, choking on the feeling of darkness flooding her throat.

She was back in her tent. She had no idea how; she had no idea what had happened. She fought free of her sleeping bag and wriggled out of the tent opening, taking deep, heaving breaths.

Had she dreamed it all? The walk to the gas station, the mirror, Aeri, the king, and her mother? No. She knew she hadn't. She never dreamed. Besides, she could still feel the pressure of her mother's hand on her back, could still hear the edge in her father's voice. *You have twenty-four hours to decide.*

It was near dawn. There was a splotchy red stain at the

horizon, a smear of sun bleeding upward, dispelling the dark. It was very cold. Dea's breath made clouds, and the ground was covered in a sheet of frost, fine as glass. When the wind lifted, it seemed to carry echoes of her mother's voice—and a faint rustling, too, as unseen animals moved together through the maze: rats, pucker-faced moles, possums fat as dogs, with long, naked tails.

Already, Dea had accepted what Miriam had told her about her birth, about where she belonged. The shock had passed and she was left instead with the dull ache of certainty, a feeling like the erratic skip of her heartbeat, both painful and familiar.

She had always suspected she was a monster; now she knew for sure.

And yet . . .

There was also a place, a world, where she belonged: an eternal world, vast as a dream, filled with strange cities and people and rivers coiled tight like snakes. She had a powerful father, a *king*, who kept thousands of monsters as soldiers for his army.

A father who wanted her back.

Twenty-four hours.

If she refused his offer—if she stayed here, in this world—he had promised her freedom. The monsters would no longer come for her; she could live like anybody else. Except that she wasn't sure what would happen to her if she couldn't walk again.

And she wasn't sure she could stand to leave her mother behind.

She knelt and began clumsily disassembling her tent, her fingers already stiff with cold, as the sun fought to free itself from the inky pull of the horizon. She had to move. She no longer had any choice. She'd stayed too long in one place and had no doubt that people would soon start asking questions—already, she'd been recognized by the guy in the gas station. How long before another family came to explore the maze and caught her sleeping? How long before someone called the cops, and Briggs showed up and hauled her back to the hospital? Or maybe he'd just chuck her in jail, as punishment for trying to escape.

The wind fell away abruptly, leaving a stillness that was like waiting. And suddenly, Dea felt—she *knew*—that something was wrong. Something was moving in the maze—not an animal. Too deliberate, too *big*, for an animal.

A person, then.

Or—her breath hitched in her chest, and despite the cold, sweat broke out along her forehead—her father had lied. He had never meant to let her go. He was just playing with her. And he'd sent the monsters to drag her back.

She grabbed her backpack and slid it silently over her shoulders. There was no time to dismantle her tent or pack up. She straightened up and slipped quietly into the darkness of the maze, wincing when her feet crunched down on dried and trampled corn husks. Instantly, she sensed a shift, a change in direction. Whoever—or *whatever*—was coming for her knew where she was.

Two lefts, and then a right. She felt rather than heard them pursue her—felt the sick heat of their breath, like the gas expelled from a dying body. Another right. She turned to see whether the monsters were behind her and stumbled, barely pivoting around the corner.

She hooked a left turn and came to a dead end. The footsteps were growing louder; she could hear heavy breathing, could practically see the monsters, rising up from the shadows, ready to grab her . . .

She turned and plunged desperately back the way she'd come from, a whimper rising in her throat. She thought she could hear them over the drumming of her feet, and the frantic slamming of her heart—slurping, sucking wetly through the holes in their nonfaces, tasting her. Her father had lied. He would never leave her alone. He would never let her be. She thought of what her mother had said—*give them faces*—but the idea skittered away. She couldn't stop. She couldn't face them. She heard a whimpering sound work its way out of her throat; *please*, she was thinking, to a god or an invisible protector or anyone who could help. *Please, please, please.*

Another right. Distantly, she thought she heard her mom calling her name. *Dea. Dea. Stop. It's all right.* But she didn't stop. She imagined the maze from above, the tangled network of turns radiating outward. She was close to the parking lot. Then what? She didn't think, just kept running, desperate and panicked. The sun rolled into the sky at last, shifting the balance of the world from dark to light, chasing the shadows across the ground.

She caught a glimpse of the parking lot ahead as she approached the final turn, the tawny color of the gravel, so normal, so real. Hurtling left, she collided, hard, with a woman in a red jacket and fell back, gasping.

"Dea?" The woman pulled off her hood. It was Kate Patinsky. "It's all right, Dea. It's just me." She put her hands on Dea's shoulders. "What happened? Are you all right?"

Dea took long, deep breaths as the fear drained from her,

all at once. Kate Patinsky. She was the one who'd been calling Dea's name—Dea had simply been too panicked to recognize her voice. No monsters had leapt. She took a deep breath and looked behind her. Nothing. Nothing but a faint wind moving through the withered corn, stained russet in the new dawn light. Nothing but the glitter of frost and the dazzle of a new day. Kate Patinsky's was the only car in the parking lot, a small VW patterned with a fine spray of dirt and salt.

And it hit her then: she really *was* free. Her father hadn't lied to her. The monsters wouldn't come after her again. She nearly laughed out loud, nearly took Kate's hands and spun around for joy.

"I'm all right," she said, gasping in the cold air, tasting the truth of what she said, sweet and new and unfamiliar. "I'm fine."

Kate Patinsky looked as if she didn't quite believe her. "Come on," she said. "You must be freezing. And hungry."

Only then did it occur to Dea to be suspicious. Kate might have been sent by Briggs. She didn't seem like she was on the cops' side—she'd helped Dea escape the motel, after all—but that didn't mean anything. Maybe Briggs had promised he would give her information for her book if she found Dea and brought her into custody. Dea didn't move, even after Kate had opened the passenger-side door and gestured for Dea to get in.

"How did you find me?" she asked.

Kate made a face, as if it were a stupid question. "How do you think?" she said. "Connor told me where to look. Well, Connor and Eleanor." It took Dea a few seconds to remember that Eleanor was Gollum's real name. "Neat little trick, calling Gollum and then hanging up right away. She was scared shitless. Thought something terrible had happened to you. She called Connor, and he called me. He would have come himself, but he has to be careful. His uncle's basically tracking him."

Dea's sense of freedom immediately dissipated. Maybe the monsters would leave her alone. But they would still exist for Connor. They would still torture him almost every time he slept. Wasn't that what her father had said? *The monsters will stay in your friend Connor's nightmares. And his memories, of course.*

And she had less than twenty-four hours to choose.

Dea licked her lips, which were dry. She was cold. *And* hungry.

"Where are you going to take me?" she asked.

Kate paused in the act of climbing into the car. "To Connor," she said, with a smile that seemed mostly sad. "Where else?"

Kate stopped at the local gas station for provisions, but insisted that Dea stay in the car. "Just in case," she said, patting Dea's leg. Dea assumed that she meant that the cops were on the lookout for her. While Kate was gone, she flipped down the vanity mirror, half-afraid that she would see a terrible face staring back at her, half-wishing to see her mom. But she saw nothing but her own reflection, her hair sticking up at crazy angles, a bit of mud streaked above her left eyebrow. She scrubbed it off and raked her fingers through her hair, wishing she didn't care that she was about to see Connor looking like a deranged homeless person. She wondered if her mother could see her, if somewhere in that other-world a mirror showed Dea's face, her breath misting the glass. She flipped the mirror back up.

Kate came back to the car with Styrofoam cups of coffee that were more like jugs, plus some packaged donuts and a lukewarm breakfast sandwich.

"Sorry," she said. "Shitty selection. Dig in."

Dea didn't care: she ate the sandwich and all three donuts, feeling only a tiny bit guilty that she hadn't saved one for Kate. When she was done, she leaned back, enjoying the taste of powdered sugar on her lips and the look of the lightening sky, the momentary sense of calm and safety. "Why are you helping us?" she asked finally.

Kate steadied the car with one hand while she ripped open sugar packets with her teeth. "I was always a sucker for a Romeo-and-Juliet story," she said, and then punched down the window, spitting out a few ragged corners of paper.

Dea blushed.

"We're not . . . I mean, it's not like that," she said, speaking louder over the rush of the wind—a wind so cold it was like metal, straight through the gut.

Kate didn't seem to have heard. She rolled up the window again. "Besides," she said, her face turning serious. "Connor has something I need."

"What do you mean?" Dea asked.

When Kate glanced at her, she looked sad. Sad, and tired, like someone who'd spent most of her life seeing shitty things and trying to smile her way through them. "Memories, Dea," she said gently.

Dea stiffened. Even if Kate was helping them, she didn't like to think of Kate poking and prying around for the sake of her book, trying to suck Connor dry of information like a mosquito feeding on blood. "He doesn't remember anything," she said shortly.

Kate only frowned. "Maybe," she said. For a moment, she was silent. Then she said: "Can I tell you a story?"

Dea knew she had no choice, so she said nothing.

"When I was three, my mom was killed by an intruder. Shot three times, point-blank range. Nearly took her head off."

Dea was so stunned she couldn't even squeak out an *I'm sorry*. Whatever she'd been expecting Kate to say, it wasn't that.

"We were living on the South Side of Chicago—a bad neighborhood. My mom was a single mother, only nineteen, liked to party. She worked as a stripper to keep the lights on and everybody knew it. Probably half the block knew she kept cash in her closet. I was staying with my grandma, like I always did on nights she worked. Some junkie busted in, shot my mom, snatched the money, and ran. Wanna know how much he took? Four hundred dollars. Four hundred dollars, for a life." She laughed, but it was without humor. "The cops caught him a week later trying to pawn some cheap shit jewelry one of my mom's regulars gave her. He spent ten years in jail."

"Good," Dea croaked out.

"Lucky," Kate corrected her. "Extremely lucky. The guy wasn't connected to my mom, didn't know her, wasn't even a regular at the club. They made sure of that first thing. They grilled every single guy she'd ever screwed—and God rest her soul, there was a long list—and every guy who'd come through the doors at Pole Dancer's in the past two months. Poor fuckers. All they wanted was a good lap dance and suddenly they're on the hook for maybe killing someone."

Again, Dea could find nothing to say. She'd never heard anyone speak the way that Kate did, and she couldn't reconcile the story with the woman who sat next to her in a bright red anorak, drinking a coffee with a billion sugars, her cheeks red from the cold. Maybe, Dea thought, she and Connor weren't the only ones with horrible secrets and dark, twisted paths. Maybe everyone was walking around carrying ugly monsters and dark little corners, nightmares and broken pasts.

"Do you know how hard it is, Dea, to catch a murderer with no connection to the victim?" Kate asked. Dea knew she wasn't expected to answer. "It's nearly impossible." She paused, letting the word sink in. "Fortunately for the police, it's also incredibly rare. The vast majority of women are killed by their partners, or by ex-partners."

"Connor's dad didn't do it," Dea said quickly. "He was away on a business trip."

Kate sighed, as if Dea were failing to see a very obvious point. "I didn't say he did. And Connor didn't do it, either. I know that." Her voice softened. "His fingerprints were found on the gun, though."

Dea felt her face heating up. "It was his father's gun," she said quickly. "Maybe he was allowed to play with it. Maybe the real killer wore gloves."

"Maybe," Kate said neutrally. Again, Dea had the sense that she was missing something. "Look, the point is, Connor's mother wasn't killed by a stranger. Sure, a window was broken. But it was a safe neighborhood, and nothing was stolen. The baby was killed but not the older brother, whose fingerprints were found on the gun. And why wear masks inside the house? Why bother with masks at all?"

The sun was slanting hard through the dirty windshield, making Dea's head hurt. She felt as if she were climbing slowly along the ladder of Kate's words, trying to make sense of them.

"They didn't want to be recognized," she said.

"Right." Kate hooked a right turn abruptly, at a sign for Chapel Hill Housing Development, and pulled over, throwing the car in park. Across a bare-scrubbed hill, Dea saw big blank houses with walls orange in the sun, many of them just skeleton structures. It was going to be a perfect day. "But recognized by who? Connor's mom was the target. Connor's brother was just a baby. He wasn't going to talk." She turned her eyes to Dea. They were a brown so dark they were nearly black. "So who the hell were they afraid of?"

"Connor," Dea said slowly. "It could only be Connor."

Kate looked satisfied—as if Dea had, at long last, resolved a complex math problem. "That's right," she said. "I'll tell you something, Dea. Connor doesn't think he knows who did it, but he does."

Dea got a sudden shock, an electrical understanding she felt in her whole body at once. "So do you," she said, knowing as soon as she said the words that they were true.

Kate deflated almost instantly. "Yeah," she said. Now she just sounded sad. "I do. I just can't prove it without Connor."

Dea looked at her. "Why do you care so much?" she said.

Kate sighed, as if she'd been waiting for Dea to ask. "The truth is hard," she said. "But the lies are worse." Then she put the car in drive again, and started slowly up the hill.

TWENTY-EIGHT

Chapel Hill was a ghost town. No workers, no Realtors, no people: just a network of cul-de-sacs, burnt into the hillside, black as tar, and houses in various stages of construction. Some were no more than skeletons, all bleached wood scraping up to the sky. Others were practically complete, though Dea noticed that none of the houses had curtains or shutters, and the blank windows gave them a haunted look, as though they were on the watch for something.

But as soon as Kate pulled into a parking space boxed out of the land in front of one of the more completed houses, Dea spotted Connor's truck, concealed behind a wall of hedgerow.

The front door was unlocked; Kate explained that she knew a guy who knew the guy who owned the development.

Inside, it was as cold as a refrigerator, with the same faint plastic smell. The house was furnished, presumably for showing. As soon as Dea opened the door, she heard voices. A moment later, Gollum flew out of the kitchen, her hair a bright fuzzy crown around her head, and catapulted into Dea's arms.

"Oh my God, Dea." Gollum was squeezing so tightly, Dea felt as if her ribs were going to crack. "I've been so worried about you. I swear when you called I almost had a heart attack. For serious. I was convinced you were getting hacked to pieces by some hitchhiking psycho killer or maybe you'd been abducted by a cult or something. *Corn maze!* Like it was some religious message from your leader."

"I'm all right." Dea pulled away, smiling for the first time in what felt like days. "No pieces missing, see? I'm still whole. And I haven't been converted to a church of crazy, either."

Connor had been hanging back a few feet, leaning in the kitchen doorway. He looked exhausted and thin, but he was smiling. Now he came forward.

"Hey, kid," he said, his voice soft, his eyes warm and bright. "Good to have you back."

He pulled her into a hug. He was wearing an old fleece so soft it felt like a blanket, and he smelled like he always did, like warm and spicy things, like a brightly lit room. In that moment her whole body felt alive and aware, electric with closeness. How could she ever leave Connor? How could she ever leave the world where he was?

How could she choose anything but him?

Gollum was still babbling. "It's been crazy, Dea. You're, like, the most famous person in Fielding. You're the most famous person in Fielding *history*. Even I'm famous just for knowing you. Connor practically has his own security tail. You want to know how we escaped this morning? Driving lessons. He's been giving me driving lessons. After yesterday when Briggs had to watch me do three-point turns in a parking lot for four hours, no way was he going to waste his time again." She took a deep breath, having temporarily run out of air. "I really did do a three-point turn, though. And Connor taught me how to parallel park."

"She only hit one trash can," Connor said solemnly. But his eyes were still smiling, softened with color.

Gollum turned serious. "What are you going to do, Dea? You can't really go on the run, can you? I mean, I guess some people do it. My dad used to love this show, *America's Most Wanted*—"

"Hey, Eleanor." Kate Patinsky was still standing by the front door. Dea had nearly forgotten she was there. "How about you and I head to the diner and pick up some real food? I nearly poisoned Dea with gas station donuts this morning. I'm thinking eggs and pancakes and bacon. You must be hungry, too. And Connor and Dea can have a breather." Her expression as she looked at Dea was almost pleading, and Dea understood then that Kate wanted something from her. But she didn't know what.

Gollum, who was a trash compactor for food, turned to her, bobbing her head. "Yeah, okay," she said. Then, as if sensing another meaning behind Kate's words, her eyes widened. "Okaaaay," she said, drawing out the word. "Yeah. Great idea. Then Dea and Connor can, um, catch up." She smirked in Dea's direction and Dea glared at her. "Just be careful, okay?" She gave Dea another hug.

Kate jogged the keys in her hand. "We'll be back in less than an hour," she said. "No need for good-byes just yet."

But Gollum still squeezed Dea tightly, as if worried she might vanish. Her hair smelled like mint. "Be careful anyway," she whispered. Then she followed Kate outside. Before shutting the door, Kate shot Dea another cryptic look.

For a moment, she and Connor stood in awkward silence. Dea felt suddenly shy.

"I'm sorry," she blurted out. "For dragging you into this. For making such a mess."

He shook his head. "Don't apologize."

"I want to," she said. "I *need* to. I—"

"Dea." The way he said her name—as if it hurt, almost—made her shut up. And before she could respond or ask him what was wrong, he crossed the distance between them, took her face in both hands, and kissed her.

For a split second, Dea froze, terrified that if she moved at all, this wouldn't be true, he wouldn't be true, and the moment—Connor, so warm, so real, the safety, the simple fact of being held, touched, cared for—would break apart. Then he shifted, barely, and she shifted with him. They moved together, finding each other through the soft pressure of their tongues. She brought her hands to his head; she leaned into him; she wanted to taste him and become him and be carried in these seconds forever.

It was different, and better, than anything she'd imagined.

It was perfect.

Then it was over. He pulled away. But she felt no sadness—only a sense of lightness and floating. He kept his hands on her face, his thumbs warm against her cheeks.

"I've been wanting to do that for a long time," he said.

"Me too," Dea said. This was where she belonged: not a dream-place of monsters and wars, but with Connor. *Kissing* Connor.

He smiled huge, a smile she hadn't seen from him in a long time. No one had ever looked at Dea like that, as if she was an unexpected present, and it made her feel happy and different and *more*. She wanted desperately to kiss him again.

"I thought I might never see you again," he whispered.

"I'm here." She nearly told him she loved him; the urge to confess it was overwhelming. Instead, she found his hand and interlaced their fingers. "I'm not going anywhere."

Connor closed his eyes. They were standing so close she could count individual lashes. Then he pulled away. His smile had vanished.

"What will you do, Dea?" he asked quietly. "Where will you go? If your mom doesn't come back—"

"She's not coming back," Dea said. All at once, the reality of what she had decided—the impossibility of it—hit her. She couldn't stay with Connor, not without getting harassed by the police, maybe stuck back in the hospital again. She had no relatives here, in this world, and barely a thousand dollars. She'd have to move, get a job, maybe even change her name. She'd lose Connor anyway. And how long would she even survive without returning to a dream? She took a deep breath. "I know where she is. And trust me, she can't come back."

Connor stared at her. He screwed up his mouth, as if he wanted to ask her a question but was swallowing it back. "Are you sure?" he said finally. Dea was glad he hadn't asked point-blank where she was. She just nodded.

"I don't want to lose you," he said quietly. And then, in a rush: "We could run away. We could get in the car and just keep driving."

Dea let herself imagine it: escaping with Connor, riding through the dark as she had done so many times with her mother. Ditching the car, changing their names, showing up in a town halfway across the country with a made-up story they'd agreed to in advance. Sleeping side by side in dirty motels, like they'd done in Wapachee Falls. But she knew it was fantasy.

"My mom spent all of her life running," Dea said. "I don't want to be like her. Besides, sooner or later we'd be caught."

Connor dropped her hands and moved to the window. When he spoke again, his voice was bitter. "You're right," he said. "Roach won't give up."

"Roach?" Dea said.

"My uncle." He shoved his hands in his pockets. "Old football nickname."

Dea felt a small chill run through her. She thought of walking Connor's summertime dream, how she had looked up and seen his mother, naked, with an enormous cockroach embracing her. It couldn't be coincidence.

"Are you . . . are you close to your uncle?" Dea asked carefully.

Connor turned back to her and stared. "I'm on your side, Dea."

"I know," she said quickly. "That isn't what I meant."

Connor sat down on the sofa, rubbing his eyes as if they were burning him. "I don't know. I used to be, I guess, when

I was a kid. Before . . ." He didn't have to finish his sentence. "He used to come around a lot more, when my mom was alive. He was living only a few blocks away. Will, too. We were best friends when we were kids. Now he won't even look at me."

She had that same creeping cold sensation. *Someone must be walking over your grave.* She remembered that expression, suddenly, from her short time in Nashville, Tennessee. For the first time, she understood it. "Briggs—Roach—used to live in Chicago?"

Connor nodded. "He helped out a lot after my mom and Jake—well, after they got killed. He was Chicago PD, pushed the whole investigation forward, told everyone I didn't do it. It didn't help much."

Something was skirting the edges of Dea's consciousness, an idea or association. It was like reaching for an object in dark, slick water: every time she seized the connection, it slipped away just as quickly. Roach and the window and Connor's mother. The faceless monster and the break-in that wasn't. Kate's funny expression, as if she knew a secret too terrible to say out loud. *Connor's mother wasn't killed by a stranger.*

"He's not a bad guy," Connor said, as if anticipating Dea's next question. "He's just . . ."

"Just what?"

"I don't know." For a second, he looked troubled, and Dea wondered whether somewhere deep in that ocean of unconsciousness, the tidal spit of memories and dreams, he was seeing something he had learned to ignore. "He just wants what he wants. He fixates on things, you know? Right now, he's fixated on catching your mom. He thinks he can get to her through you."

301

"He thinks wrong," Dea said.

"I told you, I'm on your side," Connor said sharply. Then he looked away, exhaling. "Sorry," he said. "I haven't slept in days. I keep seeing—I keep seeing horrible things. My mom. My little brother. They told me it would get better with time." His voice cracked. "They told me the nightmares would stop. But they never stopped. They only got worse." He shook his head. "Kate—she thinks I know who did it. But I don't. And you know what? After all this time, I'm not sure I even *want* to."

"The truth is hard," Dea said, reflexively parroting back what Kate had said to her. "But the lies are worse."

"Are they?" When Connor looked up, his expression was so anguished that Dea went to sit next to him and put a hand on his back.

"Yeah," she said. "Yeah, I think so." She thought about what she knew now: about her mother and father, about where she'd come from, about the city with its pickers and slaves and giant beasts yoked into service. It was terrible—but better than not knowing. Better because she could try to understand. "It's like . . . if you had to fight someone, it's better to know what you're getting into. Even if you still have to fight—if you know, you can do it with your eyes open."

As soon as she said the words, Dea knew. She what her mother had meant when she said she must give the monsters faces, and understood, too, what Kate had been trying to communicate to her. It wasn't about Kate or some book or even about Dea—it was about Connor. Connor needed to know the truth so he could be free.

And Dea could help him. More, even, than Kate knew. What

302

she could do—where she came from—wasn't just a burden. It was also a gift.

"I think . . ." Dea swallowed the sudden dryness in her throat. "I think I know a way to make the nightmares stop."

Connor's expression turned guarded. "What do you mean?"

"You'd have to let me in again," she said. Dea took a deep breath. She didn't know whether what she was about to suggest was even possible; still, she had to try. But an idea was blooming: if she could walk a dream that was like a memory, why couldn't she walk a memory like she did a dream? "Into your memories."

"No." Connor stood up. He backed away from her, looking afraid. "Forget it."

"It's the only way for you to know," she said quietly. And she thought that maybe this had been the point and the purpose of dream-walking all along: so that she could help the boy she loved. "Don't you want the truth?"

He watched her for a long time without saying anything. "Who are you?" he whispered at last.

Dea took a deep breath. She stood up. There was no longer any point in hiding or pretending. "You want the truth?"

Connor nodded.

"There's a world of dreams," she said. Saying the words out loud felt like releasing air from a balloon that had been stopping up her chest. "A world even older than this one. That's where I come from. That's where my mother comes from, too. And now, she's gone back."

Dea could hear the ticking of a clock loudly somewhere in another room. Or maybe she only imagined it, a rhythm synced to the heavy pounding of her heart. She waited for Connor to flip out, or accuse her of being out of her mind. A troubled expression passed over his face, a fast ripple.

"Are you going to go back, too?" he asked.

Dea's heart broke for him, then. He must be freaking out—he must have a thousand questions—but all he cared about was whether she would stay.

"No," she said, and she meant it. Somehow, she would find a way to stay. "But I'm running out of time to help you."

Connor moved back to the window. "I don't know anything." His voice crept higher. "I've told Kate a million times. I don't remember."

Dea thought of the men with no faces, and the ragged pant of their breathing, like deformed animals. "You said you never got a look at the guys who did it," she prompted him.

"That's right. First I was sleeping. Then I was . . . hiding." He spat the word out as if it were poisoned.

"You weren't hiding the whole time," Dea pointed out. "You crawled to the door. You peeked into the hall."

"Yeah, but just for a second." He shook his head. "Besides, they were wearing ski masks. All I could really see was a pair of mouths."

So that was where they had come from, the monsters with faces made of mangled flesh, and mouths to taste their prey: from Connor's distorted childhood memory of his mother's killers.

Give them faces, her mother had said. *They'll lose their power.*

"Take me through it again," Dea said. "From the beginning."

Connor swallowed back a sigh. "The first thing that woke me was the shot," he said, in the voice of a kid reciting multiplication tables. Dea wondered how many times he had been forced

304

to go through the same story. "Then my brother started crying. I freaked out and crawled into the closet. I heard a few . . . thuds. Wet sounding, like—"

"That's okay," Dea said quickly. "What next?"

Connor winced, as if the memory were hurting him physically. "There was another shot. That's when they . . . when they got my brother. I crawled to the door. I looked out and saw two men moving toward me. One of them—I could have sworn one of them saw me. I wet my pants. They left. The end."

"And you didn't hear anything before that first shot?" she said. "They broke a window, didn't they?"

Connor nodded. "I didn't hear it, though. Nothing until the shot." He pressed a hand to his eyes, as if gripped by a sudden headache. "Wait. That's not true. I was awake before that. They must have been talking to my mom. . . . I could hear their voices through the wall."

Dea's heartbeat quickened. "Do you remember what they were saying?"

Connor shook his head. "I wasn't really listening. At first, I wasn't frightened. But then I heard my mom start saying 'no, please, no.'" Connor's voice cracked. "Then a bang. People always say gunshots sound like firecrackers but I knew—even then I knew what it was. TV, you know?" He managed an approximation of a smile. "Even then I wasn't that scared. I didn't understand. I didn't connect the gun to my mom. But then Jacob started crying. He started screaming. And my mom was begging for her life. Then I knew." He looked down at his hands, gripped tightly in his lap. Dea could see the individual bones of his knuckles.

"Where was your dad?"

"Business trip." Connor cleared his throat. "That's why everyone thought I did it. The gun was his, you know. Whenever he was out of town, my mom kept it in her bedside table. So how did the killers know it was there? It must have been someone she knew."

Dea felt the idea, the knowledge, massing on the edges of her consciousness, a wave about to break. *The vast majority of women are killed by their partners. Or by their ex-partners.*

"You said at first you weren't frightened," she said slowly. "Why?"

"I don't know." He hesitated. "I think at first I thought my dad must have come home early from his trip. I just heard the voices and assumed . . ." He trailed off, shrugging.

"And you didn't hear them break in through the window."

Connor frowned. "I already told you that."

"Okay." Dea wiped her palms on her jeans. Even though it was cold, she felt sticky all over—nervousness, probably, and guilt. "Isn't it possible they broke the window *afterward?* To make it look like a break-in?"

Connor stared at her. "The front door was locked."

"Maybe," Dea said carefully, "someone else had a key."

She was worried he'd get angry. But he just shook his head. "No way. My uncle looked at pretty much everyone who'd ever been in the apartment—plumbers and friends and even our goddamn cleaning lady. If there was anything to find, he'd have found it."

The wave had broken, leaving the idea, the association, glittering and solid in Dea's mind. The dream of a woman enfolded by a giant cockroach; Connor mistaking the killer's voice for his

306

father's. She wanted to be wrong.

She said, "Your uncle and your mom were . . . close?"

"Very close," Connor said immediately. "Roach loved my mom almost as much as . . ." Then, abruptly, he trailed off. His whole face changed—in a split second, he turned guarded, as if someone had drawn a curtain across his eyes. "No," he said. "No. I know what you're thinking. And the answer is no."

Dea swallowed. There was a bad taste in her mouth. "He knew where she kept the gun. He probably had a key." Connor didn't correct her, so she knew she was right. "You weren't scared when you first woke up. You thought it was your dad talking. I bet—I bet your uncle and your dad sound alike."

"*No.*" Connor practically shouted it. He turned a full circle, like an animal trapped in a pen, desperate and confused. "No. Jesus, Dea. Don't you understand? He's family—he's practically the only family I have left. He *helped* us, he loved my mother, he—" Connor was out of breath, as if the words had left him physically exhausted. "Why are you doing this?" Connor's face had gone totally white. His eyes looked like twin holes. "Why are you doing this?"

Dea pressed her palms flat against her thighs, as if she could press the feeling of guilt out through them. "For the truth," she said. "For you."

TWENTY-NINE

"I won't do it." Connor backed up, as if afraid Dea might physically leap into his mind. "I won't let you do it."

"Connor," Dea took a step toward him.

"I said no, okay?" He looked as if he were about to be sick. He repeated, a little quieter, "I said no."

For a minute they stood there, staring at each other.

"Okay," Dea said finally. She held up both hands. "Okay."

Connor visibly relaxed. He turned partly away from her. He was so beautiful in the winter light. He looked almost insubstantial, like something she had imagined.

"I'm scared," he said, in a raw voice.

She came close to him. Her heart was fluttering like wings. She put a hand on his arm, reassured by the feel of him. "I'm scared, too."

He turned to face her. In that second there was nothing but him: his eyes and lips and the small scar on his chin, like a tiny moon. They were suspended together in space, in a bright white room that spoke of newness, and Dea allowed herself to believe—just for a moment—that they could stay like this forever and be happy. She put her hands on his chest and felt his heartbeat, a skimming rhythm under her fingers. Blood and bone, valves and shutters—all so easily broken, damaged, dissolved.

She stood on her tiptoes and kissed him.

I love you, she thought.

And: *I'm sorry.*

For a half second, he didn't respond. She closed her eyes and thought her way toward the soft darkness of his mind but instead felt a barrier, a rapid confusion of images that rose up like a wall. Then he let go, relaxing against her, breathing deep into her, exploring her mouth with his tongue. And she felt an inner relaxation, too—so faint, so quick, it was barely perceptible. There was a split-second gap, a fraction of a fraction of a second when the curtain parted and she felt a pull, strong as a current, toward the other side.

She pushed. Or she let go of her body and leapt. Distantly, she heard Connor cry out.

Already the curtain was closing, and for a moment she was in smothering darkness, floundering without a body, without any boundaries. She felt a sudden blast of cold wind; she fought toward the image of a winter skyline, a city blanketed in snow. With no hands, no fists or fingers, she reached out.

The darkness released her. The pressure on her chest released. Her breath was sharp and painful in her throat. The sky above her was a strange, bruised purple in the twilight, slashed like a wound above the buildings.

Across a street piled with old snow and trash, Christmas lights were blinking in the window of the deli.

She'd done it.

She was walking Connor's memory.

She didn't have much time.

Connor wanted her out. That much was clear. The air felt thick, almost syrupy, despite the cold—it was as if she were moving against a tremendous pressure, fighting just to be there. Even her body was responding slowly, as if she were a puzzle that needed to be reassembled after every step. She crossed the street with difficulty, her breath rasping in her throat. She was an infection; the memory was attacking her on all sides, exhausting her, rendering her weak.

She went, half limping, down the street. Connor's memory was significantly different from his dream. It was much darker; the snow had obviously fallen several days earlier, and was streaked yellow and gray. But the picture was badly melded, confused—in places the snow was piled high, in places it simply vanished. It was a city wrapped in the thick haze of a child's sleep, its details sketched in only afterward, in retrospect, a composite image of previous nights and other snows. Dea guessed it was well after midnight: all the apartments were dark.

She stopped to catch her breath, ducking into a darkened

doorway. She didn't want to think about how she would find the strength to fight the monsters when they came—when they finally showed themselves as men. She was being gripped by an invisible hand, squeezed on all sides; she felt that at any second she might be expelled into reality, simply popped back into the real world like a cork out of a bottle. But she wouldn't leave.

Not until she knew for sure.

Not until she gave them faces.

She would have to pick whether to watch the alley that ran along the back of Connor's apartment building or whether she should stay here, and keep her eye on the front entrance. The police believed the killers had come through the back window; they had certainly left that way. But if Dea was right, if her instincts were right, the killers had come through the front door and only made it look like a break-in later.

She stayed where she was, dragging breaths in and out, fighting to stay awake, to stay in. There was one way in which the memory and the dream were identical: she had no sense of time. It seemed to her both that she stood there for an eternity—feeling her lungs flutter against the pressure in her chest, wondering whether she had made the wrong choice and should circle around to the alley, whether she was wrong in general—and also that only a minute passed before there was a shift. The memory contracted like a heart. Everything went still, even stiller than it had been before. Dea spotted a light coming on quickly in an upstairs window; just as quickly, it was extinguished.

But it was enough. The truth hit her quickly, all at once.

The killer was already inside.

When Connor dreamed, he imagined the men approaching, sliding through the hallways, seeping up the stairs.

But in his memory, they had simply appeared. Connor was sleeping; when he woke, there they were.

She ran. Her progress was painfully slow. She had to fight for each step, each breath. She could hear her breath rasping in her ears, sharp and foreign, and every footstep sent a shudder through the sidewalk, as though the whole memory trembled at her intrusion. She was winded even before she reached the alley. She forced herself to go on, through air that felt like oil, and darkness that felt like weight.

She counted apartment buildings as she ran past them, looking for the wooden stairs stitched up the back of Connor's building. It was still quiet. There were no screams yet, but she wasn't sure there would be. Connor had never said that his mother had screamed—only that she had talked, and then begged.

More proof. She would have screamed, first and immediately. Unless . . .

Unless she knew them.

Up the stairs, her breath ragged in her throat, the wood giving way like mud, sucking her shoes down before spitting them out.

Then she was on the landing. Window closed, door locked, a trash bag heaped next to a shovel in the remains of an old snow.

She drew an elbow back and jabbed it once, hard, against the window. She heard a sound like a gunshot—or maybe it *was* a gunshot?—and the world blinked. Then she was thrown backward, as if by a giant hand.

For a second, everything was darkness and she felt herself

being pushed out, felt the heavy lines of her real body and heard Connor shouting at her to *stop, stop*.

For one long moment, she was split. She was Dea, lying on her back on a porch in the snow. She was Dea, gasping for breath in Connor's arms, her body stone-heavy, useless and abandoned.

She was neither and she was both.

Wood. Snow. Cold. She reached out, she pulled, she hauled herself back into his memory, leaving her body behind.

She stood up, shaken, steadying herself on the porch railing. A web of cracks extended across the windowpane where she had struck it, but the glass was still intact. She was changing things, screwing up the memory; and the memory was fighting back. *Connor* was fighting back.

She grabbed the shovel and used the handle to tap the glass. One, two, three times—nauseous, feeling the impact all the way to her teeth. But at last she succeeded, and the glass shattered inward, landing on the floor with a faint tinkling. Dea paused, holding her breath, half expecting the monsters to come roaring out through the broken window and leap for her throat. But nothing happened. The house was dark and still. She heard no baby crying, no footsteps, no arguments. It was terrible to enter an apartment so quiet. She was totally disoriented, and couldn't plan for what she would find.

She shimmied through the window, feeling a little bit like she was moving down into the soft dampness of an animal's throat. Her feet crunched on the glass where she landed, and she paused in a crouch, allowing her eyes to adjust to the dark, scanning every shadow for hidden movement. She was in the kitchen, and she was alone. Pale squares of moonlight fell on the tile floors. The refrigerator door was cluttered with magnets and Christmas cards, like a paper skin, and there was a high chair drawn up to the table, and a baby bib still lying, folded, on a countertop. She fought down an overwhelming sense of grief.

How easily, she thought, the ends could destroy even perfect beginnings. And just for a second, she wondered whether she could be happy living alongside her mother in a world where death didn't come for everyone; where there were no seasons and no endings.

She stood up and moved as quietly as she could around the kitchen, opening drawers until she found what she wanted: a paring knife, sharp and small and easily concealed. She curled her fist around the handle and slid out into the hall. It was hot, and the air smelled of pine needles, carpet cleaner, and something sweet she couldn't identify. It was so quiet. Had she missed them? Had the men come and vanished already?

A small part of her wished it. She didn't know if she was ready to face them. But she knew, instinctively, that they were there with her, hidden in the darkness of the apartment somewhere. They soured the air with their breathing; they made ripples in the darkness, like stones in water. Her whole body was on alert.

She no longer knew whether her heart was beating. Her chest was so tight with terror, she could barely take a breath. She inched forward, leaving the moonlight behind, in darkness so thick it felt weighty, like a blanket, gripping her knife.

Something creaked. She froze. Her hand was shaking when she raised the knife.

One of the doors on her right opened a few inches. Framed

in the gap was the white, wide-eyed face of a six-year-old Connor, his mouth opening and closing soundlessly, his expression twisted with terror.

"Shhh," she whispered. "It's all right. It's okay." Connor stayed where he was, staring, moving his mouth as if he was trying to scream. She couldn't stand to see him; she couldn't stand to have him watch. "Go back inside." She reached out and closed the door softly.

She moved on, forcing her way, doubled forward like a person fighting against a strong wind. The door of Connor's mother's bedroom was also open a crack. Dea stood for a second or for an eternity, afraid to enter and afraid to turn back. At last she pushed open the door and stepped inside, drawing a breath sharply against the sudden odor of sweat and blood. A scream rose in her throat and lodged there.

It was done. It had happened. In the corner, the lamp was shattered into pieces, and there was a huddled mass of darkness in the crib. She couldn't bring herself to go any closer. She coughed, her stomach rolling into her throat. Tears sprang to her eyes.

Connor's mom was still in bed. The covers were drawn up to the pillows, so Dea could see nothing but the vague shape of her, the swell of her body under the comforter.

She couldn't help it. She was drawn forward, as though by an external force. Without considering what she was doing—and what she would see—she reached out and flipped back the covers. She stifled a cry.

The bed was empty, except for two pillows, roughly massed together in the shape of a woman.

"You bitch."

She spun around at the sound of the voice—but slowly, too slowly, so that by the time she reacted he had already had time to push her backward onto the bed, immobilizing her under his weight. He was gripping her wrists so tightly, she couldn't begin to make use of the knife.

This time, his face wasn't made of sticky darkness. She could just make out his features, distorted by the mask—the flat plane of his nose, the cruel set of his lips, hooded eyes. The other one was standing by the door, shifting impatiently, foot to foot.

"Come on," said the second man. "Get it over with."

The man on top of Dea leaned into her, so heavy she could barely breathe. She could smell his breath, sour, faintly alcoholic. She turned her head away from him, gasping into the sheets.

"Did you really think I'd sit back and let you ruin everything?" He spat. "Huh? Did you?"

"Hurry up. The kid'll wake up."

"Please," Dea choked out. "Please don't do this." She realized, with a swinging sense of terror, of vertigo, that she was playing the part of Connor's mom: she was saying the right lines, she'd been forced into the right position. The memory was making her play the role of the murder victim. Her fingers were numb; she felt her grip relax on the knife.

He was going to kill her. Right here, right now.

"*Now* you'll beg?" He spat out. "That's funny. That's really funny." He forced his lips to her ear. She cried out. She tried to kick. But he was lying on top of her, flattening her, squeezing the air from her chest. He was too heavy and far, far too strong. She felt the stubble of his facial hair chafing her cheek.

She wanted to die. She wanted to live. She wanted out. "I told you," he whispered. "I told you I'd never let you go."

Words he had spoken to Connor's mother, years ago: words Connor, hiding, terrified, pressing his ear to the wall, had heard and buried.

Dea felt a hot surge of rage. "Get off of me." She whipped her head around and felt a blast of pain as their skulls collided with a crack. Spots of color floated across her vision. He cried out and jerked back but just for an instant. Before she could raise the knife, he had lunged for her again. She took a breath and screamed. He released her left wrist and grabbed hold of her throat. She choked on her own saliva. The scream died in her throat as he squeezed. She tried to swallow and couldn't. She tried to breathe and couldn't.

Stars were exploding in her mind; she was on the Ferris wheel with Connor again. She was floating.

Distantly, she heard someone shouting, "Jesus Christ, do it already. The kid, the goddamn kid—"

And a child, howling.

Connor?

His brother?

No . . . Connor's brother was dead. . . .

She would die, too. . . .

Her lungs were screaming. Darkness ate at the edges of her vision. Her jaw ached and there were fireworks behind her eyeballs and her head would explode. She thought of her mother's face, and the cool sensation of a wind tickling her forehead as she leaned out the window of the old VW, and watched the world whip past.

Give them faces. Her mother's voice came to her, light and laughing on the wind.

Bitchbitchbitch, the man was saying. He sounded so far away. Even the pain was passing. She was with her mother on the highway. Then she was climbing the high tower, toward a place of dreams.

No, Dea, her mother said, echoing around the stone. *Not yet. Not yet.*

In another world, she felt her left hand move. An inch. Two inches. It floated up toward his face, toward the mask pulled taut over his features. She watched it appear in her field of vision and felt nothing but curious detachment, as if she were witnessing the slow drift of a balloon from the ground.

The world was passing in jump cuts. Darkness. She curled her fingers under his mask. Darkness again. And then his mouth open, roaring, enraged: a monster's mouth.

She pulled.

THIRTY

There was the sound of a thousand shattering windows, a scream so high and terrible Dea thought her head would explode. Connor's uncle released her, staggering back from the bed, ducking his head as if he could keep her from seeing his face.

But it was too late.

There was a blast, a tremendous force of wind, and the room broke apart. The bed disappeared; the walls and floor and ceiling, gone. Connor's uncle and the man beside him went spiraling into the darkness.

"Dea!" Connor's uncle was screaming, howling her name, even as he vanished, even as he withered and dispersed, like smoke on a wind.

She let go. She let the wind carry her. She was floating in a dark pool. She just wanted to sleep. But screaming—the screaming kept rupturing the darkness, shocking her into temporary awareness.

"Dea, this is Kate. Blink if you can hear us."

A huge shock ran through her: it lit her body up all at once, toesfingerschestlungs, and she came awake, gasping.

"Come on. Wake up. Stay with us." Connor's face was hovering above hers, white and huge as the moon. It took her a minute to realize she was on the floor. Connor was kneeling, holding her head on his lap. Next to him was Kate Patinsky. Gollum was standing, talking urgently into a cell phone. Dea thought that was funny. Gollum didn't have a cell phone. A Styrofoam container of waffles was overturned on the ground, seeping maple syrup into the carpet. That was funny, too.

"Dea?" Kate was practically shouting. "Can you hear us?"

She opened her mouth and rasped a reply. Her mouth tasted like ashes. She swallowed and tried again. "Yes." Then, a little louder: "Yes."

"Stay with us, okay?" Connor's voice broke. "You're going to be fine."

Her head hurt. She could still hear screaming, a high, distant wail. Then she realized: sirens.

She struggled to sit up. But it was like forcing her way into Connor's memory. Her body was iron-heavy.

"You called the cops," she said.

"We called an ambulance. We didn't have any choice." Connor kept an arm around her. "You weren't breathing. I couldn't get you to wake up. I thought—I thought you were . . ." He couldn't finish his sentence. She noticed, for the first time, that he had been crying. His eyes were red and his voice raw.

"No." She was too tired to fight. She leaned into him. She closed her eyes. She was so tired. "No, not dead."

The sirens were getting closer. The noise reminded her of the shrill whine of an overgrown insect. But she was too tired to run anymore and she'd done what she had needed to do.

It felt nice to lie in Connor's arms. She wanted to tell him that she was sorry for what she had done, for what she'd uncovered. But she couldn't make the words take shape.

"I won't leave you." Connor ran his fingers through her hair. "I won't let anyone hurt you. I won't let him take you away."

She knew he was making promises he couldn't keep, but the words sounded so nice, she let herself believe.

"It was . . . it was Briggs," she managed to say. "It was Briggs all along. He lied. . . ."

"Shhh." Kate put a hand on Dea's knee, patting her gently, as if she were an animal. "That's all right. Just rest."

She closed her eyes, trying to ignore the sirens, trying to ignore everything in the world but the feel of Connor so close. She felt his lips skim hers—lightly, gently, as if he were afraid she might break.

"I love you, Dea," he whispered.

I love you, too, she said, or tried to say. She was drifting again, this time into the warm tide of sleep. She let go of the shore; she let herself be carried into the soft waves; she let darkness reach out its arms and enfold her.

She knew she was back in the hospital even before she opened her eyes. The smell of bleach was a dead giveaway. Distantly, she could hear the *squeak-squeak-squeak* of gurney wheels on linoleum, and the rhythmic clicking and humming of dozens of machines.

She opened her eyes and saw Connor's uncle sitting in the corner. As soon as he saw she was awake, his expression changed, became concerned and even polite. But she had seen, a split second earlier, his true face: ugly, calculating, brutal, watching her like a frog watches a fly.

"Why are you here?" she said. She wasn't afraid of him anymore—only disgusted. "Where's Connor?"

"Good morning to you, too," he said, putting both hands on his knees to stand up. His fingers were thick and patchy with hair. She looked away, ignoring the sudden tightness in her chest, the memory of choking. "Connor's at home. He's in a lot of trouble. You both are."

"That's funny, coming from you." Dea sat up. She was happy to see she was unfettered this time; no IVs, no tubes, nothing keeping her strapped to the bed. She swung her feet to the ground. "We didn't do anything wrong."

"You interfered with an investigation. You tampered with evidence." Briggs crossed his arms. "You ran away. Connor helped you."

Dea was glad, too, that she hadn't been stripped down and forced into a hospital gown. She was still wearing her own clothes. She grabbed her jacket off a peg in the corner. "Arrest me, then."

"We're not going to arrest you," Briggs said, still doing the concerned-parent act. Of course, he didn't know she knew. "I just want to have a talk."

"I have nothing to say to you," Dea said.

"I'm afraid you don't have a choice," Briggs said.

They stared at each other. Dea took a step toward him, consumed by a sudden sense of rage. "Connor knows," she said. "He remembers. He knows all about what you did."

Briggs drew back an inch. For a half second, the mask fell, and Dea knew he was afraid. Then he was smiling again, easy, condescending. "Connor doesn't know what he remembers," he said. But his voice was strained. "He's been under a lot of stress, and spending time with the wrong people."

It was a bluff. Dea knew that. Briggs was afraid because Connor was talking. He was going to tell people what he remembered. Kate would talk, too. And eventually, people would listen.

She felt a sudden ache, a longing to see Connor. She wanted to hear him say that he loved her again. She wanted to say it back.

"He's a good kid," Briggs said. "He drove himself crazy with worry over you. If you really care about him, you'll leave him alone."

Dea had nothing to lose. She said: "You should have left his mother alone."

There was a long beat of silence. A smile twitched at the corners of Briggs's mouth, like a kind of tic. At last, he said, "You're very confused." It was a struggle for him to keep the mask on, now. She kept seeing flashes of his real face—the face that had panted inches above hers, enraged, cruel. "I don't blame you. You've had a very hard time."

She was tired of playing games—tired of hospitals, tired of Briggs, tired of Fielding. It was all a big game—Briggs was pretending he wouldn't find the first excuse to chuck her in a mental ward or juvie, make sure she never got within fifty feet of Connor again. There were probably other cops standing guard outside her room, to make sure she wouldn't bolt.

And Dea was pretending she was going to cooperate.

She pulled on her jacket. "So. When are we going to have our talk?"

"Whenever you're feeling up to it," Briggs said, obviously relieved by her change in tone. "The doctor's cleared you to go."

She shrugged. "Sure. Right after I . . ." She nodded toward the bathroom, which was no bigger than a closet, and totally windowless.

Briggs made a gesture like, *be my guest.*

Dea closed the door behind her. It didn't have a lock, but it didn't matter. She doubted she'd need much time.

She ran the water in the faucet, turning the hot water on as high it would go. She barely recognized herself in the mirror. She looked skinnier, and wilder too: like a ghost.

Like someone from another world.

Her image soon began to fade, as steam rose up from the porcelain and clawed its way across the surface of the glass. Soon she couldn't see her features at all, only the vague outlines of a girl. Then even these faded. The steam looked just like fog, like a thin curtain she could pass beyond.

Briggs rapped once on the door. "You okay in there?"

Dea allowed herself to smile. "I'm fine," she answered. "Be out in a second."

She placed a palm to the mirror. The glass trembled. She felt warmth, the pressure of a second hand, reaching across dimensions.

"Hi, Mom," she whispered.

PART FOUR

Our truest life is when we are in dreams awake.

—Henry David Thoreau

THIRTY-ONE

Connor always knew when Dea would come, because the birds preceded her: two vast eagle-like creatures that swooped across the sunshine of his dreams, creating twin shadows. Then he would turn and see her.

"Hello." She shaded her eyes with a hand. Still, he could tell she was smiling.

"You came," he said, moving toward her. "I was hoping you would." She visited nearly every night. Still, he waited in agony all day, wondering whether he would see her, and when.

"Of course I did." She put her arms around his neck, stretching up onto her tiptoes to kiss him. She tasted like honey, and her skin was gold-bronze from the sun, and very warm. *No cancer in this world,* she'd told him. *I guess I should take up smoking. Except there are no cigarettes, either.*

"You're in trouble with Gollum, you know." He loved how she felt in his arms, light and heavy at the same time, solid and soft. "She says you haven't visited in weeks."

Dea wrinkled her nose, which was very lightly freckled from the sun. It was amazing how healthy she looked here, so strong and happy and confident—the same Dea but not the same Dea at all. Like a flower after a good long rainstorm, opening into the sun, full-throated and joyous. "Gollum's dreams," she said, "involve far too much horse manure for my taste. And Star Wars. Lots of Star Wars. Did you know Gollum was a Star Wars freak?"

"I do now."

"Tell her I'll come soon." She kissed him again, just lightly this time, on the very top of his chin. But he ducked, and got one on the mouth instead. She pulled away from him, laughing, but kept her arms around his waist.

"I see you have your escorts with you." He nodded to the eagles, now perched on a nearby telephone line, preening. They were enormous, but the wire stayed taut beneath their weight—details, Connor knew, didn't matter much here. Neither did physics.

She rolled her eyes. "Escorts," she said. "More like bodyguards."

He looped a finger in her hair, tugging gently—loving the feel of her, the smell of her hair, the closeness of her body to his. "Is your dad really afraid of what I might do?"

328

"He's afraid of what *I* might do." Her voice was teasing. "He's worried I might go rogue and try to escape."

He'd promised himself that he wouldn't ask her again, but now he found he couldn't help it. "When?" he said. "When are you coming back?"

"Connor . . ." She sighed and disentangled herself from him, stepping backward. Instantly, she looked much older. Like a stranger, especially in the dress she was wearing, sleeveless and white, different from anything he'd ever seen her wear in real life. "You know I can't give you an answer. It's—"

"Complicated. I know." He didn't mean to sound bitter.

She looked at him again. When she frowned, her nose pulled slightly to the left. He loved that. "You think I don't *want* to come back?" She shook her head. "My dad keeps my mom locked in a weird tower. My mom is busy plotting my father's downfall. Half my dad's army is rebelling, and now a league of monsters is marching on the city. We're talking major malfunction over here."

It was crazy how she could talk about things like monsters and towers and still sound so absolutely, so resolutely Dea: sarcastic and funny and logical all at once. All of his anger dissipated. He reached for her again, tugging on the fabric belt that held her dress closed, drawing her into him again.

"So let me come to you." He kissed her neck and shoulder. "I want to be with you, Dea."

He could feel her shiver when he moved his mouth toward her jaw. "I want to be with you, too," she whispered. "But you know it doesn't work like that."

He'd asked her a hundred times to take him to the city, to

show him the palace where she now lived and the slave pits she was determined to close down; to see the mirrors through which she could keep watch over him ("Just as long as you stay out of the bathroom," he'd said); to see the strange hybrid monsters and animals that had crawled out of or been recruited from other people's dreams. Her answer was always the same: *It doesn't work like that.* This, here, in Connor's dreams, was the only way they could be together. For now. Dea always said that, *for now,* although he didn't see what could possibly change.

"Come on." Dea kissed him again, leaving a lingering taste of sugar. "Let's be happy, okay? Let's walk and be happy and forget about all the bad stuff."

They walked through the ruins of an old fort—a place Connor remembered, vaguely, having gone to as a child. *Before.* Dea held Connor's hand, occasionally squeezing tighter when she needed to navigate uneven ground or hop over a stone. Wildflowers grew between the splintered foundations, and moss cascaded from the ramparts, half-buried in the ground. But other, random features had intruded: telephone poles, a water fountain like the kind found in school hallways, and, in the distance, a carousel. He hadn't dreamed of Chicago again, not since Dea had walked his memories.

"How's your dad?" Dea asked. She'd been avoiding the subject, letting Connor talk about it only when he wanted to, which he never did. Connor knew this was her subtle way of reminding him of his place—that there were things in his world, people, he couldn't just abandon.

"Better." For days after Connor had first said the unthinkable—*Uncle Briggs did it*—Connor's father had floated through the house like a ghost, pale and undirected. But a month later he was doing all right. He was functioning, maybe better than he had in a long time. It was as if he'd been cured of a deadly disease, something that had been eating him slowly from the inside. "He didn't want to reopen the case at first. He just couldn't deal. My stepmom convinced him. And Patinsky, of course. Turns out there's all this crazy shit—police cover-ups, misplaced evidence, all of it. My uncle's partner was the one who helped him—who stood watch. Conspiracy all the way up the chain. Or the other cops turned a blind eye." He shook his head, feeling the anger, the old sense of grief, grip his chest. "I actually feel sorry for Will. I think . . . I think he knows, though, deep down. You know he told me one time his dad cracked him over the head with a guitar? Will was playing too loudly. He didn't even take Will to the hospital. His mom did, later, because he started puking. Turns out he had a concussion."

Dea squeezed his hand so tightly he could feel all the bones in her fingers. "I heard," she said.

He looked away, toward the horizon, where the carousel had started to turn. For a moment he imagined he saw a boy there—a boy with dark hair and a wide, laughing mouth, just like Jacob's would have been, if he'd lived—but then the carousel kept turning and he realized it was just a trick of the light.

"When I was a kid, I wanted to be just like him." The anger had clawed into his throat, strangling him, making his voice sound high and tight. "He was the one who let me hold my dad's gun, you know. So I could be a real cop, like him."

Dea stopped. She turned to him and put a hand on his chest, fingers splayed, as if she was feeling for a heartbeat. "It's going to be okay," she said. *"You're* going to be okay."

He was overwhelmed by the feeling that he was going to cry. "I miss you, Dea," he said.

"You don't have to miss me." She smiled. She was so beautiful when she smiled. She was beautiful all the time. "I'm right here."

"But . . ." It was so bright outside: the kind of brightness that exists only in dreams, where the sun comes from everywhere all at once. He blinked quickly. "But it isn't real."

"Don't be stupid." Dea had to tilt her head to look up at him. He could see himself reflected in miniature in her eyes. "It's real enough."

Then promise me, he nearly said. *Promise me I won't wake up from this.*

But he knew she wouldn't—she couldn't. And maybe she was right. Maybe it didn't matter. They would be together here. They would be together forever.

She was real in his arms. Her hair smelled like lilacs.

So he kissed her again.